Also by Bili Morrow Shelburne

BLACKBIRDS AND BUTTERFLIES

CLEMMIE

COLLATERAL JUSTICE

Bili Morrow Shelburne

COLLATERAL JUSTICE by Bili Morrow Shelburne

First Edition, September 2015

Published by Wendover Press

Copyright © 2015 Bili Morrow Shelburne

Author Services by Pedernales Publishing, LLC.
www.pedernalespublishing.com

This is a work of fiction. Names, places, characters and incidents are either the product of the author's imagination or are used fictitiously, and any resemblance to actual persons, living or dead, business establishments, events, or locales is entirely coincidental.

All rights reserved, including the right to reproduce this book or portions thereof in any form whatsoever.

Library of Congress Control Number: 2015950158

ISBN: 978-0-9967430-2-0 Paperback Edition
        978-0-9967430-1-3 Hardcover Edition
        978-0-9967430-0-6 Digital Edition

Printed in the United States of America

For Ralph: my lawyer, my love

Chapter One

"Oh, jeez, Joe Bob, don't do that!" Uncle Stuart and I were buckled up in the back seat, and Bernie was doing his best to steer Joe Bob toward the car.

"When you gotta go, you gotta go," Uncle Stuart opined. His head lolled to one side, and his chin rested on his chest.

"Well, thank you there, Judge," Joe Bob said, grinning, as he zipped his fly. He fumbled car keys out of his pocket.

Bernie reached for the keys. "I'll drive," he said. "You're soused. I can't believe you just pissed right on the side of the tavern like a stray dog."

Joe Bob jerked the keys from Bernie's hand. "I don't remember askin' for your opinion, Bernard, but you're not drivin'. It's my car; I drove us here, and I'll drive us back. Git in."

Bernie got in on the passenger side, shaking his head. He seemed to push his fear of Joe Bob's driving to a back burner and launched into a recent encounter he'd had with an old high school flame. I was trying to stay awake while Uncle Stuart snored and Joe Bob piloted us down Spruce Street.

"I'm telling you, she was as broad as she was tall," Bernie said. "Remember what a dynamite body she used to have?"

"I sure do," Joe Bob said. "What a rack! She was a real fox. It all went to fat, huh?"

"Big time. Joe Bob, look out!"

The old Buick swerved, and Joe Bob slammed on the brakes. I didn't see a thing, but I felt a dull, sickening thud. Tires screamed, and the odor of burnt rubber rose from the concrete.

"What in thunder?" Uncle Stuart awoke with a start.

"Oh, no! Oh, God, no!" Joe Bob pleaded. He began hyperventilating and jumped out of the car. Bernie and I were right behind him.

A body lay on the pavement, unmoving. Joe Bob went to his knees and looked at it. He seemed hesitant, but felt the neck, then the wrist, for signs of life. He held a hand under the nostrils. With one desperate attempt after another, he came up empty. Then, he slapped the still face.

Bernie and I looked on like statues. Joe Bob sat back on his haunches and began to cry. Uncle Stuart came over to join us. The accident seemed to have had a sobering effect on him.

"Gentlemen," Uncle Stuart said, mustering an authoritative tone, "I believe we all need to settle down and collect our wits. Bernie, do you know this man?"

Bernie bent over the body.

"It's Jimmy Banks."

"Is he dead?"

"He appears to be, sir."

"Appears to be doesn't get it, son. Is he, or isn't he?"

Bernie made himself check the pulse and stood. "He's dead."

"Might you have a flashlight, Joe Bob?" Uncle Stuart said.

Joe Bob went to get it without answering. He couldn't seem to stop crying.

"We have to call an ambulance and the police," Bernie said.

Joe Bob paced back and forth beside the body, making whimpering noises and wringing his hands.

"What good's a ambulance gonna do, Bernard? The man's dead."

"That's just what you do. You call an ambulance and the police. It's the law, and we all know it, so why pretend we don't. Tell him, Judge Maxwell."

Uncle Stuart ignored Bernie. He was busy trying to examine the car.

"Matthew, take this flashlight and look the car over. I seem to be having a bit of difficulty with my equilibrium."

"What am I looking for?"

"Damage, 'course."

Automobiles meant no more to me than any other necessity. I knew this was an old Buick, but I didn't know the model. One thing was unmistakable though; it was built like a tank. There wasn't a dent on it.

Joe Bob kept pacing and crying, and Bernie was steadfast, continuing his diatribe on civic duty and the law. A man lay dead in the street of a one-horse Tennessee town, and the four men who had witnessed his demise were spinning their wheels, trying to decide what to do about it.

There were no streetlights on Spruce, and the dark night hummed with buzzing cicadas and chirping tree frogs. It was so humid the heavy air felt burdensome, but suddenly my uncle acted in such a clear-headed manner that he might have been pounding his gavel, bringing a courtroom to order.

"Get into the car," he ordered.

"One of us needs to stay here, so it doesn't look like a case of hit-and-run," Bernie said.

"You watch too much TV," Uncle Stuart said. "We're not criminals."

I couldn't think straight, but I had enough sense to know we shouldn't leave the scene of an accident.

"I'll stay here," Bernie said. "You guys go to the police station."

"Matt, you're a lawyer," Joe Bob said. "Do we have to tell the cops?"

"Well, according to the law….."

"Oh, horse manure! That's not a good idea," Uncle Stuart said. "Man's dead; no witnesses."

I didn't recall making a decision, but the three of us were in the car, and Joe Bob was behind the wheel. A pair of headlights turned onto the street. The car was about two blocks away, creeping toward us.

"Git in the car, Bernard," Joe Bob hissed.

"What?"

"Git in the car. Now!"

Bernie jerked open the front passenger door and jumped into the car. Joe Bob backed up a few yards and turned onto a side street. We barreled down the narrow street, and the old car flew over potholes like they didn't exist.

"What are you doing, Joe Bob?" I yelled.

"I'm takin' y'all back to Bernard's car."

"We can't just forget about this," Bernie said.

Joe Bob pulled up beside Bernie's Cadillac. He killed the engine and looked at Bernie.

"Why can't we?" he said. "Nobody saw it happen. Jimmy Banks never knew what hit him. He didn't have no family; lived on welfare. So what good's it gonna do anybody to turn myself in?"

I was in no condition to be a participant in the conversation. My mother's death had summoned me to my hometown. I hadn't digested the fact that she had died, and I wondered about my inability to feel grief, remorse, anything. How could I possibly command myself to be level-headed about this situation? But the fact that I was involved in a hit-and-run began to sink in.

"I think this is serious business," I said.

"Serious business," Uncle Stuart parroted.

"It was a accident," Joe Bob said. "I'm not a killer. Do you think I sit around plottin' how I'd run crazy old Jimmy Banks down and kill him?" His big hands covered his face, and he started crying again.

Uncle Stuart sighed. "It was indeed an accident," he said, "and as Joe Bob pointed out, nobody would benefit from our enlightening the police."

"Judge Maxwell," Bernie said, "what are you suggesting?"

"I'm not suggesting anything. I'm simply saying that if we so choose, this tragic mishap will be news to us in the morning."

"I can't believe this," Bernie said. "We left a dead man lying in the street like roadkill, and a judge and a lawyer think it's just fine."

"Bernard, this could ruin me," Joe Bob said. "I realize you don't think I have much of a life – compared to yours – that is. I own a run-down garage and live in a trailer, but I've got my freedom. And I always thought you was my friend."

"Of course, I'm your friend, but what if somebody finds out about this? We could all be up a creek."

"How could anybody find out about it? Nobody else saw it happen." Joe Bob leaned on the steering wheel with both arms, looking miserable. "I'm confused and I feel awful. Nobody in this world could be sorrier about Jimmy Banks than me. I almost wish I could trade places with him."

"We're all tired and more than a little drunk," I said. "Maybe we can think better after a good night's sleep."

"I know when I'm outnumbered," Bernie said. "Matt, I know it's hard for you to think straight about this with your mom's funeral tomorrow. I agree to call it a night and hope it's not a mistake." He took off his glasses, pulled out a handkerchief to mop his forehead, and got out of the car.

Uncle Stuart rolled down his window. "Now, don't mention this to your wife, son," he said. "There's no point in upsetting her."

Joe Bob drove Uncle Stuart and me home and cut the headlights. The three of us sat in the dark car, not talking. After what seemed a long time, Joe Bob broke the silence.

"Matt, do you think Bernard'll keep his mouth shut?"

"I think so."

"What if he don't? What'll they do to me?"

"I'm not sure. I'm rusty on Tennessee law."

"The best you could probably hope for would be a charge of vehicular homicide," Uncle Stuart said. "Depending on the jury, you could end up in prison for a few years, or you might be real lucky and get off with a short stay in jail and a fine. I wouldn't concern myself too much. Your friend will mull it all over and realize that nobody has anything to gain by reporting it."

"Try to get some sleep, Joe Bob," I said.

Uncle Stuart and I climbed the porch steps, and I unlocked the front door.

"Do you think we're doing the right thing?" I said.

"Hope so."

"We didn't even move him out of the street."

"No, we didn't. Good night, Matt."

Uncle Stuart headed for the guest bedroom where Aunt Lela Maude would give him a tongue lashing for leaving her to go out drinking with my old friends and me the night before my mother's funeral.

Collateral Justice

My sister had taken it upon herself to make the sleeping arrangements. She and her bean counter husband would sleep in our mother's room. She moved me out of my old room to accommodate our cousin Dave and his family. His two small daughters would sleep on a roll-away bed in the room with their parents, and I would use my sister's old room. I had always hated Sam's room; everything in it was pink: the drapes, bedspread, and a fluffy rug.

Sleep was elusive, and thoughts of my mother monopolized my mind. Her features were etched in my memory: green eyes, alabaster skin, perfectly arched brows, and not a hair out of place. She gave the impression of being airbrushed. Mother had always been considered one of the pillars of Martinsville, even after she and Dad divorced. She was active in all sorts of charitable organizations and worthy causes until the time of her death. A do-gooder to the end, she exuded goodwill, lending a helping hand and reaching out to most everyone except her family. Maybe she wasn't capable of real love. That's what I chose to believe now that she was gone.

My mother's passing would be mourned by many, unlike that of Jimmy Banks. Poor Jimmy. I didn't know how old he was. He was an adult when I was in high school. I could see him dashing into the street to stop traffic for an elderly lady or a little kid who wanted to cross. Taking no heed for his own safety, he would run into the middle of the street, arms extended so that his skinny body looked like a cross. He would stand fast until his adopted charge made it safely to the other side, then motion for the traffic to be on its way. I fell asleep with Jimmy Banks, the self-appointed traffic cop, fresh in my mind.

Everyone was still asleep when I awoke to the sound of a woodpecker hammering the bark of a tree outside my window. It was almost six o'clock. In several hours I would be attending my mother's funeral. I had disliked the custom of a visitation last night, and I dreaded the funeral even more. Staring at someone who had been alive and vibrant a few days earlier seemed barbaric to me. Funerals weren't intended to benefit the deceased; they were attempts at solace for the living.

I threw on a pair of old shorts and running shoes, then tiptoed downstairs and out the front door. I didn't feel like running, but I had to clear my head before greeting a houseful of relatives. I ran along the dirt path that paralleled the creek. It was the same trail I had used when I was in training for high school football, starting at the end of the street close to Mother's house and running all the way downtown. I tried to force myself not to think, but everywhere I looked, I saw my mother's face or that of Jimmy Banks.

Anne's Dress Shop still occupied the corner of 3rd and Main. It had been Mother's favorite place to shop. I remembered the boxes she brought home from Anne's: stark white with Anne's in script, and a big, black satin bow.

I was little—three, maybe four. Trudy, our housekeeper, had bought me a Sno Cone from the man who drove the truck that played "Pop Goes the Weasel" over and over all through our neighborhood. I was sitting on the porch steps with Trudy, sticky strawberry syrup decorating my face and hands as I drained the last of the good stuff from the paper cone. Mother pulled into the driveway and began getting white boxes out of the car. I jumped off the steps and ran to give her a hug. She stumbled and fell against the car, backing away from me.

"Gertrude, come get this child and wash his face and hands," she said.

Trudy cleaned me up; then I went looking for Mother.

"I'm going to rest for a while, Gertrude," she called through her closed bedroom door.

The window of the dress shop looked just as it always had: Anne's scripted with a flourish and signature boxes under the mannequins, resembling gifts under a tree at Christmas. I wasn't sure why I was staring at it. Maybe it was because Christmas morning had always seemed a happy time.

There must have been moments when I had felt warmth from my mother, but I couldn't pull any from my memory bank. Sometimes she read to me, and she showed up at school plays, but never came to my ball games; they were held outdoors.

When I went away to college, I didn't miss her. She and Dad were divorced then, so I made myself call her once a month. A lot had happened since then. I had married, divorced, and moved from Atlanta to Denver. There had been a lot on my plate, and Mother hadn't been high on my priority list. But being back in Martinsville and knowing that she was no longer here made me regret distancing myself from her.

As for Jimmy Banks, I hadn't seen him in years. I knew he hadn't had an easy life and that he was all alone in a world of strangers. His life had been cut short because of an unfortunate set of circumstances: he was on a street that was dark as pitch, and a carload of intoxicated men hadn't seen him until after it was too late.

As I circled the drugstore and the barbershop to head back to the house, my mind had a respite from the demons that were haunting me. For a minute, I thought I was hallucinating, but I wasn't imagining the strange sight. It was Fred Peyton, a guy who had attended school with me. He was walking along the side of the street that ran parallel to the railroad tracks with a gunny sack slung over his shoulder. And he was wearing his usual garb: an oversized topcoat. It couldn't possibly be the same gabardine coat he had worn year round so long ago, but it sure looked like it.

Fred was an idiot savant. He was brilliant in math and spelling, but all other subject areas seemed to elude him. He could spell words he had never seen or heard, and he never bothered writing numbers on paper. He computed everything in his head, and he was never wrong.

Freaky Fred lived in the worst part of town in one of several tiny red brick-sided huts lined up in a row. Everyone referred to the area as The Red Onion. It sat right beside the railroad tracks, and the only people who frequented the dirt street were those who called it home. Residents of The Onion heated their homes with wood-burning stoves, and nobody would have been surprised to see the entire area go up in smoke.

Domestic fights accompanied by a good number of injuries were commonplace, and thievery was a way of life. Unlike most folks who lived in a small community and were more than willing to lend a neighbor a hand, people who lived in The Onion wouldn't give one another the time of day. Nobody trusted anyone else; each household was wary of the others. Every now and then, one of the residents would end up in the hospital at the hand of a neighbor due to a minor dispute. I recalled an incident when a man was knifed to death for stealing a set of hubcaps from his neighbor who had lifted them from a parked car on a nearby deserted street.

I was certain that Fred had seen his share of knifings and shootings, but I couldn't swear to it. Fred didn't talk much. I hadn't hung out with him, but I hadn't shunned him. He was a loner and a victim of circumstance. I never saw a twinkle in his eye or a smile on his face.

As I started walking I felt his eyes on me. I turned in his direction and waved.

"Hi, Matt," he said, lowering his sack to throw in an aluminum can. Then, he turned his back and continued on his mission.

I walked the rest of the way back to the house, looking for

any changes in my hometown. It looked about the same, except somehow smaller. I never thought much about it until I got a taste of city life. Martinsville, Tennessee: Mayberry with a mean streak. Soon it would be no more than a memory.

Chapter Two

Trudy was in the kitchen making breakfast when I got back to the house. She came early every day, but she wasn't there when I arrived yesterday afternoon. I wasn't prepared for the way she had aged. Her shoulders sagged as she went about her task, and she looked uncommonly sad. It hurt me to see the woman who had practically reared me look so stricken.

"Trudy?"

The housekeeper stopped breaking eggs into her scrambling bowl and rushed into my arms. I held her close, and the silent tears began to fall. I knew she had held them back until I came home.

"That's it, Trudy. You go ahead and cry it all out."

"Don't know what I'll do without your mama," she said.

I couldn't come up with any words of comfort, so I just held her and offered my handkerchief.

"Put that thing away," she said, wiping her eyes with the corner of her apron. "Old Trudy feels better now. Get your sweaty self up the stairs and take a shower while I put breakfast on the table."

Gertrude Giles had been a part of our household since

I was little. Her initial job had been to clean the house one day each week, but as time went by, her duties increased. She did the cleaning, cooking, laundry, and ironing, and in her spare time, she took care of Sam and me. After Dad left, she came to the house every morning before breakfast and stayed until after dinner. Mother was capable of doing all the things she had Trudy do for her, and Trudy didn't need the job. The two of them had developed some sort of special bond that I never understood. Trudy was warm and wonderful, and I never heard my mother give her a kind word.

I went upstairs to make myself presentable and returned to the kitchen to find Uncle Stuart dressed in his funeral finest. He sat at the head of the table looking somber, but not particularly sad.

"Good morning, Uncle Stuart."

"Matt." He nodded.

"Well?" I said.

"Well, what?"

"You know what. It's now or never, Uncle Stuart."

"I'm afraid I don't have the least notion what you're talking about, Matthew."

"If we're going to take any action, we need to be quick about it."

"You make a wonderful cup of java, Mrs. Giles," Uncle Stuart said, with a satisfied smile.

Dave's children were stomping down the stairs. Everyone would be coming down to breakfast in the next few minutes, so there would be no more discussion about the accident.

"Good morning, young ladies," Uncle Stuart said, as the girls bounded into the kitchen.

I excused myself and went upstairs to finish dressing. My sister had been her usual pious self yesterday in addition to being in a foul mood. There was no reason for me to think she had changed overnight, so I wasn't anxious to be in her company.

I had been protective of Sam when we were growing up, but at some point—I wasn't sure when—she decided she could manage on her own. I never knew what I had done to incur her wrath, but she turned on me like a pit bull.

Mom and Dad divorced when I was eighteen. Sam was three years my junior. I knew she was hurting; I was, too. Our mother simply wasn't meant to be nurturing, so she was no help. Sam stayed in her room most of the time. She never asked for affection and never received it. I don't think she ever forgave our father for leaving, but I did. I understood his position completely.

I was standing before my sister's dresser mirror, working my tie into a perfect knot, and noticed a book lying on the pink bedspread. Funny. The bed was made, but I hadn't made it, and my high school yearbook was propped on a pillow. I didn't know when she had a chance to get upstairs, but I could see those loving black hands making Sam's bed and leaving me a memory book. Trudy had a reason for everything she did, but this left me stumped.

I sat down and opened the book, thumbing through its pages to the fresh faces of the senior class. Looking at my class photo made me feel old. Then, I turned the page to see Beth smiling up at me, exposing her slightly crooked tooth. She and I had been inseparable our senior year. I thought she was breathtakingly beautiful, and I knew I wanted her by my side forever.

We had both been accepted at the University of Tennessee in Knoxville. All during college we focused on our career goals and impending marriage.

We were married back home in Martinsville, then returned to Knoxville and leased an apartment. I began law school, and Beth landed a job as administrative assistant in a mortgage company. She worked at being the perfect wife, and I studied hard. Beth learned to cook and run a household while holding down a demanding job, and I was enormously proud of her.

Shortly before graduation I flew to Atlanta to interview with an impressive law firm. The interviewing process was a team effort and took two full days. Each of the four partners in the firm talked with me individually, and I was drained by the time it was over.

Returning to Knoxville and my bride, I waited three weeks. I was certain the interviews had been in vain, but a few days later I was offered the job. Beth and I celebrated with a dinner and champagne we couldn't afford.

I was still staring at the picture of my ex and recalling the day we decided we could afford the braces Beth insisted she needed to straighten her teeth when my peripheral vision registered movement. One of Dave's daughters dashed into the room and closed the door behind her. She was breathless from running up the stairs, and her small frame was pressed against the door. The child noticed me, and the look she gave me said I was interfering with her plans. She brought a chubby finger to her lips, warning me to keep quiet, and tiptoed toward me with panic in her blue eyes.

"Hide me fast!" she said.

"I'm afraid there's not a good hiding place in here."

"What's in that cedar chest?"

"I don't know. I haven't been in this room for a long time."

"Open it," she said.

I lifted the lid. There was nothing in the chest but a couple of quilts.

"This is perfect," she said, climbing in and curling into a fetal position. "Put the top down and sit on it."

"That's not a good idea; it could be dangerous."

"It'll only be for a minute or two. Sit on it and look at your book some more. There's money riding on this."

I could hear the girl's sister coming up the stairs, counting to a hundred.

"Quick! Here she comes," the child said, brushing a flaming red curl away from her eyes.

"I'll do it, but only for a few seconds."

The sister opened the bedroom door without knocking, and I looked up from the yearbook.

"Hi, there," I said.

"Hi. Have you seen my sister?"

"Your sister?"

"Oh," she said, with a wave of her hand, "you haven't seen her, or you'd 'member. She's got fire engine hair. Bye."

She left the room, and closed the door.

I got up and lifted the top of the cedar chest to see the pint-sized redhead smiling and giving me a thumbs-up sign.

"Good job," she said, as I helped her out. "I'm Leah, and that was my sister, Becca. You just helped me make a quarter."

"I'm Matt. How did I help you make a quarter?"

"Becca and I think kids' games are boring, so we bet on them."

"You bet on a game of hide-and-seek?"

"Sure. We bet on everything, but don't tell our mom. She'd kill us if she knew."

"Okay, I won't tell, but I doubt your mother would kill you."

"She'd kill us or make us learn about ten new Bible verses. She's real churchy; so is your sister, but we like her a lot. She did our makeup and found some high heels so we could play dress-up. I think she likes Becca better than me, though."

"Oh?"

"I can tell she does. She wanted Becca to sit on her lap while

I took my turn in the high heels. Becca's five-and-a-half; her feet touched the floor, but Samantha treated her like a baby. I think it made Becca feel funny."

I didn't think the child had hatched such a story, but that was weird behavior, even from my sister.

I heard Dave speaking to his younger daughter. "Becca, go find Leah. I told Aunt Sally we would be dropping you girls off in a few minutes."

"I can't find her," Becca whined. "I've looked everywhere."

"Sounds like you'd better head on downstairs, Leah," I said. "If you don't show up, they might send out a posse to find you."

"You're right," she said, and took off.

Sam and Ron, her husband, who would appear rumpled in a five-thousand-dollar suit, were holding forth in the living room. My sister was spouting orders to Trudy while Ron assigned seats in the Lincoln Town Car he had rented. I wouldn't have been surprised if he refused the limousine service to the cemetery after the funeral, so he could chauffeur the family in the Lincoln. He seemed awfully proud of the car. I would try to keep from making any waves on the day of my mother's funeral. If Sam threw one of her infamous tantrums over some insignificant thing that didn't fit her game plan, the day would be intolerable.

As soon as I received my orders, I followed Trudy to the kitchen.

"Your sister hasn't changed much," Trudy said with a chuckle that sounded like it had a smirk in it.

"I'm afraid you're right. I'm going to try to stay out of her way. Listen, you don't have to do anything here at the house after the service. I've already lined up a place for that. I'll let the funeral director know as soon as we arrive. He'll announce it right after the service so people will know where to go for the celebration of Mother's life. There'll be wine, coffee, tea, and hors d'oeuvres."

"Mattie, are you sure? What if Sam pitches a fit?"

"That won't happen; she won't have an opportunity. Besides, she would never embarrass herself in public."

Ron played the sentry beside the Lincoln, making sure we sat in the seats he had assigned. We rode in silence to the funeral home where we were greeted by the director and ushered into the flower-filled room where my mother lay still and beautiful. The half hour before the service was reserved for the family to spend a last private moment with the dearly departed.

My sister, martyr that she was, stood before the casket, dabbing at her eyes. She and our mother had never been close. My brother-in-law stood by his grieving wife's side with a supporting hand on the small of her back. I stood by the door, waiting for them to say their goodbyes. The air was smothering with the perfume of an overabundance of flowers. My sinuses were beginning to clog, and I was about to step outside for a breath of unadorned oxygen when Uncle Stuart placed a firm hand on my shoulder.

"Go ahead, son; do your duty," he said.

I didn't know what my duty was, but I knew I wanted to get out of that room. Staring at my dead mother wasn't going to bring her back to life, and I didn't have any tears to shed. I wanted my mother to rest in peace. Then, I wanted to be on my way, back to my real life. I would bury Martinsville, Tennessee along with my mother.

Uncle Stuart nudged me, and I made myself move forward to stand beside Sam. She must have taken my presence as her cue to leave, because she turned and headed for a chair with Ron trailing behind her. I looked down at my mother's face and tried to send her good vibes via this barbaric ritual. I needed to let her know that I didn't harbor resentment; that I had always loved her in my own way. Then, Aunt Lela Maude was squeezing my hand, making little snorting noises, and Uncle Stuart put a hand on my shoulder. My aunt began speaking to my mother; it was surreal.

"My precious little sister, we're all here, everyone who loved you: Samantha, Mathoo, Stuart, and me. Oh, and Gertrude is here somewhere. I don't see her right now."

"I think it's time for us to take our seats, Aunt Lela Maude," I said. "The organist is playing 'Beyond the Sunset'."

My attempt to focus on the minister's words was unsuccessful. I was sitting between Sam and my aunt, and the only sounds I heard were my sister's quiet sniffles and Aunt Lela Maude's overt ones. Then, people were filing out of the room, each one stopping to touch us in some way. They squeezed our hands, or put just the right amount of pressure on our shoulders to let us know they felt our pain, and whispered words of comfort. Their stony faces were set in grim, but kind expressions. Most were like robots, but every now and then, one of them lingered longer than the rest to let us know he cared the most.

The burial service was short and unattended, except for our family. Everyone else had gone to the hall I had rented. When we arrived, people were milling about, balancing small plates and drinks. I knew they were sharing anecdotes about my mother.

For some reason, the celebration of my mother's life angered me. It amazed me how some of the attendees were capable of turning a somber occasion into a party. They were laughing and drinking wine, having a high old time. An obese woman I didn't recognize was telling someone else the ingredients for an *easy as pie* peach cobbler. Well, that was how people celebrated, wasn't it?

I allowed strangers to pump my hand and praise my mother. Bernie wasn't smiling when he shook my hand. He looked distressed, but I could tell it didn't have anything to do with grief.

"You're here alone?" I said.

"Yeah. Lee Ann thought it would be best to keep the baby at home. She sends her condolences."

"Thanks for coming, man. I appreciate your support."

"Matt, I know this isn't appropriate, and forgive me if I'm too out of line, but do you think you might go with me to see Joe Bob later? He's a wreck."

"Sure, and you're not out of line. I only have this place rented for a couple of hours. As soon as I can get away from the house, I'll call you."

"Thanks, Matt. I'll let him know we're coming."

I didn't know what we could do for Joe Bob, but I wanted to support him. For all I knew, he had decided to go to the police.

Chapter Three

The house was quiet. Sam and Ron had gone to their room, Trudy and Aunt Lela Maude had both dozed off in the living room, and Uncle Stuart had disappeared. I pushed myself back and forth on the front porch swing, waiting for Bernie.

The gray Cadillac slid up to the curb like silk.

"You drive like an old lady," I said, sliding into the passenger seat.

"Yeah, I know. Fasten your seatbelt. Everything changes when you become a dad. There's nothing I wouldn't do for my baby girl; I worship her. I'm probably more cautious than I need to be, but I have to be responsible, you know?"

"I'm sure you're a great dad, and you've done real well in your dry cleaning business. That's important for a guy with a family."

"Enough about me. I'm concerned about Joe Bob. When I went to pick him up to go to your mom's service he was pacing back and forth in front of his trailer. He had on a suit, so I knew he planned to go, but when I got close enough to see his face, I saw that he was biting his nails and crying. He's a real mess."

"I haven't seen him today. I didn't know he was at the service."

"He wasn't. He was so upset I had to leave him there. When I turned on my cell after the service, I saw that he had left two messages for me to call him. I don't know what we can do for him."

It was nearly six o'clock when we pulled into the trailer park where Joe Bob lived. There were lots of shade trees, a stream ran around the perimeter, and several neatly tended patches of grass passed for small front lawns. But some of the residents must not have been too impressed with the natural beauty of the place. They seemed to have found all sorts of tacky ways to bring it down to their unfortunate nickname. A few had affixed crude porches to their trailers. Others opted for remnants of Astroturf in lieu of grass. The worst offender was a sprinkling of vehicles that must have been deemed beyond repair and left to rust, propped up on concrete blocks minus their wheels.

Joe Bob resided in a double-wide tucked at the end of a cul-de-sac. It was situated so that two big sugar maples offered it an abundance of shade. The grass was trimmed and edged, and there were long beds of rose begonias that ran from each side of the front steps to the ends of the trailer. Bernie approached the trailer like a cat walking on wet grass and knocked on the door.

Joe Bob appeared in a white terrycloth robe. His long, dishwater blond hair was dripping wet.

"Hi, guys," he said. "Come on in. Don't look too hard. I didn't have time to clean the place up."

We were standing in a living/dining room area. A big screen TV took up most of the wall space across from a huge leather recliner. Part of a sectional couch was wedged into a corner. In front of it was a coffee table covered with copies of *Sports Illustrated*, *Modern Mechanic*, and *Playboy* magazines.

A big yellow cat sat on a Formica table, nibbling at the remains of what looked like last night's supper, switching its tail. Joe Bob took notice of the animal and swiped it off the table. The cat landed on all fours and dashed out of the room.

"Wonder why cats do that?" he said.

"Do what?" Bernie said. "Eat?"

"Why do they think they have to git on the table and on top of the refrigerator; weird places like that?"

"Who knows?" Bernie shrugged.

It was beyond me why we were discussing animals and their habits when our reason for being here was because Joe Bob was hurting. I figured he must have changed his mind about going to the cops and wanted us to know his intentions.

"Y'all want a beer?" Joe Bob asked.

"Sounds good," I said.

He went to the fridge and returned with a couple of longnecks.

"Where's yours?" Bernie said.

"I don't want one. I'm gonna throw on some clothes. Make yourselves at home. I won't be long."

Bernie and I made a halfhearted attempt to brush some of the cat hair off the couch and sat down.

"Here's to old friends," Bernie said, touching his bottle to mine.

"To old friends," I said. "What do you think he's going to do?"

"I know what he should do, but I doubt that'll happen," Bernie said. He looked around the smoke-filled room and took a long pull on his beer.

When Joe Bob came back to the living room he had donned an expensive-looking pair of slacks and a white dress shirt with rolled-up sleeves, unbuttoned halfway down his hairy chest. A wide, gold chain graced his thick football player's neck. I thought he looked like an out-of-place, modern-day Adonis. He lit a cigarette, then as an afterthought, picked up the dirty dinner plate and put it in the sink.

"Shoes," he said. "Gotta find my shoes."

He disappeared into the bedroom and returned with his bare feet stuffed into a pair of Gucci loafers.

"I'm flat starved," he said, stubbing out his cigarette. "Want to go grab a bite somewhere? I couldn't eat all day. My stomach's been in knots."

"Sure," I said, thinking he needed to take care of his basic needs before telling us he was ready to pay the penalty for ending someone's life.

A black Ford pickup was parked in the graveled drive beside the trailer.

"That your truck?" Bernie said.

Joe Bob nodded.

"Where's your Buick?" I said.

"At the garage."

"Let's take my car," Bernie said.

We climbed into the Cadillac, and Bernie rested his hands on the wheel.

"Where to?" he said. "Do we want real food, or grease?"

"I think I need grease if that's okay with you guys," Joe Bob said.

"How about Morgan's?" Bernie said. "They have fairly decent grease."

"Yeah, sure," Joe Bob said.

Morgan's Restaurant was located on the north side of town just inside the city limits. It was nearly deserted when we got there. The exterior of the building was constructed of fieldstone, and the only visible window was in the front door.

A skinny, middle-aged woman wove her way through the empty tables.

"How many in your party?" she asked.

"You're looking at it," Bernie said.

She led us through the maze to a sunken dining room and seated us next to a faux window with curtains which extended halfway down the wall. Slats of open wooden shutters filled the space inside the curtains, and patches of bright blue paint with intermittent daubs of white jumped out at us.

Joe Bob took a seat and reached for a box of Marlboros in his shirt pocket.

"Uh, Joe Bob, do you mind holding off on the cigarettes while we're at the table?" Bernie said. "I don't want to cramp your style, but my eyes are still burning from sitting in your living room."

"Not a problem. Why didn't you say somethin'?"

Bernie shrugged.

A waitress appeared and handed out menus.

"What can I get you guys to drink?" she said.

Before we had a chance to answer, she leaned closer.

"Well, Joe Bob Kincaid, I didn't know that was you," she said. "Where you been keepin' yourself?"

"Hey, Lucy. I been around."

Joe Bob wasn't a student of the rules of etiquette, but I had never known him to be deliberately rude.

"Y'all remember Lucy Combs," he said. "Lucy, you know Bernie Zuckerman and Matt Stevenson."

We nodded, and Lucy peered down at me.

"Matt Stevenson!" she said, her mouth stretching into a smile. "The same Matt Stevenson used to live over on Mulberry Street?"

"In the flesh, Lucy," I said.

"If that don't beat all." She slapped herself on an ample thigh.

"Hey, Lucy, did you ever break the chain?" I asked.

"Sure did." She laughed and shot a glance at Joe Bob.

"Hey, how about bringin' us three beers," Joe Bob said.

Lucy nodded. "Be right back with 'em," she said, and headed for the bar.

"I figured Lucy would have found herself a rich white man and moved away from Martinsville a long time ago," I said.

"What's this *break the chain* stuff?" Bernie asked.

"It wouldn't have meant anything anywhere else," I said. "The rest of the world had been integrated forever. Don't you remember how Lucy was always asking me to break the chain of segregation and go out with her?"

"Come to think of it, I do remember she was hot for you. Too bad we lived in Old South Martinsville, Tennessee. She's still a looker."

"Ditto that, except for that bleached blond hair," I said. It looks sort of incongruous on her."

"I like it," Joe Bob said.

"What crippled her?" I asked.

"Oh, you mean the foot thing," Bernie said. "I think I heard she was in a wreck a few years ago."

Lucy brought the beers and took out her pad and pencil.

"Know what you want?" she said.

"Well, we're here at a greasy spoon, so we might as well eat grease," I said. "I'll have a burger and fries."

"I believe I'll have a chef salad," Bernie said.

"Know what you want, Joe Bob?" Lucy asked.

"Yeah. Bring me the chicken-fried steak, mashed potatoes with gravy, and green beans."

"Talk about a heart attack on a plate," Bernie said.

"We're too young for heart attacks," Joe Bob said.

The hostess ushered two rough-looking men down the stairs and seated them at a table near us. Both men lit up, and Bernie began fanning the air.

Our food arrived, and Bernie looked up at the waitress with eyes that begged.

"I hate to be a bother, but could we please sit in a non-smoking section?" he said.

Lucy set her tray down and whisked the ashtray off our table.

"Okay, sugar," she said. "You're sittin' in it."

Joe Bob laughed and started scarfing down his fat food. When he had cleaned his plate, he looked at Bernie.

"You gonna turn me in, Bernard?"

Bernie labored with a mouthful of salad and at length, swallowed.

"No, I'm not," he said.

"I don't want you to keep quiet because of our friendship," Joe Bob said. "I know you wanted to go to the cops. What changed your mind?"

Bernie put down his fork and took his time to answer.

"I'm not sure," he said.

"Did you guys save room for dessert?" Lucy asked.

We declined, and she laid the check on the table.

"It was good to see y'all," she said. "By the way, did you hear what happened?"

"Well, I don't know," I said. "What happened?"

"Somebody run old loony Jimmy Banks down las' night; killed him."

None of us said anything. We just looked up at Lucy, wanting her to leave.

"Ain't no doubt he needed to be locked up in a nut house," she said. "Standin' out in the street, tryin' to be a traffic cop and all. But he wuzn't mean, or nothin'. I heard the county's gonna have to bury him. Sad thing. Um, um, real sad."

"Yes, it is. Sad things happen every day," I said. "Are we ready to go, guys?"

We drove back to Joe Bob's place in silence. The Cadillac's tires crunched the pea gravel as Bernie pulled in behind Joe Bob's truck.

"I'd better be getting home," Bernie said.

"No, don't go yet," Joe Bob said. "It's still early."

He led us around the side of the double-wide to a wrought iron table and chairs, then went to get three more beers.

"It's nice out here," I said.

"I come out here a lot at night," Joe Bob said. "There's always a breeze, seems like. The cat comes with me. He catches bugs, and I think about things."

I assumed he was about to drop his bomb.

"I think about you guys sometimes," he said.

"Get out," Bernie said.

"Yeah, I do every now and then."

"I appreciate that, Joe Bob, and I'm sure Bernie does, too," I said.

"Sure I do, but I need to know your final posture on the problem at hand," Bernie said. "I have to get the matter settled in my mind once and for all."

"I don't want to go to prison," Joe Bob said. "I just want to live my life."

Chapter Four

I was about to climb the porch steps when I heard someone call my name; it was almost a whisper. Beth was hurrying across the street toward me. She was wearing short shorts and tennis shoes. She walked under a streetlight, and I could tell she wasn't wearing a bra.

"Beth, what are you doing here?"

"I called earlier, and Samantha told me you were out with your old buddies. I've been waiting for you, because I thought you might need someone to talk to."

"Thanks, but I'm fine."

"Go for a walk with me?" she said.

"Why not."

"Matt, I know you weren't close to your mom, but I also think I can tell when you're hurting. I saw it in your eyes at the funeral."

"I'm fine. Mom's death was a shock. Now there's this void. I guess that's natural."

Beth took my hand and laced her fingers with mine. That had

been a habit of hers back when we had just started dating in high school. I remembered that her hands had always been warm and soft. It was something I had always liked about her.

"I still care for you, Matt."

"You didn't seem to care for me when you told me you wanted a divorce."

She stopped and faced me. Nobody could look as sincere as Beth when she put on that face.

"I miss you," she said, and slid my hand under her tee shirt. "I'm lonely."

"I'm sure you'll get over it," I said, retrieving my hand.

"Kiss me for old time's sake."

I wasn't sure why I did it, but I pulled her to me and kissed her. She leaned into me and returned the kiss. I had forgotten how much I liked the way she did that, and I was almost lost in the moment. Then, my common sense returned.

"This is ridiculous, Beth! If you're lonely, go find someone who can make you happy. That obviously isn't me."

"How do you know?" she said.

"This conversation is over. I can't imagine why you're behaving this way, but you can forget it. In case it's slipped your mind in the last few seconds, my mother has just been buried. I'm not in the mood to play games."

"I'm not playing games, Matt. I miss you. There's been a hole in my heart since our divorce. You can't imagine how lonely I am. I need you."

"I'm sure you haven't been sitting at home, watching television with your mother every night since you came back to Martinsville."

"I've had dates, but none of them meant anything. Accepting an invitation to dinner or a movie just meant getting out of the house; something to do."

"Well, maybe you'll get lucky and your Prince Charming will come along when you least expect it."

"I hate it when you're sarcastic. I guess this means you're involved with someone."

"No, I'm not. My dates are strictly social. I have no desire to be in a serious relationship now. I may never want that again."

"I see."

"I don't think you do see. You killed everything inside me, Beth. You were my life, and then you were gone."

"I hardly saw you. You were never at home. All you did was work, or so you said. How could I have been your life when we were never together?"

"That's a cheap shot. You knew how demanding my job was. It was either work like a dog, or get out. I wasn't going to do it forever."

"You did it long enough for me to wonder what you were doing late at night. I decided nobody could keep up that pace, and that you must have been having an affair. Were you?"

I shook my head. "I was working my ass off for us; for our future."

It puzzled me that she hadn't mentioned any of this to me when she told me she wanted a divorce. She had simply told me that our marriage wasn't working.

"I had an affair, you know," she said.

"No, I didn't know, but I suspected it. I couldn't imagine what I had done to make you turn so cold."

"It lasted for nearly a year, but it didn't mean anything. I was just trying to get back at you. You made me feel unwanted. I needed to feel desirable, and I was afraid I was going to lose you."

"That makes sense. You had an affair to keep that from happening."

"I should have known I'd be wasting my time trying to talk to you," she said.

"Let's call it a night, Beth. I'm tired and I don't want to argue."

Beth had opened old wounds—wounds that had lost some of their hurt over the past three years, but hadn't completely healed. I just wanted her to go away and leave me alone. It was difficult to look at her, even under a dim streetlight, and to feel her slightest touch without feeling that raw pain anew. I walked her back to her car and turned to leave.

"Goodnight, Matt," she said. There were tears in her voice.

"Take care of yourself," I said.

Damn, I wanted to be in Denver. I was miserable for too many reasons to count, and I was stuck here in Podunk Junction with all its misfits. Kicking off my shoes, I went out onto the patio. I had loved to camp out back here when I was a kid. The back yard was screened from the stars by interlocking branches of old maple trees, and it was dark as pitch.

I heard something on the far end of the patio, and ventured a little closer. A night light in the hall leaked a dim stream through a window, and as I got closer I realized the source of the noise. Two nude bodies writhed on a chaise lounge next to a big pot of geraniums. I started backing away as quietly as I could, but I stumbled over a wicker ottoman.

"Damn you, Matt," my sister hissed.

"I'm sorry," I said, trying to feel my way back to the kitchen door.

"There is no privacy around this place," she said, grabbing her robe.

"I said I was sorry."

"Oh, no!" Ron said.

"What's the matter?" Sam sounded as if she wanted to slap her husband.

"I think I just stepped on my glasses," Ron said.

I hurried into the kitchen. Sam was right behind me. She flipped on the light, and her eyes spat fire at me. Her hair was a rat's nest, and she had fastened the buttons of her robe in the wrong holes. I couldn't help grinning at her.

"I hope you realize I had no idea you were out there," I said.

"I don't know anything of the kind. All I know is that you've shown nothing but disrespect for our mother from the minute you got off the plane."

"What does this have to do with our mother, and what did I do that was disrespectful?"

"For starters you went out drinking and carousing with the scum of the earth. And you took Uncle Stuart along and got him smashed. Aunt Lela Maude was beside herself. She needed her husband, but you took him out drinking."

"Uncle Stuart invited himself. And who are you calling scum?"

"That piece of trailer trash, your grease monkey buddy and Bernie Zuckerman who should have been at home with his wife and child."

"We were not carousing, and Joe Bob's not scum."

"I'm ashamed for my husband to see how my brother behaves. He couldn't believe you left the family the minute Mom's funeral was over to go out and do the town again."

"I'm going to bed."

Sam grabbed my arm.

"I'm not through talking to you. You had no right to sneak up on Ron and me. We thought we were alone. How would that make you feel?"

"Good night, Sam."

Chapter Five

My sister was still on her tirade the next morning. She didn't like the way Trudy had cooked her eggs, and she was mad because Uncle Stuart and I were a few minutes late coming down to breakfast.

"Good mornin', Mathoo," Aunt Lela Maude drawled. "Did you sleep well?"

"Yes, thank you, I did."

"You probably passed out from guzzling so much liquor," Sam said.

"Give it a rest, Sam," I said.

"I will not give it a rest," she spat. "You need to show your family some respect. Your behavior is deplorable! And don't think I don't know about your little rendezvous with that witch you were married to, because I do. She called here, and when I told her you were out, she drove here and parked across the street to wait for you. Did she try to seduce you?"

"This is uncalled for," I said. "I think we're all in shock over Mom's death. I admit that I'm a little on edge. I apologize if I've been terse with any of you, and for not being as attentive as I could have been, but my family doesn't hold a monopoly on feeling low. My old friends matter, too."

"Your old friends being that piece of trailer trash and Bernie Zuckerman who thinks he owns Martinsville. He should have stayed up north; nobody likes him, pushy little bald Jew."

"You don't know anything about my friends, Samantha, and when did you become such a bigot?"

Ron hadn't said a word; neither had my aunt or uncle. The three of them were looking down at their plates.

"I think it would be best for everyone if I stayed somewhere else until it's time to meet with the lawyer," I said, and got up from the table. "You have my cell phone number if you need me."

"You'll need a ride," Uncle Stuart said. "I'll drive you wherever you're going."

I threw a few things into a bag and met Uncle Stuart on the front porch.

"That girl needs help," he said. "She's too young to carry on that way."

"I'm afraid she came by part of it honestly," I said.

"Ah, Matt, you can't tell me anything about your dear mother that I don't already know," Uncle Stuart said. "Eloise was a beautiful woman; she definitely was that. Samantha resembles her a great deal, I think. Eloise was very well thought of, as you know, and she did, indeed, deserve accolades for the hard work she did for Martinsville, but she had a streak, as they say. I'm sure you were quite aware of it, growing up under her parenting."

I shouldn't have made a statement that led my uncle to believe I wanted to hear him criticize my mother, so I changed the subject and got into the car.

"I guess I'll go to The Greystone," I said. "It's downtown on Main Street."

"I've stayed at The Greystone," Uncle Stuart said. "It was a long time ago. Back then, it was topnotch."

"I don't care what it's like as long as it's clean. It's within walking distance of a couple of decent restaurants, and I'll be leaving in a few days."

"I suppose you're right. If I didn't think I'd catch it from Lela Maude, I'd check in with you."

I had no doubt that my uncle would have enjoyed a respite away from the house. At The Greystone, he would have been free to drink his bourbon and smoke his cigars with nobody to interfere, but Uncle Stuart was a man steeped in tradition. He would return to his wife and her family to assume the role of benevolent patriarch and take the helm to keep things on an even keel until he could escape that unpleasant duty in a respectable manner.

I checked in, bought a newspaper, and took a rickety elevator up to the third floor. When I opened the door to my room, I was almost overwhelmed by the strong air freshener that permeated it. The window air-conditioning unit hummed and was doing its job, but I had to open the other window to get rid of the choking floral smell. I looked down on Main Street and watched the slow, lazy movement of the small southern town. Nobody hurried down the street with briefcase in hand. The few pedestrians strolled at a leisurely pace, some stopping to pass the time-of-day with people they knew. No horns honked, and nobody yelled obscenities. I was bored, and I missed the city.

Several things nagged at me. I knew it was ridiculous, but I was angry at my mother for dying. The way Sam was behaving grated on my nerves, too, but there was something else that was eating away at me. I needed to leave The Greystone and go someplace away from Martinsville to digest everything that had happened.

Joe Bob answered his phone with a mouthful of something. "Kincaid's Garage."

"It's Matt, Joe Bob. You must be eating lunch. I'll call back later."

"I can talk and eat at the same time. What's on your mind?"

"I was wondering if your uncle still has that cabin at the lake, and if you think he might rent it to me. I have a few days before I meet with Mother's attorney, and I was thinking it would be nice to get away from town."

"Yeah, he's still got it, but he won't rent it to you. He sold his house in town and moved into the cabin about a year ago, but there's plenty of room. Would you mind if I tagged along? It might do me some good to git away from this place for a few days; settle things in my head. I promise to stay out of your way and let you do all the cogitatin' you want to, or whatever it is you lawyers call thinkin'."

"You won't bother me at all. If your uncle gives the okay, maybe Bernie'd like to go, too."

"I'll call Uncle Jake right now. He'll be glad to have us, and he won't bother you neither. You call Bernard, and y'all come by my place. I'll drag out the fishin' gear."

Bernie picked me up at The Greystone a few hours later. I could tell by an offhand remark he made that he'd had to be pretty crafty to get approval for this guy trip. I had the impression that his wife kept him on a fairly short leash.

Joe Bob had the fishing gear and two large coolers loaded into the back of his pickup when we pulled up in front of his trailer.

"I'm almost ready," he said. "Just let me put out food and water for my cat and grab my good luck cap."

I didn't think he sounded like a guy who needed to clear his head. He sounded more like an excited kid who was about to take off for summer camp.

He tended to the cat, stopping to stroke its fur a time or two, then donned an orange cap with a big black "T" on it.

"That's your good luck cap, huh?" I said.

"Yep, it's my Bill Dance cap. Y'all know who he is, don't you?"

We admitted that we didn't, and Joe Bob looked astonished at our ignorance.

"He's only the bass fishin' champ in the whole U.S., and he happens to be from Tennessee."

"Interesting," Bernie said, rolling his eyes.

We finished loading the truck and headed for the lake. I was hoping this short hiatus with no distractions would be beneficial to all three of us. We would be able to share our thoughts about the accident until we were all on the same page. Then, maybe we could heal.

"We'd better stop and stock up on supplies," I said. "We can't just drop in on your uncle empty-handed."

"We'll stop at McCauley's General Store," Joe Bob said. "It's real close to the lake, and it'll have everything we'll need. Oh, I almost forgot to tell you guys, Uncle Jake's not at the cabin. I caught up with him on his cell. He told us to make ourselves at home and said he was sorry to miss us."

The general store was much bigger than it looked from the road. It reminded me of the shotgun houses built in the early twentieth century in cities—long, straight, and narrow. The store extended back into the woods, and was surrounded by tall pines. It was divided into sections: grocery items, hunting and fishing gear, and hardware.

The proprietor stopped what he was doing when he saw Joe Bob enter the store.

"Well, Joe Bob Kincaid, I haven't seen you in a coon's age."

"Hey, Mister McCauley; how you been?" Joe Bob and the storekeeper shook hands.

"I can't complain. Business has been real good lately. How about yourself?"

Joe Bob shifted his weight from one foot to the other.

"I'm fine as frog hair." He laughed. "You seen Uncle Jake lately?"

"Matter of fact, I saw him yesterday morning. He and another fellow stopped by the store on their way to Knoxville. Said they were going to see a bass boat exposition. They won't be back until Sunday."

"Yeah, I knew he wasn't here," Joe Bob said. "I hate to miss him, but we decided to come at the last minute."

The storekeeper glanced at Bernie and me. He seemed to be waiting for an introduction.

"Oh, uh, Mister McCauley, these are my old friends Matt Stevenson and Bernard Zuckerman."

"Glad to make your acquaintance. You fellows plan to stay at Jake's place, do you?"

"Yeah," Joe Bob said. "He told me where he keeps a spare key in case I happen to show up when he's not here."

Mister McCauley laughed. "I'm sure that key's long since rusted. You know he keeps it under a flat rock. You'd better take mine. I'll give you the key to the shed, too. You do want to use the boat, don't you?"

"Sure thing," Joe Bob said, pocketing the keys.

We filled the coolers with ice, and loaded soft drinks, beer, and perishables. Then, we headed for the cabin.

"Here comes the fun part," Joe Bob said.

He took a hard left turn onto a dirt road. Deep tire tracks had dug into the road when it was muddy, leaving a high ridge in the center. There was nothing resembling a shoulder on the sides of the trail. Tree branches and bramble bushes brushed the pickup unmercifully as we chugged along.

"I think you missed a hole back there," Bernie said.

Joe Bob had just driven into a deep one, bouncing us all off the seat, and Bernie's wire-rims had been knocked off.

"Sorry, Bernard. You're welcome to drive the rest of the way if you think you can do a better job."

When we reached the cabin, it wasn't what I had expected. It was crude, built of wood with a tin roof, but it had some interesting touches. The front porch ran the width of the cabin. Four rough-hewn rocking chairs were scattered across it, and colorful plant baskets hung from the rafters. A fieldstone fireplace covered an entire wall of the living room, and over the mantle was one of Uncle Jake's prize catches: a big-mouth bass that must have weighed nearly ten pounds. The kitchen was equipped with all the necessities, plus a solid oak table and four matching chairs.

Bernie surveyed the place. "Where do we sleep?" he said.

"Well, there's Uncle Jake's bedroom, and there's twin beds up in the loft," Joe Bob said, nodding toward the open stairs. "Oh, and this sofa makes into a bed. Take your pick."

"You take your uncle's room. Bernie and I will sleep in the loft," I said.

We put everything away and pulled the boat out of the shed. Joe Bob hitched it to the back of the pickup, and we took off for the lake, determined to catch our supper.

It wasn't until we were about to put the boat into the water that Bernie showed his ignorance of fishing. I had figured he would watch Joe Bob or me and play it by ear, but no.

"We seem to have a small problem here," he said.

"What?" Joe Bob said.

"I don't know if you've noticed, but there are three fishermen and only two seats."

"It's a bass boat, a stump jumper, Bernard. Don't worry about it; we'll all fit. You guys take the seats, and I'll sit on the cooler."

Joe Bob steered the boat into the water, and when he came to a spot where he thought the fish might be biting, he cut the motor.

The setting was serene. The water was calm, and the only sounds to be heard were the light lapping of water at its banks and hushed sounds made by creatures of the woodsy lake habitat. It seemed to me the perfect place to broach the subject that I knew was haunting the three of us. I was trying to think of the best way to introduce Jimmy Banks's unfortunate demise when Bernie decided to develop an interest in fishing.

"What's that fancy lure you have there, Joe Bob?" Bernie said.

"This, Bernard, is a Charlie O. It's hand-carved. You want to try it?"

"No. I'll just use the one that's on my line. The fish might prefer this lure over your fancy one."

"Y'all cast over there around some of them stick-ups," Joe Bob said. "I guarantee you'll git a bite."

I felt a tap on my line almost instantly, and reeled in the slack, giving my rod a deliberate jerk. The fish jumped out of the water, flashing silver in the sun, and the lake glittered. I was afraid it was going to outmaneuver me, but I was living in the moment without a single care. I must have done things right, because seconds later, Joe Bob scooped the fish into the net and held it up for Bernie to see.

"This smallmouth'll weigh upwards of six pounds," Joe Bob said.

We caught our limit in less than an hour. Joe Bob and I had been catching fish as fast as we could throw our lines into the water, but Bernie couldn't land one no matter how hard he tried. It seemed he was simply out of his element.

Chapter Six

We cleaned the fish and went about preparing our meal. Joe Bob cooked, and I set the table. Then, Bernie and I plopped down on a couple of bar stools and drank beer while Joe Bob proceeded to fry everything in sight.

"I think I'll toss a salad," Bernie said. "That fried stuff smells good, but I have a feeling the grease is going to do a number on my stomach."

"What are you talking about?" I laughed. "We only have fried fish, fried potatoes, and fried corncakes. It's a feast fit for kings."

And indeed, it was. The three of us ate like prisoners on death row. We cleaned up the kitchen, and Joe Bob and I retired to the rockers on the front porch. Bernie took a fishing magazine and headed to the bathroom.

Joe Bob pulled the red and white box from his shirt pocket, shook out a smoke, and lit it. He inhaled deeply, then blew out twin trails of smoke through his nostrils.

"You doin' okay, sport?" he asked.

I could feel him looking at me, so I turned to let him see the truth in my face.

"I'm alright. I was never very close to my mom. It's hard to explain, but I really miss her. Empty inside, I guess, is the best way to describe the way I feel."

"I know what you mean. My mama was a saint, and I reckon I'll miss her until I die. You remember what a mean bastard my daddy was; how he used to beat the hell out of me. He left a hole in my heart just like Mama did when they died in that wreck. I don't think I shed a tear at the funeral, but nothin' ever hurt me that much. I still miss 'em, and it's been twelve years."

"Dad didn't come to Mother's funeral," I said. "He called though; talked to Sam. She probably told him not to come."

Joe Bob didn't say anything. He just continued to rock and smoke.

"Do you believe in God?" I said. I wasn't sure why I asked.

"Well, yeah, I do. Just look around you."

"How about heaven and hell?"

Joe Bob took a deep drag of the Marlboro. "Yeah, I believe there's a heaven and a hell, but I'm not much in the mood to discuss the hereafter right now."

The screen door spring squeaked, and Bernie came out on the porch.

"Everthing come out okay, Bernard?" Joe Bob said.

"You know, you can be downright crude when you really try," Bernie said.

"Listen," I said.

Everybody got still.

"I don't hear anything," Bernie said. "It was probably the wind."

What sounded like moaning, followed by shouting echoed up from the hollow through the trees.

"What could that be?" I said.

"I'll tell you what it is," Joe Bob said. "It's them crazy snake handlers."

"Snake handlers?" I said.

"There's a snake cult down the road a piece. It's not far from the store. We drove past it on our way up here. It's not easy to see 'cause it's stuck back in the woods off the road."

"Get outta town," Bernie said.

"I'll prove it to you," Joe Bob said. "Come on."

We jumped into the truck and started down the hill toward the noise. A few minutes later we were pulling into a graveled parking lot crowded with mud-spattered cars and pickup trucks.

The church was a white clapboard structure. It wasn't very large, and the exterior looked like many little country churches. Bright lights shone through open windows. We sat in the truck, listening to the strange noises pouring out into the night, blending with the guttural croaks of frogs and the hum of insects.

"What do you say we go inside?" Joe Bob said.

"I don't see how we could pass it up," I said.

"Wait a minute," Bernie said. "Do you think they really do handle live snakes?"

"I'm bettin' they do," Joe Bob said. "Mister McCauley told Uncle Jake the state police have raided 'em three or four times. Let's go see."

"Guys, I'm not sure about this," Bernie said.

"You sound like a little girl, Bernard. Come on."

Bernie took a deep breath and climbed out of the pickup.

We threaded our way through the maze of vehicles toward the church. The double doors were propped open. We walked in and sat down in the back pew.

There was a dais down front where four men were sort of wandering around, waving their arms in wild gestures. They seemed to be taking turns shouting out strange things to the congregation at large.

"Come on, holy ghost!" shouted the one wearing a seedy-looking black suit slick from wear. I took him to be the ringleader, a preacher of sorts.

Bernie jumped and sucked in his breath.

"I feel His presence!" yelled a different man. He looked about eighty years old, and he was dressed in a short-sleeved, plaid shirt and denim overalls, sporting neatly pressed creases.

"I feel the spirit! I feel it!" screamed an adolescent girl who sat a couple of rows in front of us.

She sprang from her seat and ran out into the aisle where she started yelling indistinguishable utterings and crying. She began flailing her arms and fell to the floor, rolling around as though she were having a fit. Then, she became quite still. She lay supine on the floor, and her head lolled back toward us. I was sitting next to the aisle, so I had a bird's-eye view. Her eyes rolled up in her head, and saliva dribbled from the corner of her mouth. For a minute I thought she was dead. Then, suddenly, she wiped her mouth with the back of her hand and smiled. She got up and returned to her seat beside an older woman who embraced her.

Joe Bob wore a fixed stare, his mouth agape.

A guy down close to the front stood and began speaking in tongues. He was staring up at the ceiling and waving his arms.

Bernie leaned closer to me, craning his neck to get a better look.

"I see the snake box," he whispered. "Look down there at the base of that platform."

I saw the wooden box and guessed that it probably did contain the snakes. There was so much going on that I nearly missed the reference made to the state police by yet a different leader.

"He thinks we're the fuzz," Joe Bob whispered.

About that time, two more people jumped up and started yelling and carrying on like maniacs. Amid this chaos, the fourth leader decided it was his turn to speak. He pulled a rumpled handkerchief from the breast pocket of his worn navy suit and mopped his face.

"I feel the presence of lost souls!" he thundered over the din. "Don't let this opportunity pass you by, sinners. Tomorrow may be too late."

"He means us," I said. "He's looking straight at us."

Bernie squirmed in his seat like a three-year-old.

Just then, a man sitting directly in front of me turned to face me. His dark eyes bore into mine.

"Brother, are you saved?" he said.

The question startled me, but I managed to assure him that I was. He nodded and turned around as though my answer pacified him.

A guy about our age jumped from his seat and ran to the front of the church.

"The spirit's with me!" he shouted. "I feel it!"

"Hallelujah! Praise the Lord!" the preacher bellowed.

He raised his hand heavenward, and a hush fell over the congregation.

"We've been prayin' for you in earnest, Brother Harold," he said, his voice cracking with emotion. "Praise God! And now you're ready to test your faith?"

"I am."

"Good Lord, they're really gonna do it," Joe Bob whispered.

"Let's get out of here," Bernie said.

"Wait a minute," Joe Bob said. "I've gotta see this."

"Brother Harold, do you truly believe?" the preacher said.

"I do."

The preacher bent down and raised the lid of the wooden box. This couldn't really be happening, but it was. He lifted up a diamondback rattler. The snake jerked and writhed; it began winding itself around the preacher's left arm.

"Prove your faith," the preacher said to the now frightened-looking man, thrusting the agitated snake toward him.

The young man extended his arms to take hold of the snake, then jerked them back.

"Remember, this is your testimony, a test of your faith," the preacher said in a calming voice. "There's nothin' for you to fear."

The young man reached for the snake again, and the preacher disentangled it from his own arm, allowing it to wrap around that of the newly-saved.

"I can't!" the young man cried.

But it was too late. The rattler had already struck him on the neck.

"I'm dyin! I'm dyin!" the young man shouted, and fell to the floor.

The preacher looked down at the young man, then out at the congregation. Tears glistened in his dark eyes. Then, stark anger shone in his face as he began berating his flock. Opening the box, he reached in and started grabbing snakes.

"Blasphemers and sinners will all surely go to hell!" he trumpeted.

He began slinging snakes in every direction. People were screaming, and everybody was scrambling for the door. Bernie stood stock still.

"Move your ass, Bernard," Joe Bob hissed.

Bernie had somehow gotten in front of us and was blocking the aisle. He clutched his chest, then started hyperventilating.

"Go, Bernie!" I said.

Bernie was frozen to the spot, so Joe Bob grabbed one arm, and I grabbed the other, and we hauled him out of the church. We had barely stuffed Bernie into the truck when the mad preacher reached the front steps and threw the last snake into the crowd.

Joe Bob sprayed gravel getting out of the parking lot. He sped up the blacktop and swerved onto the dirt road that led to the cabin. It seemed to take forever to get to the circular drive in front of our safe haven.

Nobody had said a word on the ride back. I think I had been holding my breath. Joe Bob heaved a sigh and got out of the pickup.

"We're home, children," he said. "Let's go inside and try to settle our nerves."

I had to practically pull Bernie out of the truck and drag him into the cabin. He was hyperventilating, and crying at the same time. I deposited him on a couch in the living room, and Joe Bob found a paper sack for him to breathe into until he was back to normal.

"I could use a real drink," I said. "We don't have anything but beer, do we?"

"We don't, but I'll bet Uncle Jake does," Joe Bob said, taking off in search of spirits.

Bernie was finally breathing normally. He curled into a corner of the couch and hugged himself like a shy child.

Minutes later, Joe Bob returned with a bottle of Wild Turkey and three jelly glasses. He did the honors. Bernie came off the couch and grabbed the first glass with a trembling hand before Joe Bob had a chance to fill the others. He downed it in one gulp and slapped the glass on the coffee table like cowboys in saloons did in old movies.

"Hit me again," he said.

Joe Bob accommodated him.

"I didn't think you indulged in hard liquor," I said.

"I don't, but I need this," Bernie said.

Joe Bob pulled a rubber band from his pocket and put his hair into a ponytail.

"I tell you, I just can't get that little girl's face out of my mind," Bernie said. "That sweet looking little girl couldn't have been more than thirteen or fourteen years old."

"That was awful," I agreed, "but what about that guy on the floor? Do you think the snakebite killed him?"

"I'd say he's got a helluva good chance of bein' dead. What a bunch of lunatics," Joe Bob said.

"If somebody didn't rush him to an emergency room, I think he has to be dead," I said.

"You know, I think he really wanted to handle that snake," Bernie said.

"Oh, you bet he did," Joe Bob said, "but them people ain't gonna change. That crazy religion, or whatever you want to call it; it's their way of life. It beats anything I ever seen."

"The whole bunch belongs behind bars," Bernie said. "They murdered that guy just the same as if they'd shot him."

"I gotta have a smoke," Joe Bob said. "Let's take this party outside. I wouldn't want to foul the air in here. Bernard might not be able to sleep."

We took our glasses and the bottle of Wild Turkey out to the porch. Joe Bob poured more bourbon, and we claimed our respective rockers. We were sitting in what I thought was communal silence for a few minutes, sipping bourbon, each with his private thoughts. Then, things seemed to get nasty for no apparent reason.

"You changed when you got married, Bernard," Joe Bob said.

"Changed? I haven't changed. What are you talking about?"

"Yes, you have. You used to go along with anything me and

Matt wanted to do. You're a different guy. Everthing's gotta be done right by the book. Tell him, Matt."

"Hey, leave me out of this. I don't live here anymore."

"Bernard, when you moved down here, you was kinda shy. You was a real nerd 'til me and Matt decided to save your butt. Then, you turned into a regular guy, and we did everthing together; just the three of us."

"I might remind you that we're not in high school anymore. Men in their thirties don't usually do everything together. They have responsibilities."

"When's the last time you called me to meet you for a beer? Never. If Matt's mom hadn't passed away, we wouldn't be sittin' here together."

"Guys," I said, "this is ridiculous. We're not here to argue. Let's relax and enjoy one another's company."

"It's difficult to relax when one is being ridiculed for having a family, running a respectable business, and doing things by the book," Bernie said.

"Don't be gittin' your panties in a wad, Bernard. Have another drink," Joe Bob said.

"No, thank you," Bernie said. He scooted his rocker out of the semicircle we had arranged for easy conversation, and stared into the night.

"Come on, Bernard. Forgit I said anything."

"What kind of man wants to spend his leisure time with a damn cat?" Bernie said.

"You guys stop it right now," I said. "We went our separate ways after high school, but we're friends; we haven't seen one another in a long time. I value our friendship."

"Let's turn in," Joe Bob said. "It's been a weird night."

Chapter Seven

I had to help Bernie up the stairs. Neither of us was feeling any pain. We bunked down, and I turned off the lamp between our beds. I had started to drift off when Bernie decided he wanted to talk.

"I wasn't really alive until I married Lee Ann," he said. "She's the best thing that ever happened to me."

"That's great, Bernie."

"Yeah, she keeps the books for my business, she's a wonderful mother, and a great little homemaker."

"Pretty, too," I said.

"And on top of all that, she teaches ballet at Miss Audrey's Dance Studio two afternoons a week."

"She sounds like a keeper," I said, wishing he would be quiet and go to sleep.

"You know, we toyed with the idea of leaving Martinsville and moving back to Philly. That's where she's from, too. To be honest with you, learning that she was from my hometown was what sparked my interest in her; well, that and the fact that she's Jewish."

"Is that right?"

"Yeah, but after the baby came, we decided Martinsville would be an ideal place to rear a child. I can't think of another place so sheltered."

"That's for sure," I mumbled, feeling myself fade out of the conversation.

"Just listen to me, will you." Bernie said. "I'm probably boring you stiff."

"Not at all," I lied.

"Matt?"

"Yeah?"

"I don't know why Joe Bob decided to bash me tonight, but I should have shrugged it off. He's a good guy, and he had a shitty childhood. I shouldn't have made that remark about him and his cat. It was juvenile; I just wanted to sting him back."

"Maybe he just needed something, or somebody to bash. He probably has a lot of different feelings at war inside him, and lashing out at a handy target was a release. He'll be in a better mood in the morning."

"I hope you're right."

Bernie began snoring, and that was precisely what I wanted to do. But now I was wide awake. Events of the last few days were standing in line to keep sleep at arm's length. My mother's death and Sam's acerbic attitude made me sad more than anything. Then, there was the revelation that Beth wanted me back. But the thing that bothered me most was being a party to the unintentional killing of a human being. I knew Joe Bob's pain was real, and that he was trying to push it away. A moral conundrum was eating away at my old friend.

Another thing about small towns: unpleasant things got swept under rugs. Things like closet alcoholism, wife beating, small-time embezzlement, and adultery were hush-hush. If a young unmarried woman became pregnant, she was sent away on a lengthy vacation. Who would care how Jimmy Banks died? It seemed to me there was no truth in small towns.

I tried meditation techniques I had read about to make my mind go blank, to relax and feel that I was light; maybe floating. Finally, I was lulled by the rhythm of Bernie's snoring, and I was gone.

Birds heralded the dawn, and minutes later daylight showed itself through the window across the loft. I shook myself awake, got into a pair of shorts, and went down to make coffee. The stronger, the better for me, so I put in an extra scoop. Gulping a cup of the brew and a little juice, I slipped out the front door.

I jogged down the dirt road, feeling sluggish. It was a terrible place to run; riddled with ruts and holes. If I didn't watch what I was doing, I'd end up with a sprained ankle. By the time I made it to the blacktop, I decided it wasn't worth the effort. A little creek meandered through a meadow that paralleled the dirt road, and I decided to climb a padlocked gate and follow the stream, taking the scenic route back to the cabin.

I trudged along a cow-path that ran along the creek bank. After a while I realized I would have to make a pretty sharp left to get back to the cabin, so I headed across the meadow. A herd of cows lazed under some shade trees. They ignored me as I walked past them toward the fence I would have to negotiate.

I heard a muffled noise behind me and turned to see what it was. A huge Hereford bull was snorting and pawing the ground. I sensed that I was the source of his disgruntlement, because he started toward me, shaking his head and going into a fast trot. Common sense told me not to make a false move, but when he let out a bellow, panic struck, and I dashed toward the fence, barely beating him. I couldn't possibly jump it; it was too high. Grabbing a metal post, I jammed one foot into the woven wire and pulled myself up. I slung one leg over a strand of rusty barbed wire that guarded the top of the fence and heaved myself forward. Hitting the ground in a run and looking back just once, I saw the bull pawing up a cloud of dust and banging his horns into the fencepost. With my heart hammering and legs pumping, I didn't stop until I reached the cabin. I dropped down on the porch steps to catch my breath, and that was when I saw a gash on my left inner thigh.

"Hey!" I yelled.

"Hey, yourself," Joe Bob called.

"I could use a little help," I said. "Do we have a first aid kit?"

That brought both of my cohorts outside. They stood on the porch, staring at my bloody thigh like it was some sort of novelty.

"How'd you do that?" Bernie said.

"I caught it on a strand of barbed wire, trying to outrun a mad bull."

"Uncle Jake don't have no bull," Joe Bob said. "He don't have any cattle."

"Maybe I was on somebody else's property. Do we have a first aid kit, or not?"

Joe Bob went into the cabin and came back with the kit. He knelt down to examine my wound.

"I don't think you'll die from this," he said. "Looks like just a scratch."

He pulled out a bottle of alcohol and some gauze pads.

"This'll prob'ly hurt more than the barbed wire did," he said, and began cleaning the wound.

"Oh, shit! That smarts!"

"It'll stop in a minute. When'd you have a tetanus shot?"

"I don't remember."

"Try hard. I'd hate to cut our fishin' trip short 'cause we had to take you to a doctor."

He poured iodine on the wound and bandaged it.

Bernie seemed to have lost interest in my injury. He sat in his rocker, eating a plate of fruit. There were a few small things about Bernie that annoyed me, and his self-absorbed attitude was one of them.

"You sure you can't remember?" Joe Bob said.

"Not for certain. I think I had one several years ago. Do you think I need to see a doctor?"

Joe Bob scratched his head and frowned. It was clear that he didn't like what he was about to tell me.

"Yeah, I reckon you'd better. Let's go down to the store and see if Mr. McCauley knows where to find one."

Bernie was miffed. He had wanted another chance to try his luck at fishing. But he had to settle for the privilege of calling his wife from Mr. McCauley's landline. Reception out here in the boonies was so poor that he had given up trying to call her from his cell phone.

None of my family had called me, so I pushed down my pride and called Sam to make sure everything was all right at the house.

"Well," she said, "are you enjoying your stay at The Greystone?"

"I'm not at The Greystone. I'm at Joe Bob's uncle's cabin. We've been fishing."

"I suppose you kidnapped Bernie, too."

"He's here."

"Well, don't rush back. The attorney called and rescheduled our appointment for Monday."

"What? He can't do that! I need to get back to Denver."

"He did do it, so I guess you'll have to wait like the rest of us. And by the way, everything's fine here in case you're interested."

"Glad to hear it. I'll talk to you later."

Mr. McCauley told us there was a clinic about forty miles north of where we were.

We were leaving the store when he called after us.

"Say, did you fellows happen to hear about the fracas up the road here last night?"

"What fracas?" Joe Bob said.

Bernie's ears started turning red the way they always did when he was caught with his hand in the cookie jar; this indiscretion being nothing more than feigning ignorance.

"Surely you remember when those so-called snake handlers were raided by the state police several months ago, Joe Bob," Mr. McCauley said.

"Yeah, seems like Uncle Jake did mention somethin' about that."

"Well, they're not so-called anymore. They brought a box of rattlers to their meeting last night. I could hear them yelling and carrying on something awful from my house. A young fellow supposedly took a leap of faith and missed his mark. Word is the diamondback struck him, and he dropped dead on the spot. Must not have been a true believer according to the guy they've got locked up."

"You said one guy," Joe Bob said. "How many was there?"

"I'm not sure. Somebody said there were three or four. I understand the police had a hard time getting into the church. Everyone was trying to escape at the same time. The guy they arrested was throwing snakes into the crowd all the way out to the parking lot. A few people got trampled, and there were several fender benders."

It was obvious to me that Joe Bob and Bernie were determined to play dumb, and I was anxious to get to the clinic, so I decided to put an end to the charade.

"Man, it's too bad we missed out on all that excitement," I said.

Mr. McCauley shook his head and laughed. "Never a dull moment out here in the sticks," he said. "You can't miss the clinic. Good luck to you."

"Why do I always get stuck sitting in the middle?" Bernie said.

"We put you there because we love you so much," I said.

He punched me.

"We saw a man get killed last night," he said.

I nodded. "That's two in one week."

Joe Bob turned on the radio.

The clinic sat right on the highway. It was a plain building with a gravel parking lot. The glass front door wore what appeared to be a permanent thick coat of white dust.

I filled out the form a receptionist passed through a glass window and took a seat in one of the straight-backed chairs. Bernie sat next to me and started working a crossword puzzle. Some small children were playing with blocks and plastic toys in a corner of the room. Joe Bob watched them for a few minutes, then gave me a pained look.

"I've gotta git out of here," he said, and left.

"Where do you think he's going?" I said.

"I don't know," Bernie said. "Maybe he just wants to be by himself to think. He might be about to change his mind."

"I've got to tell you that he's not the only one who's having a tough time with this. We should have gone to the cops, and we didn't. Now, I think it's too late. We could go to jail. All of our lives could be ruined, including Uncle Stuart's."

"Listen, Matt, you've got to stop talking this way. I didn't want to, but I've accepted Joe Bob's decision. My family means the world to me. I'm not willing to lose them, or my business. You and

I walked into this mess. If we had obeyed the law that night, we wouldn't be in this up to our necks."

"You're right. Let's drop it. Talking about it isn't getting us anywhere."

I certainly didn't want to talk about it, or think about it. My marriage had been a failure. Now, my career could be shot down because I was in the wrong place at the wrong time. The best thing to do for all of us would be to let sleeping dogs lie.

Chapter Eight

The clinic didn't make appointments. Patients signed in when they arrived and waited their turn. Lunch was whatever one bought from the vending machine down the hall, because nobody was willing to leave and take a chance on being skipped.

It was late afternoon before I was ushered into an examination room. A nurse who cleaned my wound wasn't as gentle as Joe Bob had been. She grasped the tape and ripped off the bandage in one fluid motion, and I knew she hadn't thought twice about yanking all the hair off my thigh. A tired-looking doctor examined the gash for all of five seconds. Then, he and I had the tetanus shot conversation. He ordered Nurse Ratched to dress my wound and give me the shot.

Bernie and Joe Bob had their eyes glued to the waiting room television, watching an infomercial when I returned. I had expected Joe Bob to be upset, but he appeared calm and in a decent mood.

"It's too late to go fishin'," he said. "We don't have anything to cook at the cabin. I found us a restaurant down the road that has a good-lookin' menu. It don't have a dress code, so we can go like we are."

"I usually dress better than this," Bernie said, "but I'm starved. This is a good idea."

"Sounds good to me," I said.

The name of the restaurant wasn't fancy: Ned's Place. I figured that was what made Joe Bob check it out. It was a sprawling affair. One large open room held a long bar in front of a mirrored wall and a dining room crowded with sturdy, wooden tables and chairs. A portable dance floor and a small stage with microphones filled a space at the end of the dining area.

"There must be some kind of floor show," I said.

"That should be a real treat," Bernie said.

There was a hostess stand but no hostess. We stood inside the door, waiting for someone to show up and seat us. Minutes later, a barmaid with Mae West white-blond hair and bosom to match swayed her hips toward us, balancing a tray of drinks. She funneled a puff of air from the corner of her red lips to dispense with a wisp of her mane.

"You boys been here before?" she said.

"No, we haven't," I said.

"You can grab any empty table you want," she said. "Get as close to the stage as you can. The show starts in a half hour, so the place'll be fillin' up in the next few minutes."

When the blond came to take our drink orders, I told her I'd like a Wild Turkey and club soda. Uncle Jake's bourbon had tasted pretty good to me.

"We don't have any hard liquor," she said. "You'll have to settle for wine or beer."

"Bring us a pitcher of beer while we look over the menu," Bernie said.

"Menu's over there on that chalkboard," she said, nodding toward it.

"Well, well," Bernie said, "grilled sea bass with fresh vegetables. That sounds good."

"I thought you was tired of fish," Joe Bob said.

"Perhaps I didn't make myself clear. This is hardly the same as breaded pan-fried fish. But I wonder where they got it; it can't be fresh."

"I think I'll have the chicken Florentine," I said.

"You two don't realize it, but you're gonna die whenever you're gonna die," Joe Bob said. "You drink your sissy bottles of water, and you exercise. I know you think a fried pork chop's got death and destruction wrote all over it. Speakin' of which, that's what I'm gonna have."

"Who's ready for some suds?" I said.

They shoved their mugs toward me, and we drank our beer and watched the room fill. The crowd was an eclectic bunch. I couldn't tell whether the group to our right was having a business dinner or a family reunion, but they filled three large round tables. The women were dressed to the nines, and the men wore suits. Other diners were attired in traditional country garb: house dresses, jeans, cutoffs, and overalls.

We were all pleased with the food and the bottle of chardonnay Bernie had ordered. Ned's Place had turned out to be a delight. I had expected the piped-in music to be rock or country, but it was old standards, just the thing for dinner background music.

Our conversation ebbed as we enjoyed the meal, and I began thinking how we had all changed since our teenage years: Joe Bob had developed into even more of a weird duck. His formal education had come to an abrupt halt upon his high school graduation. He was a self-taught mechanic, and from what Bernie told me, a very good one. His lifestyle and taste seemed to be at odds with one another. He had never married and seemed to enjoy the freedom of being single. I wasn't really sure I still knew who he was.

Bernie had gone to an Ivy League school, returned to Martinsville, and worked diligently to build his dry cleaning shop into a lucrative business. No more wild oats for him; he was a real family man, and if it were possible, he had grown more conservative than ever.

And me, I couldn't see that I had changed much since my high school days. Time and experience had added a modicum of sophistication, but that was about it. I didn't know how fate would treat me from now on, but I wouldn't look back.

"Wonder what the entertainment's gonna be?" Joe Bob said.

"Probably some fiddlers, sawing their arms off and a bunch of clodhoppers, dancing the Virginia reel," Bernie said. "They might even have some old guy, blowing into a jug."

"We might be surprised," I said. "My dinner was very good."

The lights dimmed, and a spotlight focused on center stage. An old geezer in cowboy attire stepped up to the microphone. Lifting the brim of his hat with a thumb, he smiled out at the audience.

"Hello out there," he said.

He waited several seconds and, cupping his ear, he said, "Is anybody there? Am I talkin' to an empty room?"

"Hello!" came from the back of the room.

A broad grin deepened the laugh wrinkles around his mustache; he was in his comfort zone.

"How y'all doin' tonight?"

Several jokers called out various responses.

"You're in for a special treat, boys and girls," he said, "because tonight we have with us a whole slew of Elvis impersonators."

Applause broke out, and he had to hold up his hands to quiet the crowd.

"I gotta tell you I've listened to every one of 'em, ladies and gents, and they all sound so much like the King that if you'll close your eyes, you'll think you're listenin' to Elvis hisself."

"I don't believe this," Bernie said.

"Quit bein' so high and mighty, Bernard. Give 'em a chance."

"Sorry, sorry," Bernie said.

The first entertainer wore Elvis threads, and his thick shock of dark hair was cut like that of a latter-day Presley. He hooked the strap of his guitar over his head and adjusted the mike. Strains of "Are You Lonesome Tonight?" filled the room, producing gasps of delight. This guy must have spent hours training himself to sing in the Elvis mode.

The emcee strolled back on stage, waiting for the applause to die down.

"What'd I tell you, folks?"

People were shouting for more, but the old cowboy held up his hands, letting it be known that he was still in charge.

"We're gonna hear just one song from each of these talented young men," he said. "Then, we're gonna vote on 'em."

He pumped the entertainer's hand and sent him off the stage to bring out the next contestant.

The next three singers were just okay, but the last of the tryouts was fantastic. He sang "Blue Suede Shoes". He looked like a very young Elvis, puffing out his cheeks with air and belching out the word "blue" with just the right emphasis. I figured he would be a shoo-in.

Two scantily-clad young women lugged a big applause meter onto the stage and struck sexy poses.

"Okay, boys and girls," the kicker shouted. "Y'all know how we do this."

He called each of the contestants out individually and asked for applause. The first contestant won hands down.

"I thought the last guy was a clear winner," I said.

"It wasn't the singer that won," Joe Bob said. "It was the song. Look at all the women in this room. They just love them slow songs."

"Well, what do you say, gentlemen?" Bernie said. "Have we had all the excitement we can stand for one evening?"

Nearly everyone had left except the well-dressed group. They were engaged in quiet conversation, sipping wine. One of the gentlemen went to the jukebox, dropped in some coins, and pushed a few buttons. Then, the lazy melody of "Mood Indigo" settled over the room, and I found that I was in no rush to leave.

"I'd be willing to share another bottle of wine if you guys are up to it," I said.

"That's all the wine I can handle," Joe Bob said. "Too much of that stuff gives me a headache, but I'll drink another beer with you."

"Bernie?"

"Okay, I'll go with the wine. It's too early to go to bed, and there's nothing to do back at the cabin."

A few couples were slow-dancing to romantic music, and I was relaxing for the first time since my plane landed.

"Now, you see, Bernard, this place didn't turn out to be so bad," Joe Bob said.

"No, it didn't, but you have to admit there are some strange people in this neck of the woods."

"You mean them people at the church. That's true enough, but this ain't our bailiwick, so we can't talk about 'em. Let the locals do that. It was okay for Mr. McCauley to tell us about it. People around here look up to him. He knows everthing that goes on around here; that's how folks git the news. We just listen. Okay?"

"You're the boss. Hey, check out that couple. They look like they just finished a crash course at an Arthur Murray studio. Lee Ann can dance like that, but she doesn't have much of a partner."

Collateral Justice

I was about to go drop some change into the jukebox, but a guy I assumed was one of the locals beat me to it. A nasal female voice started filling the room with a tearjerker. I glanced toward the guy's table. He and a couple of other men, all wearing wife-beaters, were sitting with a girl who might have been pretty if she'd had some grooming. All four wore lots of ink.

I was pouring more wine when one of the rough-looking guys and the girl got up. I thought they were headed for the dance floor, but they came over to our table. They were both giving Bernie the eye.

"Hey," the man said.

Bernie looked up. "Hello."

"My sister wants to dance with you."

"Me?" Bernie pointed to himself with a thumb.

"Yeah."

A nervous laugh bubbled from Bernie's throat.

"I'm flattered by the compliment," he said, looking at the girl, "but I'm afraid I'm not much of a dancer."

The girl looked disappointed. She shifted her weight from one foot to the other, calling attention to her hourglass figure which had been stuffed into a pair of dirty jeans. Her long, greasy hair hung down to her décolletage, and she curled a hank of it around her index finger, staring wantonly down at Bernie with pleading eyes.

"Aw, that don't matter," the brother said.

"No, really," Bernie said. "I honestly don't know how to dance. I'm sorry, but thanks for asking."

"Now, listen, I asked you nice-like. Eva here's got her heart set on dancin' with you."

"I always just loved bald-headed men," Eva said, then giggled. "Ain't nobody here but us. It's okay if you step on my toes. Honest."

"Why don't you go ahead and dance with her, Bernard?" Joe

Bob grinned. "I got a feelin' you ain't leavin' here 'til you do."

Bernie looked miserable, but he pushed back his chair and got up. He escorted Eva to the dance floor. Big brother appeared pleased as he watched.

The song coming from the jukebox was worse than its predecessor, and the girl wrapped both her arms around Bernie's neck and drew him into smothering range. Bernie stared past Eva's head into space and stumbled around the floor until the song finally ended. Then, he walked her back to her table and thanked her.

"We'd better go rescue him," I said.

"Yeah, I reckon we better," Joe Bob said.

Eva's brother got up and gave Bernie's hand a heartfelt pump. "Thank you kindly," he said. "We like to make sure our little sister gits everthang she wants."

Bernie nodded and backed away, bumping into a grinning Joe Bob. His exit from the restaurant was the fastest I had ever seen him move.

As soon as we were outside, he began taking in large gulps of air as if he had been swimming underwater.

"You looked like a real professional out there dancin' with that pair of tight jeans, Bernard."

"Very funny. Did you guys get a whiff of her?"

"Yep, and I didn't envy you a bit," I said.

"Well, this has been an interesting little getaway, but I'm looking forward to getting back to civilization and my family," Bernie said. "I wonder what my baby girl has learned to do while I've been gone."

Chapter Nine

The night was alive with sounds that could only be heard away from the hubbub of traffic. Joe Bob had flipped on the living room light when we got back to the cabin, and it shone through the screen door—a bright rectangle in the dark. We rocked in our chairs on the porch, watching hard-shelled bugs bang into the screen and fall on their backs. Their legs clawed the air in an effort to right themselves; only a few managed it. If Joe Bob noticed, he assisted the frantic insect. Bernie would have no part of it. He either scraped the bug off the porch with his shoe, or stepped on it.

"It was nice of your uncle to let us use his place," I said. "It's a different world out here."

"Oh, Uncle Jake was happy to let us stay here," Joe Bob said. "And you're right. It is different. Bein' out here's kinda like runnin' away. A guy can relax; not think about stuff."

It seemed to me that was exactly what we had been doing: running away. What should have been a meeting of the minds had turned out to be a fishing trip, an unbelievable church service, and a fiasco at a restaurant stuck out in the sticks. We were afraid to broach the subject that haunted us. I had thought we would replay the night of the accident, lay out all the pros and cons of facing the truth, and agree on what the next step should be. There was no way I could go back to Denver and pretend nothing had happened.

"Well," Bernie said, "since this is our last night here, I think we should have a nightcap. We'll replace the bottle of Wild Turkey and send your uncle a gift for the cabin. Lee Ann's good at choosing things like that. She'll come up with something that's perfect."

"That's a good idea," I said.

Joe Bob went inside and came back with the whiskey and three glasses.

"Where do you plan on stayin' when we git back to town, Matt?" he asked.

"I guess I'll try staying at the house and see how it goes. I'll be flying back to Denver on Monday."

"Well, if that don't work out, you're welcome to bunk at my place," he said.

What sounded like a muffled moan came through the screen.

"What was that?" I said.

"This place is beginning to spook me," Bernie said. "There are way too many strange things happening."

Joe Bob hurried inside, looking for the intruder. I put down my drink and followed him. He stood beside the bedroom closet, clutching a heavy brogan, poised to floor whoever was hiding inside.

"You'd better show yourself fast!" he said.

He flung open the door and waited.

"Am I gonna have to come in there and drag you out?"

Bernie had mustered the nerve to come inside and watch from the bedroom door.

We heard a sob from inside the closet, and Joe Bob dropped his weapon, knelt down, and stuck in his head.

"What the hell?" he said.

"What is it?" Bernie asked.

"A girl."

He crawled inside, and I could hear him making comforting noises. Then, he backed out on his knees, carrying a whimpering, very pregnant girl. He took her to the bed and carefully lowered her to it.

"Don't be afraid," he said. "We ain't gonna hurt you."

The girl pressed a fist to her mouth and stifled a scream.

"We got ourselves a problem here," Joe Bob said, looking up at us from his kneeling position.

"Should I drive down and wake Mr. McCauley?" Bernie said. "She needs a doctor right now."

"Too late," Joe Bob said. "Look at her dress. Her water's done broke."

"Don't look at me," I said. "I don't know anything about delivering babies. I've never even held one."

A nervous giggle slipped out of Bernie. "You sound like Prissy talking to Scarlet in *Gone With the Wind*," he said.

"Go boil some water, and git a bunch of clean towels out of the bathroom," Joe Bob said.

Bernie headed to the kitchen, and I took off to get the towels.

When I got back, Joe Bob was doing his best to calm the girl. Tears ran down her dirty face, and she was squeezing his big hand as though it were her lifeline.

"You just hold on tight, darlin'. Everthing's gonna be fine," he said.

He looked up at me.

"Stay with her while I wash up," he said.

I figured that was the least I could do since I didn't know how to do anything else in this situation. Joe Bob pried the girl's fingers from his hand and pulled my hand close to hers. She grabbed it and squeezed so hard it hurt. I didn't think she looked nearly strong enough to hurt me. Then, she let loose with a scream that could rattle the rafters.

Joe Bob went to the closet and grabbed one of his uncle's belts. He folded it in half and knelt beside the bed.

"Let's put this between your teeth," he said. "You can clamp down on this soft leather all you want to. It'll help."

The girl nodded, and he slipped the belt between her teeth. Whether it helped or not, she thought it did, because she relaxed her grip on my hand. I didn't like being left alone in the room with a pregnant woman and willed Joe Bob to hurry back. Bernie didn't have to stay in the kitchen, waiting for the water to boil. He could have at least been with me for moral support.

Joe Bob came back all scrubbed with his shirtsleeves rolled up. He had a pair of scissors in his hand.

"I'm gonna have to cut your dress," he told the girl, "so I can see what I'm doin'."

The girl had stopped crying. She kept her teeth clamped on the leather and closed her eyes. Joe Bob cut the front of her dress all the way up to her breasts, exposing her enormous belly. She wasn't wearing underwear.

"Now, what I want you to do is let me turn you over on your left side," he said.

"Why?" I said.

"It makes the delivery easier. I read about it."

I didn't know whether that was factual or an old wives' tale, but I wasn't going to argue about it.

"Maybe I should go check on Bernie," I said. I didn't want to see any more.

"You do that."

Bernie was standing watch over the boiling water.

"How's it going in there?" he said.

"I don't know how it's going, Bernie. How could I?"

"I hope Joe Bob knows what he's doing," Bernie said. "You know, if anything goes wrong, he could have a lawsuit on his hands."

"Nothing's going to go wrong. Besides, this girl's from the Tennessee sticks. She wouldn't know how to file suit. Wonder why she came to this cabin?"

"Well, she looks awfully young. My guess is that she's a runaway."

"If that's the case, why would she wait until time for the baby to be born to run?"

"Go figure," Bernie said. "Hey, what do we do with the boiling water?"

"Beats me."

Just then, Joe Bob came into the kitchen with the scissors.

"Sterilize these," he said, handing them to Bernie.

Bernie looked dumbfounded.

"How?" he said.

"Burn 'em with a kitchen match. Then, clean 'em with alcohol. I'll need 'em to cut the cord."

"What do we do with the boiling water?" I said.

"Don't do nothin' with it. Add some more water to the pot, and leave it on the stove for now."

The way Joe Bob looked at Bernie and me told us that he knew we were going to be useless. He shook his head and turned to leave.

"Tell you what," he said, "you two go out on the porch and have yourselves another drink. I'll holler if I need you."

He didn't have to repeat the offer. We were out the door before he had a chance to change his mind.

Bernie poured each of us a drink and raised his glass.

"I propose a toast to our brave mechanic friend turned obstetrician; a man of many talents."

"To our good friend," I said.

My idea to take off for the woods had turned out to be a comedy of errors. Every time there had been an opportunity to air our thoughts about the accident, some outlandish thing had occurred to derail it. Bernie seemed to have come to the conclusion that we should simply forget it ever happened, but I didn't think Joe Bob felt that way. He didn't want to talk about it, but I knew him well enough to know that he hadn't resolved the issue.

I had also hoped to be able to feel a genuine emotional attachment to my mother. The lake was a perfect setting, and I could have made use of quiet moments alone to make that happen, but for some reason, Jimmy Banks's death took precedence.

I certainly didn't want to discuss childbirth with Bernie, and I didn't think he would understand my inner turmoil, so I began telling him about my law practice. When I had exhausted that subject, I switched to skiing and the laid-back Denver lifestyle.

I was describing my favorite killer run at Aspen when Joe Bob swaggered out onto the porch. He rubbed a hand across his face.

"The little girl's got a little girl of her own," he said.

He lit a cigarette, pulled the smoke into his lungs, and blew out a thick cloud, looking satisfied.

"Yessir. A pretty, pink little baby girl. And old Doc Kincaid pulled off that little operation without a hitch."

"So the kid's got all its fingers and toes?" Bernie said.

"Yes, she does," Joe Bob said. "Now, the big question is: what are we gonna do with the two of 'em in the mornin'?"

"We'll take them to a hospital, of course," Bernie said.

"Bernard, how're we gonna take 'em to a hospital? There's three of us, our fishin' gear and stuff, and we're in a pickup. Sometimes I wonder about you."

"We'll go down to the store and explain the whole thing to Mr. McCauley," I said. "Surely, he'll be willing to drive them to a hospital."

"Now, that's a good idea, Matt," Joe Bob said. "That's what we'll do."

Joe Bob bunked on the couch in the living room in case the new mother needed assistance during the night.

Chapter Ten

"Hey, guys!" Joe Bob stood at the bottom of the stairs, looking bewildered.

I glanced at my watch; it was 7:15 a.m.

"On my way to make coffee," I said, pulling on my jeans.

"Forgit coffee. Y'all come down here."

"What's the matter?" Bernie said, fumbling around for his glasses.

"The girl's gone; took the baby with her. I didn't hear a thing. I've got Indian blood; I hear everthing."

"We'd better take a look around to see what else she took," Bernie said.

"She's not a thief, Bernard," Joe Bob said. "She took Uncle Jake's bathrobe and a couple of towels. That's all."

"What do you call that?" Bernie said. "When you take something that doesn't belong to you, you're stealing."

"Guys, you're wasting time and effort," I said. "She can't have gone very far, barefoot and carrying a baby. And I'd think she would be pretty weak since she just gave birth."

"That makes sense, Matt. We'll branch out and search the woods around the cabin," Joe Bob said. "Meet up back here in twenty minutes."

Our search was uneventful. The girl and her baby had simply disappeared.

"Now, what do we do? We can't just leave them out there in the woods," I said.

"Well, we could," Bernie said. "We're the only ones who know the girl was here."

"That's awful coldhearted," Joe Bob said. "She's just a kid; prob'ly don't know how to take care of a baby."

"This conversation sounds vaguely familiar," I said.

"Yeah, it does," Joe Bob said, and swallowed hard.

"I suppose we could tell Mr. McCauley when we return the keys," Bernie said, "but he might not want to get involved."

"Good idea," Joe Bob said. "He knows everbody around here. It'll be real easy for him to git the word out."

We packed our things, locked the cabin, and headed down the hill to the general store.

"Good morning, gentlemen," the storekeeper said. "I take it you had no trouble finding the clinic."

"No trouble at all," Joe Bob said.

"I'm all patched up with butterfly clips and a tetanus shot," I said.

"Uh, Mr. McCauley, I don't guess you seen a young girl with a baby this mornin', have you?" Joe Bob said.

"Why, no." A look of concern crossed the proprietor's face.

"Somethin' awful strange happened last night. When we got back to the cabin after supper, we heard a noise. It come from a closet in my uncle's bedroom."

"Those darn raccoons! They've gotten into every building

around here. I had to call animal control to come and trap one that took over my storeroom not long ago. They're real pests; smart little critters. But what does a raccoon have to do with a girl and a baby?"

"You see, it wasn't a raccoon, or any other kind of varmint. It was the girl, and she was mighty pregnant."

"You don't say."

"Yessir, she sure was. That baby was so ready to come out, I had to deliver it—all by myself."

Bernie and I nodded to support Joe Bob's story.

"Well, I must say I'm impressed," Mr. McCauley said. "So, what happened? Are you telling me the mother and child just disappeared?"

"That's exactly what I'm tellin' you. I slept on a couch in the room next to her. When I woke up, she'd took off with the baby; didn't make a sound."

"Wonder how she got into the cabin?" Mr. McCauley said.

"We don't know. I guess we coulda forgot to lock the kitchen door. We was thinkin' about gettin' Matt to a doctor when we left."

The storekeeper looked thoughtful. "I'll bet she's one of those gypsies," he said.

"Gypsies?"

"Well, I don't know what they are. I call them gypsies. They come through this area from God knows where, usually in old beat-up trucks, and camp out in the woods close to the creek for a few days. Then, they're gone. The ones who stop in here to buy a few groceries impress me as the kind who would just as soon steal me blind, or stick a knife in me."

"Well, you might ask your customers if they know anything about the girl. We don't know anything else to do. We searched the woods around the cabin."

"I'll do that, Joe Bob, but I wouldn't worry about her too

much. If she's one of them, they'll look out for her. She was probably running away, but had a change of heart and went back to her people."

"I guess we'd better be gittin' back to town," Joe Bob said. "Thanks for all your help."

I didn't want to go back to Martinsville. Nothing would have changed. My sister would still be in a rotten mood, because that's how she chose to be. Uncle Stuart would still have to sneak behind his wife's back to feed his vices, and Trudy would still be pulling slave duty in my mother's house. But the thing that bothered me most was that Joe Bob, Bernie, and I were stuck in the same place we were the night of the accident. We were simply doing nothing.

"Hey, Joe Bob," Bernie said, "you afraid you're going to break the speed limit?"

"Huh?"

"You're driving forty-five in a sixty-five mile per hour speed zone."

"Oh. I'm tellin' you guys, my mind's not workin' right."

"What do you mean?" I said.

"It just seems like there are so many helpless people; I can't stand it. Kids who grow up in that crazy snake cult like that little girl, rollin' around in the aisle, slobberin' like a bulldog, and that guy the snake bit. They're taught that foolishness from the time they're born. How can they ever git away from that life?"

"Buddy, there's nothing you can do about all the strange people in the world, and you have no control over what they teach their children. I'll admit that whole experience was mind boggling and upsetting, but we don't ever have to witness it again," Bernie said.

"And what about the girl and her baby? They're prob'ly lost in the woods. There's all kinds of danger out there: poisonous snakes, brown recluse spiders, maybe even a black bear, or two. Wolves could git 'em. Things like that worry me. She might not be able to find her way back to her people."

I didn't know what to say. My friend was a real mess.

We rode in silence then, watching the beauty of the southern landscape without appreciation as we bumped over lines of tar on concrete. On the outskirts of town, commercial buildings took the place of barns and farmhouses, and we were back in familiar territory.

Joe Bob cleared his throat.

"Would you guys mind if we made a little stop?" he asked.

"Of course not," I said.

Joe Bob pulled in at a strip shopping center and went into a florist's shop.

"What do you think he's doing?" Bernie said.

"I'll hazard a wild guess: buying flowers."

"For whom?"

"I have no idea for whom. I don't know anything about his private life."

Joe Bob came out of the shop, carrying a gorgeous bouquet and thrust it at Bernie.

"Oh, for me?" Bernie said.

Joe Bob was solemn-faced. "No, Bernard. They're not for you."

He drove to the other end of town and turned on the street that led to the county cemetery. Then, we knew the recipient. Bernie held the flowers and stared at the dashboard. Joe Bob gathered the bouquet into his big hands, sighed once, and got out of the truck.

"Do you want to be alone?" I said.

"I don't care one way or another. He won't either." Joe Bob sounded as though he were mad, but I didn't know why.

Bernie and I followed as he walked along the side of the cemetery until he came to the pauper's section. He stepped over the short, rusty wrought-iron fence. The grass needed mowing and was riddled with weeds and thistles. The new grave was easy to spot. It hadn't been sodded and looked like nothing more than a pile of dirt. It didn't have a marker.

"This has to be it," Joe Bob said.

He stood very still and looked down at the grave for a long time. Tears poured silently from his eyes. Then, as if shaking himself back into the present, he knelt beside the mound of soil and placed the bouquet on it.

"I'm so awful sorry," he said as though speaking to a ghost. "Just so damn sorry."

Chapter Eleven

My aunt and uncle were in the living room when I made my grand entrance, looking like a refugee. I had been living in the same pair of jeans since I left the house and hadn't bothered to shave the entire time I was at the lake.

Aunt Lela Maude tugged her eyes away from the television screen.

"Welcome home, dear," she drawled. "My goodness, you boys must have really been roughin' it from the looks of you."

"Yeah, pretty much."

Uncle Stuart roused from his nap, throwing off his newspaper blanket.

"So, the great outdoorsman returns," he said. "Did you catch any fish?"

"Yes, we did. We ate some and gave the rest away."

"Well, I'm glad you had the opportunity to get away and relax for a few days," my aunt said. "You've been under a lot of stress. I know you're grievin' somethin' awful, and stayin' in this house must be terribly painful for you. Then, there's your poor little sister."

"Is she here? I didn't see the rental car."

"No. She and Ron went out for a while. They'll probably be back soon."

"I guess I'd better get cleaned up so Sam won't throw me out," I said, and started up the stairs.

"You know, I think your sister is takin' her mother's death unusually hard," my aunt said.

"I'm sorry. I'll try to be more understanding."

"Oh, it's not your fault, dear. It doesn't seem to matter what anyone says, or does. Samantha's simply overwrought. If someone bids the child good mornin', she begins to either weep, or rage."

"Maybe I'll have a talk with her," I said.

"I certainly wouldn't advise it. She'll probably bite your head off. Stuart and I have learned to steel ourselves against her harsh attacks. I suppose everyone has their own way of dealin' with grief, and it seems Samantha has chosen to be meaner than the devil himself. I'm hopin' it'll pass in time."

"I hope so, too."

I didn't relish the thought of having a heart-to-heart with my sister. It wouldn't do any good. Everything had to be Sam's way or no way. Maybe I would just try to be as laid back as possible, and refuse to let her get under my skin.

I got dressed and called my office to let Jack know I had been delayed.

"You'll cry when you see your desk," he said. "It's stacked knee-deep, but I'll try to whittle it down as much as I can this weekend. I don't have any plans, so I'll tackle this mess."

"I appreciate it, partner."

"How are things in the sunny south?" he said. "Did my flowers get there in time for the service?"

"The flowers were really nice. Thanks. As for Martinsville,

I can't wait to hightail it out of here. I've got the small town blues."

Ron and Sam walked in just as I hung up.

"How was the fishing trip?" Ron asked.

"Relaxing."

My sister didn't bother to speak to anyone. She headed for the kitchen and returned with a tall glass of milk.

Of course, I couldn't keep my mouth shut. "I didn't think you liked milk," I said.

There was no reason for me to remark on her choice of beverage, so why did I do it? Was I subconsciously trying to antagonize her?

"I don't," she said.

Trudy told us that lunch was ready. I knew Sam had instructed her to prepare all of the family's meals while I was out of town. Although that wasn't supposed to be a part of her job, I knew Trudy would have done it without being asked.

We sat down to homemade clam chowder and stuffed tomatoes from the garden.

"This chowder is superb, Mrs. Giles," Uncle Stuart said. "Why don't you break your self-imposed rule and come have lunch with us?"

"Thank you, Judge, but I'm not hungry just yet."

I had tried over the years to talk Trudy out of her old school habits, but she had grown up in the south, and subservience was ingrained in her; I knew she would never change.

We turned our attention to the meal, and all table talk seemed to cease. It was clear to me that this group had absolutely nothing in common. We were sitting at my mother's kitchen table, pretending to be a real family until the attorney read the will. Then, we would go our separate ways.

"Looks like it might rain," Uncle Stuart said.

"There's a forty percent chance," Ron said.

Sam was gobbling her food in a most unladylike manner, and didn't appear to care whether anyone thought she was eating like a starved animal. She finished her meal and excused herself, announcing that she was going to take a nap.

"Let's adjourn to the livin' room," Aunt Lela Maude said.

Uncle Stuart and I followed her into the room that was my mother personified.

"That piano was your mother's pride and joy." My aunt gestured to the polished Steinway. "She loved music from the time she was a little girl."

"What was she like as a child?" I asked.

"Well, she was beautiful." Aunt Lela Maude smiled. "She was even a pretty baby. Quite frankly, I've always thought most newborns look a great deal like monkeys, but not Eloise. She was gorgeous the day she came into this world."

"But what was she really like? Did she have a sunny disposition?"

"Your mother was probably the most self-centered child who ever lived. She wanted the world to do her biddin'. Mother and Daddy doted on her, of course, because she was the baby. She could be a little charmer at times, but she had the ability to turn mean quicker than the wink of an eye."

"Did the two of you get along when you were growing up?"

"We did, but it was only because our parents forced me to give in to her every whim. I loved her, but I also resented her. I don't suppose I should be tellin' you these things."

Uncle Stuart was snoring on the sofa. I was sure he had heard all about the unfair childhood his wife had endured. He probably knew every detail.

"Do you like my dad, Aunt Lela Maude?"

"Oh, my, yes. Why, your father is a true southern gentleman. He's one of the most delightful men I've ever known."

"Do you think he and Mom were ever happy together?"

"Yes, I do, but it didn't last. You see, your father wanted a family, but your mother wanted to play. She wanted to be free to flit about whenever she pleased."

"I see."

"Oh, don't get me wrong, dear. Eloise loved you and Samantha in her own way. She was simply caught up in her own world; she lived in one big social whirl. It was even that way when she was a child."

"I don't remember ever feeling close to her, even when I was a kid, but I always wanted to make her proud of me. I never could."

"Oh, darlin', you're wrong. She talked about you constantly, braggin' about your high IQ and all of your academic awards."

"That's news to me."

"Well, it's true, and she loved you."

"She had a strange way of showing it. I don't remember her ever being affectionate toward me."

"That would have been a pipe dream, dear. She simply wasn't capable of givin'. That's why your father left her. He finally came to the realization that she wasn't goin' to change. Your mother was a cold fish, as they say."

The phone rang; it was Joe Bob.

"I gotta talk," he said.

"Where are you?"

"At the garage, but I can't git my mind on my work. I don't think I've got enough sense to change a tire."

"I don't have any wheels," I said. "Maybe I can borrow my uncle's car."

"I'll come pick you up. Give me ten minutes."

Aunt Lela Maude had turned on the television.

"I have to go out for a while," I said.

"That's fine, dear. My favorite program is just comin' on."

"Aunt Lela Maude, thank you for being honest with me."

She smiled at me, but it didn't reach her eyes.

"We don't always get the answers we want to hear," she said, "but everyone deserves to know the truth."

The leaden sky had started to drizzle when I saw Joe Bob's truck round the corner. I hurried to the curb to meet him. We had looked equally scruffy when we got back to town, and Joe Bob obviously hadn't gotten around to his personal ablutions. His eyes were bloodshot, and his face was a mask of pure misery.

Neither of us spoke on the way to his place. We had barely gotten inside when it started raining hard.

Joe Bob offered his predictable opening line: "You want a beer?"

"No, thanks. I'm about beered out."

"Matt, I'm goin' crazy. I can't git Jimmy Banks off my mind no matter how I try."

"A thing like this is going to take time, Joe Bob. You're feeling responsible for a man's demise."

"I am responsible. I killed Jimmy Banks. That's the long and the short of it."

"I can't give you any advice."

"Oh, man, I been over there in the garage down on my knees prayin' ever since we come back to town, not that it done a lick of good."

"You're going to have to get your head on straight and think it through. There are only two options: either tough it out on your own, or turn yourself in. I'm afraid you're going to be miserable either way."

Joe Bob shook his head. "You know, when I was bringin' that little baby into the world, I forgot all about it just for a little while."

"If you hadn't been there, that baby might well not have made it."

"I'd sure like to believe that, but I know better. It was a real easy birth. I'd like to think helpin' that little girl come into this world would make up for the life I took, but I know I can't do that."

Joe Bob's cat padded into the room and began rubbing its hair on my pants. I've always thought of felines as sneaky creatures. They recognize those of us who aren't particularly enamored of them, and we're the unfortunates they choose to pursue. I could tell that this one was really spoiled, and that it wanted me to do something, because it was throwing all of its weight into the rubbing, and began yowling as though it were in pain.

Joe Bob reached down and scooped the cat into his lap. He stroked its fur until it got quiet.

"Cat's scared of storms," he said. "He sleeps in a chair in the bedroom most of the time, but if he hears thunder, he gits in bed with me."

Rain was pounding the top of the double-wide, and we practically had to shout to make ourselves heard.

"Joe Bob, I need to know what you've decided to do. You can't let this guilt consume you. Do you think being punished by going to prison would ease your pain?"

"I don't know, but I don't think I can go on like this. I'd almost rather be dead."

I couldn't imagine how torn he felt, and I didn't know what I would do if I were in his shoes.

"I think Bernie has a right to know you're still undecided," I said. "He thought you had made up your mind to drop it, and I hate to say it, but your decision affects all of us."

Joe Bob nodded.

I called Bernie at work and told him that he needed to come to Joe Bob's place. He sounded tired, and tried to shut me down before I said another word.

"Lee Ann's cooking dinner, and she'll be upset if I don't show up to eat it."

"It's important, Bernie. Call and tell her you're going to be a little late."

He finally agreed and showed up about a half-hour later, dripping wet and looking mad at the world. Joe Bob tossed him a kitchen towel.

"So, what's all this about?" Bernie said, drying his glasses.

"We think maybe we should go to the police after all," I said.

"Not you, too!" he said. "You do realize you could lose your license to practice law, I'm sure. Opening this thing up won't just ruin one life; it'll destroy ours, your uncle's, and my family's."

"I feel awful about it," Joe Bob said, "but I can't live like this. I'm goin' crazy!"

"You know what?" Bernie said. "You're being a selfish prick. It's plain to see that you're thinking only of yourself. I tried to get you to go to the police the night of the accident, but you whined like a little kid. You cried, and made me feel like the bad guy."

Bernie's words echoed in my head. I realized that everything he had said was true. Our lives would never be the same. I wasn't an indecisive person, but I had never been in a predicament like this.

"Let me talk to Uncle Stuart again," I said. "I don't know why he encouraged us to keep quiet that night, but he knows everything about Tennessee law. There might be other options."

"I'm going home," Bernie said, and he went back out into the rain.

Chapter Twelve

I headed straight for the stairs when I got back to the house, because I had made up my mind to avoid my sister whenever I could.

"Matt," she said, "would you come in here for a minute, please?"

I was wary, but I backtracked and went into the living room where the rest of the family had gathered.

My sister actually wore a pleasant expression.

"I have something to tell all of you," she said. "Ron and I are going to have a baby."

Then, she genuinely smiled, the kind of smile she used to give me after I let her have my last bite of dessert.

"Wow!" I said. "So when am I going to be an uncle?"

"December," Ron said. He beamed at his wife.

"Isn't this wonderful news, Stuart?" Aunt Lela Maude said. "A new baby in the family."

"It certainly is. The young ones keep us oldies on our toes."

"This explains your strange behavior, dear," Aunt Lela Maude said, smiling at Sam. "I was beginin' to be terribly concerned about you."

Sam surprised me by taking the remark in stride.

"I'm afraid I have rather severe mood swings," she said. "I was already experiencing them before Mom died, and I've been on a downswing ever since."

"Now, don't you worry about a thing, sweetheart," my aunt said. "We understand."

The phone rang, and I went to answer it. I was surprised to hear Beth on the other end of the line.

"Matt, we got off to a bad start the other night," she said, "and to make up for it, I'm taking you to dinner tonight."

"That's nice of you, Beth, but I'm having dinner here with my family tonight. Besides, I don't think it's a good idea for the two of us to get together. Let's just leave things the way they are and part friends."

"Please don't turn me down, Matt. I realize I overstepped my bounds, and I regret it. Give me a chance to apologize and make up for it. I promise to be a good girl, and the reservation has already been made."

"Since you put it that way, I'll go, but I'm serious; this is just going to be dinner."

"You won't be sorry, Matt. I'll pick you up at 6:30."

"Who was that?" Sam said.

"It was Beth. She wants to take me to dinner as an apology for trying to rekindle the old flame."

Anger flickered in my sister's eyes for just an instant, then disappeared.

Beth pulled up to the curb in front of my mother's house promptly at 6:30. She was sitting behind the wheel of a new gunmetal-gray Lexus. I slid into the passenger seat, and she smiled, showing off her perfectly straight pearly whites.

She took me to one of Martinsville's pricey new restaurants

I hadn't known existed, and we were led to a window table which looked out at a gorgeous man-made lake flanked by a manicured landscape. The menu was extensive, and the wine list resembled a tome.

Over cocktails, Beth went into great detail about her new job as hospital administrator at St. Luke's. She seemed very excited about it.

"The people I work with are awfully nice. And Matt, the salary is sweet. I never dreamed I could make this kind of money in a little town like Martinsville."

"I assume you're living here because it's where you want to be," I said.

"I didn't know where I wanted to be after our divorce. My initial reason for coming here was that my mother was all alone since Dad passed away, and I knew she would expect me to come here. I thought she was probably feeling helpless and needed me to be strong for her. That wasn't the case; she was fine. I came home, and she nursed my wounds. Then, I landed the job at the hospital."

"Well, you seem none the worse for wear, and you have the perfect job. I'm happy for you."

"What about your practice?" she said. "Are you still struggling to survive?"

"I'm afraid so. It's going to take a while to build a clientele, but Jack and I are both working hard to make that happen."

"I know you will."

"Hey, guess what? Sam's going to have a baby."

"How wonderful! I'm sure she's pleased."

We had finished our meal and were running out of comfortable table talk. I was glad to see the waiter bring the check. Beth reached for it.

"I invited you. Remember?" she said.

"All right," I said. "It's a good thing you make so much money."

She gave me a tour of Martinsville after dark to point out some of the changes that had occurred since we left. Then, she took me to her house.

We were sitting in the driveway, and I could see lamplight through the living room window.

"It's too late for me to barge in on your mother," I said.

"You won't be barging in on anyone. Mother's not here. She went to visit her sister in Charlotte this morning."

Little Beth wanted more than a dinner date. I should have known. She hadn't been able to seduce me the other night when she came on so strong, but she hadn't given up. Beth was never a quitter.

"Beth, you promised. I should know better than to believe anything you say."

"Don't be so dramatic, Matt. Surely you're not afraid to come in for a nightcap."

"One drink," I said.

Beth kicked off her high heels as soon as she got inside the house.

"Make yourself comfy," she said. "I'll be right back."

I sat down in a chair. If I got anywhere near her, I was afraid she would start putting the moves on me again. I would have one drink, then leave. There was no reason we couldn't part friends.

I heard a pop. A minute later Beth padded into the living room with a bottle of champagne and two flutes. She poured the champagne.

"Beth, you know I can't drink champagne."

"It won't hurt you just this once. Besides, it's all I have. Mother doesn't like having hard liquor in the house."

"Well, just one glass."

She patted the seat beside her and held up a glass of champagne.

"Come over and sit beside me," she said. "I promise I won't bite you."

"I'm fine right here."

"You didn't used to be such a party pooper," she said, bringing me the drink and going back to the sofa.

"Cheers," she said, raising her glass.

"Cheers."

After my initial sip I knew I couldn't finish the drink. We had ordered cocktails before dinner, polished off a bottle of wine and after-dinner ports. I was already three sheets to the wind, and now she wanted to pour champagne down my throat.

I straightened up in my chair and tried to look sober.

"How's your mother?" I said.

"Mother's quite well. She keeps asking when we're going to come to our senses and get back together."

"That's not going to work, Beth."

"Don't worry. I'm not suggesting anything, but there's no harm in talking about old times, is there?"

"Maybe not, but there's no reason to talk about them."

I didn't remember finishing my drink, but my glass was empty. Beth uncurled her lithe body and eased over to refill it.

"Please come sit on the sofa, Matt. You're awfully far away."

"What the hell," I said, and let her lead me across the room on unsteady legs.

"Remember the time we left that party in Knoxville at two in the morning, searching for a hotel with satin sheets?" She grinned.

"As a matter of fact, I do. As I recall, we had been drinking champagne that night, too."

"You seemed to enjoy it."

"Everybody does some pretty foolish things when they're

young, and I was no exception. I knew I shouldn't have been behind the wheel of anything that moved that night."

"When we finally found a place that had the sheets, we checked in and made love like there was no tomorrow." She smiled.

"Yeah, I remember. The next morning we had no idea where we were." I laughed.

Beth poured more champagne and snuggled closer.

"I miss us, Matt," she said. Her speech was garbled.

"Me, too."

My vision was fuzzy, and I could tell I was running my words together. I was afraid it would only be a matter of time before I upchucked, but for the moment, I was serenely happy.

Beth set her glass on the coffee table and clumsily extracted mine from my hand, spilling the contents on my pants.

"Take off your coat and stay a while," she said.

She started undressing me. It was with considerable effort that she managed to get me out of my jacket. She slung it in the direction of a chair, and missed.

"Do you really miss me, Matt?"

"Sometimes."

"What do you miss about me most?"

"I donno."

"You gotta know."

I started laughing, but I wasn't sure what was funny.

I had slid down so far that I was lying, rather than sitting on the sofa, and my butt was hanging over the edge. Beth leaned down and gave me an inordinately sloppy kiss.

"This?" she said.

"Or this?"

She began fumbling with my fly.

"Hey," I said, "the big guy's resting."

"Don't be so mean."

"Okay. I won't be mean."

"I know what we need," she said.

She got up and started down the hall. The tail of her blouse was hanging out.

"Where are you going?" I said, pulling myself back on the sofa cushion. "I think I'd better go home."

"I'll be right back," she said.

She was weaving from one side of the hall to the other. I didn't know how long she was gone, but I was asleep when she returned.

"Here we are," she said, rousing me from my catnap. "I have a treat for us."

"You do?"

She had shed most of her clothes, and I thought she was awfully easy on the eyes. I had forgotten how sexy she was.

"Sure do." She grinned. "I been saving this for a special 'casion."

She delved into her black lace bra and pulled out a book of matches. And like magic, she produced a cigarette from somewhere and placed it between her lips. She struggled with the matches until she finally struck one and lit the cigarette.

"Beth, you're smoking! We don't smoke, do we?"

"'snot a cigarette." She coughed.

Suddenly, the acrid aroma of marijuana filled my nostrils.

"Oh, Beth, you have to put that out right now. You could lose your job."

"Nah." She waved the possibility away.

"I'm serious."

"Here," she said, holding the reefer toward me. "Take a hit."

"No. I haven't done this for years, and I don't miss it a bit."

"Do it!" she said.

I must have been in a vulnerable state of mind, because I

accepted the joint and took a deep drag. Suddenly, I started coughing and thought I might never stop.

"Now, wasn't that nice?" she said, smiling like a benign benefactor.

I grabbed the champagne bottle and downed a few gulps.

"Gotta go to sleep," I said. "I'm destroyed."

"Poor baby."

I thought that if I could stand up and grab my coat, I would be home free. Neither Beth nor I was capable of driving, but I knew I had to get home. I wasn't hitting on all eight cylinders, but I figured if I could manage to get away from my ex and out the door I could walk the four blocks to my mother's house.

I sat up as straight as I could, and pushed myself to a standing position. Then, I stumbled toward my coat.

"Don't leave," Beth wailed.

Then, the floor came up to meet me.

Chapter Thirteen

I was naked in my ex's bed with my hands cuffed to a sturdy spindle in the headboard. My head was splitting, and I felt pretty sure I was about to throw up.

"Beth!"

No answer.

I wondered how a hundred fifteen pound woman could lug me down a narrow hall and into this bed.

"Beth!"

"Patience, sweetheart. I'm on my way."

She was dripping wet from the shower, wearing nothing but a sexy expression.

"Welcome back, precious," she said, and slithered seductively toward me.

"This isn't funny, Beth."

She smiled. "I find it terribly amusing."

She climbed onto the bed and stood over me on her knees. The dim light from a bedside lamp shone on her bare skin and made it look like shiny plastic. She did a pouty thing with her mouth and began shaking her head, sprinkling me with water droplets.

"Stop that, and get me out of these handcuffs, Beth."

"Oh, Matt, I can't do that. It would ruin all the fun."

Then, her long legs straddled me, and she sat on my stomach and bent down to kiss me.

"Quit it," I said, and turned my head away.

The cuffs were digging into my wrists, and it hurt like hell.

"You're mean to me," she said in a little girl voice.

She got up and crawled to the foot of the bed, reaching for something on a cedar chest. Then, like lightning, she was facing me with what looked like a riding crop clenched between her teeth. This wasn't the Beth I had fallen in love with and married. It wasn't even the Beth who broke my heart a few years ago. She took the crop from her mouth and began caressing it. I wasn't sure what she had in mind, but I knew I wasn't going to enjoy it. Pulling my knees up to protect myself, I closed my eyes and waited for the pain. It ripped through my right buttock like fire.

"Stop it, Beth!"

"Shhh, you'll wake the neighbors," she said, delivering another sharp rap I was sure had drawn blood.

"You're crazy," I said.

"Crazy for you, and you want me just as much as I want you, Matt; you just don't realize it."

She put down her weapon and began caressing me all over. Her breathing had grown heavy, and she was making little sighing noises. My hip was killing me, and I could feel the handcuffs cutting deeper into my wrists. I was still pretty drunk, but I knew I had to somehow get away from Beth.

She looked down at my manhood with a disgusted sneer.

"You're going to have to do a lot better than that," she said. "It's obvious you're not even trying to cooperate. Let's see, I know what we'll try next."

I was so glad to see her get off the bed and leave the room that I almost didn't care what else she had planned. At least I would have a short reprieve. I tried using my feet to push myself toward the bedpost, because I had slid down so far the circulation in my hands was being cut off.

Beth padded into the bedroom, carrying a small silver bowl.

"What's that?" I said.

Smiling, she reached into the bowl with a delicate thumb and index finger, coming up with an ice cube. She deposited it on my stomach, dangerously close to my genitalia. I rolled to one side, and the cube slid onto the sheet.

"Now, Matt, you get to choose our toy. Do you prefer the riding crop, or the ice, Mr. Big Shot Attorney?"

"You've lost your mind, Beth!"

"You're going to make love to me, Matt. You're going to make love to me for the rest of the night, just like you did with your whore all those nights you said you were working."

"I was working, and I did not have an affair. Beth, I was faithful to you; I swear it."

"Sure you were, Matt." Her pretty face twisted into an ugly mask. "I'm not in the mood to listen to any more of your lies. Pick a toy!"

"No!"

"Pick one, you bastard!"

She lunged at me, and my reflexes must have taken over, because I kicked her in the stomach as hard as I could, sending her across the room. She crashed into the wall, and slid to the floor.

At that moment, I didn't care whether I had injured her or not. I just knew that I had to get away from her.

The leather crop was lying on the foot of the bed. It was all I could do to inch myself away from the bedpost to reach it with my foot. My wrists were killing me, and I felt my hands going numb. I had to free myself and get the hell out of this house. My ex-wife had gone crazy. I didn't know her, and I didn't want to.

I finally managed to lay my foot across the riding crop and drag it toward me, but it still wasn't close enough. Thirty-five isn't that old, but I found that I wasn't the contortionist I was as a kid. After twisting myself into unimaginable positions, I was able to maneuver the riding crop close enough to my face to pick it up with my teeth.

Thankfully, a phone was on a table beside the bed, and I could tell that I would be able to push the buttons with the riding crop. Then, I realized I would have to lift the receiver. I never considered giving up. After several attempts, I was able to knock the receiver off its cradle. I held my breath, praying it wouldn't fall to the floor. Good luck comes to those who keep the faith. I meticulously punched in the number for information, and then I breathed.

"Please give me the number for Joseph Robert Kincaid," I said. "It could be listed under J.R."

"I have a Joe Bob Kincaid on Chriswell," the operator said.

"That's it."

"Could you please dial the...?"

The receiver clicked in my ear, and I had to rest for a few seconds before punching in the number.

Joe Bob must have been enjoying the sleep of the dead. I thought he would never answer.

"Joe Bob, this is Matt. Sorry to wake you."

"Who?"

I could tell he was still half asleep.

"It's Matt."

"I can't hear you."

"Don't hang up! It's Matt, and I need your help."

"Oh, Matt. What time is it?"

"I don't know what time it is. Can you hear me now?"

"Just barely. You okay?"

"Yes, I'm okay, but I need you to get up and do me a favor."

"Sure, man."

"Listen carefully," I said.

"I'm listnin'."

"Do you remember where Beth lives?"

"Yeah. Why?"

"I'm at her house. I want you to come over here in a hurry and bring your toolbox."

My friend didn't ask any questions.

"I'm on it, buddy."

"Joe Bob, you might have to break in if the door's locked."

"I can do that. Anything else?"

"No. Just hurry."

I tried to get in the most comfortable position possible until Joe Bob came to rescue me. Beth hadn't moved, or made a sound. I was afraid she would come to before he arrived.

I wasn't sure how long it took Joe Bob to get to Beth's house. He called my name in a loud whisper from the living room. I was afraid to answer for fear of waking Beth, so I just let him wander around, looking for me. The heels of his boots made thumping noises as he clumped down the hall on the hardwood floor. The noise stopped at the open bedroom door, and Joe Bob stood in the doorway, open-mouthed, trying to digest what he was seeing.

"Dang!" he said. "Now I seen it all."

Stepping into the room, he peered down at my ex-wife.

"Wow!"

"You think she's okay?" I said.

"Oh, yeah. She's a ten if I ever seen one."

"Is she hurt?"

He bent down to check her out.

"Looks like she's just got a goose egg on her head."

"Get me out of these things," I said.

Joe Bob seemed to notice my predicament for the first time. He stood at the foot of the bed, scratching his head and looking amused at his old high school pal naked, curled into a fetal position, and handcuffed to a bed.

"Hey!" I said, "How about a little help?"

"Oh, yeah. Where's the key to the bracelets?"

"I don't know. Where's your toolbox?"

"In the truck. I'll git it."

Minutes later, he was back with his tools. He opened the toolbox, and looked at its contents.

"These bolt cutters oughta do the trick," he said.

Joe Bob Kincaid was strong as an ox, but cutting the steel chain between the handcuffs produced a few loud grunts and a sweat-slicked, red face.

"Damnation!" he said as the cuffs flew apart. "That little operation was touch and go there for a while."

"Let's get out of here," I said.

"We just gonna leave her here on the floor? I mean, she is your ex-wife."

"You can pick her up and put her into bed. Just hurry."

Joe Bob took his time lifting Beth and posing her in a sexy position on the satin sheets; I threw a blanket over her. She was just beginning to come around and made little moaning noises.

My clothes were strewn all over the place. We gathered them up, and I got into my shirt and pants. Joe Bob grabbed the rest of my clothes and my shoes, and we got out of the house fast.

"You've got to get these cuffs off me somehow," I said.

"I know a locksmith who'll take care of you. He's gonna be mad as hell when I call and wake him up, but he'll do it."

Joe Bob pulled into a grocery store parking lot and wrestled his cell phone from his jeans pocket. He went to his contacts and found the guy's number. It made me wonder how many times he had found it necessary to call a locksmith.

Joe Bob had been right on the money about the guy's temper. I hadn't heard a string of expletives that long and loud since high school on a Friday night.

Money won out over sleep, however, because a few minutes later we were sitting in front of a small whitewashed cinder block building bearing the sign: ***Willie's Locksmith Shop.***

We could see Willie coming down the stairs from his apartment through the dirty plate glass window. He had on a pair of baggy pants and a wife beater. I didn't think he looked too happy about getting business at four in the morning.

We got out of the pickup and started toward the door.

"Let me do the talkin'," Joe Bob said, knocking on the door.

"It's open," the locksmith hollered.

"Hey, Willie," Joe Bob said, thrusting his hand toward the locksmith.

Willie ignored the gesture and glared at me.

"We hate to git you up at this hour," Joe Bob said, "but as you can see, we need your expertise right now."

Willie motioned with his head for me to step over to where he stood under a spotlight. I walked across the room and held out my wrists for him to do his magic. The cuffs were off in seconds; Willie knew his stuff.

"You ain't broke out of jail, or nothin', have you?" Willie said with a little grin.

"Nah," Joe Bob was quick to say. "We was just foolin' around. Put these on my buddy here for a joke and somehow misplaced the key." He laughed.

Truth be told, I didn't think Willie gave a hoot in hell why I was wearing steel bracelets. I paid him, and we left.

"Now what?" Joe Bob said.

"I'm tired, but I'm starved. Let's get something to eat."

"That puts us back at Morgan's, the place with the interestin' *no smokin'* section."

The restaurant was open twenty-four/seven, but the only options in these early hours were breakfast or burgers. I ordered ham and eggs with black coffee.

"Bring me some of them huevos rancheros," Joe Bob said, "and a cold brew."

Then, I knew he had a stomach made of cast-iron.

"You gonna tell me how you got yourself in such a fix, or do you just want to leave it to my imagination?" he said.

"You probably won't believe it, but I'll tell you since you bailed me out."

I told him what had transpired, leaving out very little, and it didn't even seem real in the telling.

"She must be one wild, sexy woman," Joe Bob said.

I glanced down at my watch and noticed that the crystal was broken.

"There's no doubt about it," I said.

Chapter Fourteen

I crashed on Joe Bob's couch. He offered to give up his bed, but there was no way I was going to accept it. My old friend was the most unselfish human being I knew, and I didn't want to take advantage of him. I had already done that earlier tonight.

The aroma of coffee brewing introduced the day. I reached for my watch on the coffee table, and found it nestled between a *Playboy* and a *Sports Illustrated*. Remnants of last night's activities were clear and present on my hip and thigh where red marks lingered. I cursed Beth as I eased myself off the couch and got into my pants.

"How about a cup of java, sport?" Joe Bob said. He was standing in the tiny kitchen, smoking a cigarette and petting his spoiled cat.

"Sounds good. Do you happen to have any mouthwash?"

"In the john. Help yourself."

I splashed cold water on my face and gargled mouthwash thinking I couldn't possibly look like the bum I saw in the mirror. How could I have been so weak as to be taken in by my ex? I vowed it would never happen again.

Joe Bob made coffee strong enough to run a footrace, just the way I liked it. We sat at his Formica table and stared first at one another, then at our steaming mugs.

"Well, that was quite a night, huh?" I said.

"It's been quite a week."

"So it has. I guess I've been shoving part of it to the back of my mind."

"You're a better man than I am if you can do that."

"Did you decide what you're going to do?" I said.

"No, but I do know one thing for sure."

"What's that?"

Joe Bob lit a cigarette.

"I come to the conclusion there's no reason to drag you and Bernard and the judge into this thing."

"I'm afraid leaving us out of it isn't an option. You were driving when the accident occurred, but the three of us are just as guilty as you for leaving the scene."

"Listen, Matt, nobody seen it happen. As far as I'm concerned, you guys was all tucked in your beds fast asleep."

"That's noble of you, but it won't fly."

"I knew you'd be stubborn. You lawyers don't think like normal people. You know what I think? I think the law is unfair; honest to God, I do. There's lots of things that are legal, but they're not fair. Don't ask me to name one right this minute, but you know I'm right. There's all kinds of loopholes lawyers know about that the average guy don't."

"This is different, Joe Bob. It's not unfair. The three of us knew better, but we left the scene of the accident. We're guilty of a crime."

Joe Bob sighed. "Let me think on it some more."

"You do that," I said. "I'd better get home and let you go to work."

It was nine o'clock by the time Joe Bob dropped me off at the house. Aunt Lela Maude was in the rose garden, cutting my mother's beauties for a bouquet. She had on a floppy straw hat and gloves which came up to her elbows. It was such a familiar sight, coming up the front walk and seeing Mother selecting and cutting the perfect roses for her dining room table. She and my aunt were nearly the same size and build, and for a moment I felt a lump in my throat.

My aunt looked up from her work. "Good mornin', dear." She smiled.

"Good morning, Aunt Lela Maude."

I expected her to question me as to where I had spent the night, but she resumed her rose snipping as if she weren't the least bit curious.

I felt sluggish and stupid to boot. The food I had consumed since I left Denver had added at least six or seven pounds, and I felt it. I'd gotten fat because my discipline had forsaken me, and I had been stupid to come within a mile of Beth. There was no time like the present to take action, so I put on shorts and running shoes. Things were going to change starting right now.

Trudy was in the laundry room off the kitchen.

"Hey, Trudy. How's my girl?"

"I'm fine, just sad," she said, putting the last of the wet laundry into the dryer and pushing buttons.

"Where is everybody?"

"Miz Lela Maude's in the rose garden, and the young ones took off about an hour ago."

"What about Uncle Stuart?"

The housekeeper pointed out the window toward the back yard.

"See that cloud of smoke?" she said.

I nodded, seeing the curly wisp drifting upward behind the japonica bush.

"He's out there smokin' cigars; thinks nobody knows what he's up to."

I grinned and went out to catch him off guard. He was perched on a wicker footstool he had copped from the patio, looking immensely content.

"Good morning, Uncle Stuart."

"Ah, top 'o the mornin' to you, Matthew," he said, tapping ashes from the end of a fat stogie.

He looked at his vice appreciatively. "There's nothing like a good cigar," he declared, sticking the well-chewed end between his teeth.

"It smells good," I said.

"I suppose you're wondering why I'm hiding out in the back yard."

"Well, no."

"Of course you are. It's Lela Maude. She won't let me smoke in the house. Says it stinks everything up. That woman doesn't want me to enjoy any of life's little pleasures. She says smoking's bad for my health and drinking's sinful. At my age, what else is there?"

"Well, as long as you don't overdo."

"Going for a run, are you?"

"Yeah, I've put on a few pounds since I got here."

"Ah, thank God for the resilience of youth, my boy," he said wistfully. "I wish I could still run. Enjoy your youth, Matt. It'll be gone before you know it."

If he knew how I felt this morning, he wouldn't be singing youth's praises. I had the feeling that I was wasting some of my best years. My practice was pretty much of a joke. Building a clientele shouldn't be as hard as my partner and I seemed to be making it.

Most of our clients didn't produce much income. We needed to land a case good enough to give us a jump start. And my marriage had turned out to be a flop. I didn't realize it was going down the pipes until after the fact. At this point I wasn't sure what I wanted to do with the years I had left, but I knew I didn't want to spend them behind bars.

I ran until I didn't think I could take another step, and then I ran some more. Finally, I got my second wind, and started to feel a little better. I jogged for a few minutes and slowed to a walk when I came to a shady picnic area. Then, I walked around in the grass and checked my heart rate until it slowed to something resembling normalcy.

I couldn't get Beth out of my mind. Thoughts of her seeped in through the cracks whenever I had an idle moment. How could she have changed so drastically? I wondered who she had been keeping company with since she left me. The sweet, naïve little Beth I had married right out of college, filled with dreams of our future together, was gone. She had insisted that we attend church every Sunday morning, and she refused to watch X-rated movies. Vulgarity and violence were taboo.

Two squirrels were playing tag up and down the trunk of a hackberry tree. They were carefree like children, and made me think about how long it had been since I had felt that lighthearted. My ex-wife, my family, and my friend were burdensome to me, and all I wanted to do was escape Martinsville, Tennessee, leaving them all behind.

A few years ago, I attended a seminar on the art of compartmentalizing. I was working for the firm in Atlanta then. One of the partners had touted it as a surefire timesaver, so the other newbie and I were told it was a command performance. After practicing some of the strategies from the seminar, I began to think it was a good idea; it appeared to prove helpful in the workplace. It was several months later that my marriage began to fall apart. I didn't realize what was happening; I simply thought I was overworked.

I started back to the house, recalling the strategy that had worked best for me. As I put one foot in front of the other, I looked at the trees, the flowers in neat beds on front lawns, and tried to rid my mind of everything but enjoying a walk in the sunshine. It didn't work.

I was feeling sorry for myself; I had been an unfortunate victim the night Jimmy Banks lost his life. It was a case of my being in the wrong place at the wrong time. My mind was in a state of confusion because of my relationship with my dead mother. The family expected me to feel sad, and I didn't. If my mind hadn't been in such a state, my good sense would have told me that none of us could leave the scene of the accident. Now, I could go to prison.

My conscience bothered me because of Joe Bob. He was good to the core. I knew it was against his nature to think only of himself and to break the law. He had always put himself last. My friend was an anomaly to me. He grew up on the wrong side of the tracks, and my folks had been less than excited when I hooked up with him during our teenage years. My mother considered him a ruffian who wanted to edge his way into a social set where he didn't belong. She thought he was using me, riding on my coattails to get into the right crowd. But I had admired him from the minute we met.

Joe Bob had more common sense than anyone I knew. His grammar was atrocious simply because it wasn't high on his priority list. I often thought he spoke like an uneducated hick because he wanted to own it as a part of his persona. Everyone knew he was smart, and I had never heard anyone correct him, or even mention his poor grammar. He was a problem solver, someone who was innately competent at figuring out how things worked, and he had a good understanding of what made people tick. He studied personalities and knew when the odds were good enough that he could work a crowd to get something he wanted. He also knew when to walk away. Joe Bob picked his friends; they didn't choose him. If he was your friend, you knew that you could count on him to be around if you needed him, no matter the circumstance. Knowing Joe Bob Kincaid made me feel inordinately fortunate.

Chapter Fifteen

I couldn't believe what I was seeing. Beth's car was parked at the curb in front of my mother's house. What could she possibly be doing? Surely, she hadn't come to tell my family anything about our so-called dinner date last night. She came out onto the front porch, carrying the wicker basket she had used to bring food to my grieving family. I breathed easier, thinking she had come by to pick it up so we wouldn't have to return it to her. She had probably called to make sure I wasn't home before she came by.

Aunt Lela Maude and Trudy were in the porch swing, drinking iced tea. I waited for Beth to deliver an air kiss to my aunt's cheek and press Trudy's hand between her small palms before walking down the steps and to her car. She smiled and waved as she drove away.

The swing squeaked as I approached the porch. Both women were smiling and animated as I came up the steps.

"You two look cool and refreshed," I said.

"Oh, Mathoo, we're so happy for you," my aunt said.

Trudy looked the way she had the day Beth and I married. She wore the same satisfied smile, and a tear slid down her cheek.

"Oh?"

"There's no reason to be secretive, dear," Aunt Lela Maude said. "Elizabeth told us all about it."

"All about what?" I said. If she had told them anything about last night, they certainly wouldn't be smiling.

"Sweetheart, she told us that the two of you have buried the hatchet, and that you're gettin' back together after all."

"What?"

"I must say, you don't seem very excited," Aunt Lela Maude said.

Trudy's expression changed to one of concern. She wiped away her tear of happiness with the back of her hand.

"What's the matter, child?" she said.

"This whole thing is unbelievable," I said. "Beth and I are not getting back together, and I can't imagine why she told you such a thing."

Aunt Lela Maude paled.

"Elizabeth told us about your delightful evenin' together, and how you both decided that you missed one another somethin' awful. She said that you both owned up to the mistakes you had made in your marriage and forgave each other, and that you were plannin' to remarry."

"She lied. The woman's gone mad!"

"Oh, dear, I'm so confused," my aunt said.

"That makes two of us," Trudy said. "Honey, I think you'd better have a talk with Beth before she spreads the rumor all over Martinsville."

"Don't worry. I'm going to set her straight right now," I said. "I never want to see her again."

I didn't want to call the house in case Beth's mother answered, and I didn't want to go through her secretary while I was so angry, so I called her cell phone. She didn't answer, so I had to leave a message. I had to put a stop to her insanity:

"Beth, this is your ex. I don't know what you think you have to gain by making up lies about our relationship, but you must stop it immediately. And you had better stay away from my family. I can't imagine what kind of demented scheme you're trying to cook up, but leave me out of it. This is goodbye."

I tried to make my mind go blank while I showered. If I could get through the next few days without any more craziness, I would be on my way back to Denver and the real world.

Sam and Ron had baby clothes spread out on the kitchen table when I came downstairs. Trudy and Aunt Lela Maude were admiring the tiny pastel outfits.

"Oh, just look at these precious little things, Mathoo," my aunt cooed. "Samantha was so smart to buy unisex colors."

"Cute," I said, glancing at the tabletop. "Where's Uncle Stuart?"

"He said somethin' about trimmin' the shrubs," Trudy said.

I found my uncle on the patio, lounging on a chaise. He brandished a pair of pruning shears while staring at the uneven hedge that surrounded the back yard.

"Getting ready to do some yard work?" I said.

Uncle Stuart pulled his gaze away from the hedge to look up at me.

"Yes, in the fullness of time. I'm trying to decide whether I should do this the correct way and take out the superfluous branches, or just lop off the rough edges to make the hedge look neat."

"That's easy," I said. "The latter; it's just a hedge."

"I suppose you're right. The other way would take too long and be a great deal more work."

I wasn't a fan of yard work, but I was willing to do most anything to keep from being cooped up in the house, listening to the women ooh and aah over baby clothes. It would also be a chance to bring up the subject of the accident when nobody else was within earshot.

I tagged along like a dog following my uncle as he headed for the hedge, and he turned to look at me with an expression close to that of annoyance.

"If you want to help, go get a trash bag for the clippings," he said.

I found a leaf and lawn bag in the garage and hurried back to my uncle. He seemed to be taking his task seriously.

"We're considering going to the police," I blurted.

Uncle Stuart turned to face me. His piercing blue eyes bored into mine.

"It's a little late for that, don't you think?"

"That's true, but Joe Bob's having a real hard time with the situation. The guilt is killing him."

"Yes, I expect it is," Uncle Stuart said, and turned back to his work.

Ron came out to tell us lunch was ready.

"Well, what do you think?" my uncle said.

My brother-in-law pushed his glasses up on his nose.

"Since you asked, you're going about it all wrong," he said. "You see, you're supposed to take out some of the branches back close to the main stem and...."

"I asked you how the hedge looks, not the proper procedure."

Ron cleared his throat.

"It looks fine," he said.

I wondered if he had ever stood up to anyone in his life. No wonder my sister treated him like her little carpet.

Sam sat at her place at the table scowling, and I assumed she was having another of her mood swings.

"I understand your ex is out to get you," she said.

"Something like that," I said.

"I wish I'd been here when she came over this morning. You can bet I would have set her straight."

"It's been done," I said.

"She's one of those women who won't take no for an answer. You really shouldn't have gone to dinner with her last night. I'm sure it encouraged her. She's probably spread rumors about you all over town by now."

"I told you, Sam, I took care of it. Let's drop it, shall we?"

"I swear, Matt, you don't have to be so testy."

I knew she was itching for another fight, and no matter what I said would add fuel to the fire.

"I'm sorry," I said, thinking refusal to argue was the best way to deal with her.

Uncle Stuart winked at me from across the table.

"One of these days, you'll look back on this with longing, Matt. What I wouldn't give to have beautiful women chasing after me," he said with a grin.

"It's just this particular one who's a problem," I said.

"Just forget it, my boy. You'll only be here for a couple of more days. No harm done."

"That's true, dear," Aunt Lela Maude said. "And I'm sure there are lots of delightful young women in Denver. You have plenty of time to find the right one. You and Elizabeth were just babies when you married."

"I'm not actively seeking a relationship right now, Aunt Lela Maude."

"No, of course not," she said.

Ron must have wanted to escape from the women, too, because he accompanied Uncle Stuart and me to the back yard after lunch. He stood out of the way with his hands stuffed into his pockets, nodding approval as Uncle Stuart switched from his lazy method to pruning correctly.

Trudy stuck her head out the back door to tell me I had a phone call. Bernie was on the other end of the line, and he sounded strange, like maybe he was reading from a script.

"Matt, I feel awkward about this," he said. "I know you haven't had much time to spend with your family. I'll understand if you feel you shouldn't accept, but Lee Ann and I would really like for you to come over to the house for dinner tonight. No hard feelings if you don't think you can get away."

It didn't sound like an invitation he had really wanted to issue, and I had an inkling that it might not be strictly social. But being curious by nature, I told him I would come.

Uncle Stuart and Ron had finished with the hedge by the time I got off the phone, so I showered and stretched out on Sam's bed in the pink room, dozed off, and dreamed:

It was the evening of the visitation at the funeral home. Joe Bob, Bernie, Uncle Stuart, and I decided to go for a nightcap instead of going straight home. We were in Joe Bob's old Buick, but Joe Bob wasn't driving; I was. I had turned to say something to someone in the back seat. Before I could return my eyes to the road, I felt an impact and heard a thud. Jimmy Banks was standing in the middle of the street with outstretched arms; he was smiling. Then, the scene shifted to the cemetery. I was holding a bouquet of flowers, the one that Joe Bob had sent to the funeral home to honor my mother. I laid the flowers on Mom's grave; it was in the pauper's section.

Chapter Sixteen

Bernie and his wife lived on a cul-de-sac in a neat bungalow with a manicured lawn. I parked on the street and took my time approaching the house. Bernie opened the door before I had a chance to ring the bell. He had on an old pair of cut-offs and a faded tee shirt. His arm circled a beautiful little girl who sat on his hip with both of her chubby arms around his neck.

"Well, hello there, cutie," I said to the child.

"Hey, Matt, come in," Bernie said. "Lee Ann'll be out in a few minutes. This is our little Claire."

"She sure is pretty," I said.

Claire stared at me, and drooled around the finger she was sucking.

"Fix you a drink?" Bernie said.

"That'd be great."

"What'll it be?" Bernie said, depositing the child into a playpen filled with toys.

"Bourbon and soda, if you have it."

"Coming right up," he said, heading for a bar in the corner of a large family room.

"Great house, Bernie," I said.

"We enjoy it. I'll give you the nickel tour later."

I was in my old friend's house, making the kind of small talk I hated, because I didn't know what else to do. Bernie sounded like a stranger, maybe a realtor, showing a house to make a few bucks. It was clear to me that the two of us had been thrown into an uncomfortable situation, and I wasn't sure why, or who had been the instigator.

Lee Ann made her entrance as Bernie handed me my drink, and I stood to greet her.

"We're so glad you could make it," she said, and put on an affected smile.

I had been around this woman for all of ten minutes the night of my mother's visitation when I realized she wasn't going to be one of my favorite people. She was indeed quite attractive with large dark eyes and an olive complexion, and her smartly bobbed hair looked shiny and healthy.

"What would you like to drink, sweetheart?" Bernie asked his wife.

"A glass of chardonnay, thanks."

Claire began making little whiny noises as soon as she saw her mother. She stretched her arms over the rim of her cage to be liberated.

"You're fine where you are, sweetie," Lee Ann said, smiling at her offspring.

The doorbell rang, and Lee Ann excused herself to answer it. Moments later, she returned with a couple about our age.

"Susan and Dick Tripley, I'd like you to meet Matt Stevenson." She called up another smile.

I stood to be introduced and shake hands with the newcomers, and Bernie resumed his duties as bartender. Then, we all sat down to watch the baby try to climb from her confinement while making unhappy noises.

"Be a good girl, or daddy will have to lock you in the closet again," Bernie said.

"Stop that, Bernie," Lee Ann said. "You say things like that so often that people will start to think you're serious."

We all offered indulgent smiles.

"It's nearly Claire's bedtime, and she's ready for her bottle," Lee Ann said.

"I've been hearing what a wonderful cook you are, Lee Ann," I said.

The young mother went to the playpen to pick up the child.

"I really should have prepared something special," she said, "but Bernie's grilling tonight. He does a pretty decent job."

"Speaking of the grill, should I be lighting it?" Bernie said.

"Yes. You do that while I feed Claire. Make yourselves comfortable and get acquainted," Lee Ann told her guests. "I won't be long."

"I understand you and Bernie are old friends," Dick said.

"Yes. We've known one another since we were teenagers."

"We've only known Lee Ann and Bernie for about six months," Susan said. "Our house is just down the street."

The doorbell rang again, and I wondered if the Zuckermans had invited the entire neighborhood.

"Would someone please get the door?" Lee Ann called.

"On my way," I said.

I opened the door to find myself face-to-face with my ex. She wore a white sundress that showed off her golden tan, and she looked gorgeous.

"Beth?"

She seemed to ignore my shocked expression.

"Matt, this is a surprise."

Bernie hadn't said a word about having invited her to dinner. I would never have thought he would be one to try his hand at matchmaking. Maybe his wife had roped him into it.

"May I come in?" Beth said. "I promise I'm an invited guest."

I knew all about her promises, and they weren't worth the breath it took to utter them.

"Certainly."

She breezed past me into the family room and introduced herself to the Tripleys.

"I'm Beth Stevenson," she said. "Matt and I used to be married."

"Now we're just friends," I said, managing a weak smile.

"That's good," Dick said. "It's always better to part friends."

Bernie came in from outside.

"Hello, Beth," he said, and pecked her on the cheek. "Don't you look smashing."

"Thank you."

"Scotch and soda?" Bernie said.

"Please."

Beth had obviously been here before, and Bernie seemed to be aware of her cocktail preference. I couldn't imagine why he would want to corral the two of us in the same room.

Bernie suggested we have our drinks on the patio while the grill heated.

"That's a good idea," Susan said. "I adore your back yard."

The others agreed. I was definitely the outsider in this group. I wondered how many times Beth had been here, and if she and Lee Ann had some connection.

Our hostess came out to join us.

"Beth, it's so good to see you," she said.

"Oh, I wouldn't have missed it. Have I arrived too late to see my little Claire?"

"I'm afraid so," Lee Ann said. "I just put her to bed."

"I think I must be predisposed to be late," Beth said. "Ask Matt."

She smiled and took a sip of her drink. I thought she appeared to be looking at me for confirmation.

"Sorry. I don't remember," I said.

Bernie gave me what I took to be an apologetic look.

"I hope everybody likes salmon," he said.

Lee Ann looked at her watch.

"I'd better go finish up inside," she said.

The other women went with her, and Dick went to freshen his drink.

"I know what you're thinking," Bernie said. "It was none of my doing. I would never have invited Beth without checking with you. You didn't mention her even once during our fishing trip, so I knew you didn't have any coals left for her."

"You don't know how right you are about that," I said. "Are Lee Ann and Beth good friends?"

"I wouldn't call them close friends. They met at some charity thing. Lee Ann's an incurable matchmaker. She's been trying to fix Beth up for months, inviting her for dinner and parties to meet every unattached male we know."

"I see. Did Beth know I was going to be here tonight?"

"Not until she ran into Lee Ann at the supermarket today. Actually, she sort of invited herself."

"That figures."

"What do you mean?" Bernie said.

Dick came through the sliding glass door to join us.

"Later," I said.

It appeared the Zuckermans had managed to time everything perfectly: Bernie was taking the salmon off the grill and sliding it onto a platter just as Lee Ann stuck her head out to tell us the vegetables were ready.

The meal was delicious, and dinner conversation didn't suffer, because everyone at the table had interesting tidbits about Martinsville to share except yours truly. I not only felt left out; I had no interest in their small town gossip, politics, or the butts of jokes I didn't know.

The time spent having coffee and dessert in the living room was nearly more than I could take. No matter what anyone said, Beth seized the opportunity to make reference to something similar that had occurred during our married past. So as soon as I thought I could escape without appearing blatantly rude, I made a feeble excuse about family business and left.

I drove to Joe Bob's and found him watching a bowling tournament on his big screen TV.

"This is not exactly an exciting way to spend a Saturday night," I said.

"It's about as excitin' as it's gonna git."

"You should have had dinner with me," I said. "You could have been surrounded by beautiful women."

"Maybe you'd like to explain that."

"I've been at Bernie's. You know his wife."

"Not very well. I've been around her a few times. She's not exactly friendly."

"I think she's a knockout," I said. "Sexy, too."

"Yeah, she's that all right, but I gotta tell you, that woman rules the roost. She tells old Bernard to jump, and he asks, 'how high?'"

"I got that impression, too."

"What other women?"

"The Zuckerman's neighbors were there, and the wife wasn't too shabby."

"Yeah?"

"And then there was Beth."

"You're kiddin'," Joe Bob said, grinning.

"I wish I were. Bernie said she invited herself after she found out I was going to be there."

"That woman wants you bad."

"I don't understand her," I said. "She was the one who wanted a divorce. Now, all of a sudden, I'm on her *must have* list."

"Looks like." He grabbed the remote and turned off the TV. "Let's go outside and have a beer."

We leaned back in our chairs with longnecks, feet on the table, and studied the star-studded sky. Joe Bob lit a cigarette.

"If I had a cigar, I'd smoke with you tonight," I said.

"Well, why didn't you say so? I've got cigars. How about a Macanudo?"

"That'd be fine."

He went inside and came back with the cigar.

"I keep 'em on hand in case somebody wants one," he said.

He fished in his pocket for a knife, unwrapped the smoke, and sliced off the end, then handed it to me with his lighter.

The idea of smoking reminded me of the previous night. I hadn't told Joe Bob about the joint.

The cigar tasted good. I hadn't smoked one in ages, and I was enjoying this one.

"Do you ever see Beth around town?" I asked.

"Once in a while. Why?"

"I just wondered what her friends were like. She had some grass last night."

"Yeah?"

"Yeah. She was pretty nonchalant about it."

"Now I know how you got so wasted."

"That and a whole lot of alcohol. I told you, I'm not used to it."

"You think she's turned into a pothead or somethin'?"

"I don't know, but she's not the Beth I married."

Joe Bob was an expert at changing the subject.

"How's that cigar?" he said.

"Great. Hey, would you be interested in playing a round of golf with Uncle Stuart and me tomorrow morning?"

"Well, sure. What time do you want to play?"

"I'll have to call The Meadows and see when I can get a tee time."

"No, you don't. I'll call the club. We can play whenever we want."

"When did you join the country club?"

The man was one big contradiction. He lived in a trailer and belonged to an exclusive country club.

"Coupla years ago," he said. "I love golf, but I only git to play on weekends. Work at the garage keeps me right busy."

"Are you sure you can get a tee time on such short notice?"

"You bet. Wonder if Bernard would like to play?"

"You'll have to call him and find out. I'm not about to call his house."

"You think it's too late to call?" he said.

"Nah."

Joe Bob dug out his phone and typed in the number.

"I hope his wife don't answer," he said.

"Hang up if she does," I said, feeling like a kid.

"Bernard, my man, how's your golf game?"

Pause.

"That don't matter. I'm off my game, too. We're gonna meet at the club at 9:30."

Bernie must have asked who would make up our foursome.

"Matt and the judge."

Joe Bob grinned. "He's checkin' with the missus," he said.

Then, he was back on the phone. "See you then."

"I take it she said Bernie can come out and play," I said.

Joe Bob nodded. "You think old Bernard's happy?"

"He seems to be."

Joe Bob stretched his long arms over his head, returned them to the table, and methodically cracked his knuckles.

"I don't think I could take a woman like her no matter how much of a looker she is. Can't see myself askin' for permission to go to the can."

"Whatever floats your boat, I guess," I said.

"I reckon. That's prob'ly why I never got married. I do what I want when I want to do it, but sometimes I git downright lonesome. Everbody else goes home from work to somebody who cares enough about 'em to cook their meals, and I come home to a cat and a TV dinner."

I puffed my cigar. "That's by choice, I assume."

"Yeah, it is, but sometimes I wonder what I'm missin'."

I stubbed out my cigar.

"I guess I'd better be getting back to the house," I said.

"I'll come by to pick you and the judge up about 8:30."

I stood and shook my friend's hand. He had a handshake that said a lot about him.

I smiled to myself as I turned on the ignition.

Chapter Seventeen

The house was quiet. I went upstairs and undressed to go to bed, but I wasn't sleepy. Maybe a glass of warm milk would help. I went down to the kitchen in my underwear. When I opened the refrigerator door to get the milk, I saw a bottle of good chardonnay which appeared to be missing no more than a few ounces. Whoever had indulged had put a stopper in the bottle. Suddenly, a glass of wine sounded better than milk, so I poured some into a goblet and took it out on the patio.

I stood just outside the kitchen door, waiting for my eyes to become accustomed to the dark before going any farther. After a few minutes I could see the length of the patio; I was alone. I could see the birdbath and the outline of stones surrounding the lily pond. Everything looked small: the house, the patio, and the entire backyard. It had all seemed larger when I was growing up.

I stretched out on a chaise lounge and sipped my wine, feeling something akin to peaceful, but not quite. The things that had been cluttering my mind were not crowding one another to be my top priority. Come Monday, Mother's attorney would read her last will and testament. I was certain there would be no big surprises. My sister and I would hear what we already knew: the bulk of the estate would be divided equally between the two of us. Oh, she would probably have left a modest sum of money and maybe a piece of jewelry to Aunt Lela Maude, and I was certain that she had remembered Trudy in her will.

I wondered what Sam would want to do with the house. The smart thing for us to do would be to sell it, but knowing my sister, I wasn't sure she would agree to that. If I weren't so broke, I'd give it to her, and she could do whatever she wanted with it.

Poor Sam. She was never content as a child, and I was sure she never would be. I had to admit that she was quite an actress though. She gave the appearance of being happily married to Ron, but I knew better. After a while she would tire of his letting her push him around; then, she'd dump him. If he had been privy to her past record, he probably never would have married her.

When Sam was a little girl, she never had more than one friend at a time. She was always the one who called all the shots, and the friendships never lasted long. It was the same after she started dating. She chose boyfriends who allowed her to walk all over them, and it didn't take long for her to cast them aside like so many pairs of worn-out shoes. Her husband was just like all of the boyfriends, except that he had married her and now he was the father of her child. I had feigned happiness upon learning of the pregnancy, but I was truly sorry about it. Sam would have to consider her innocent child. I wondered how that would affect her behavior.

My eyes were getting heavy. I sipped the last of my wine and put down the glass. There was a light breeze, and I was very comfortable. I could feel myself dozing off. Then, Beth crept into my mind in a dream:

I could see her walking toward me, and she seemed to grow larger with each step. Her beautiful face was masked in an evil grin as she looked down at me.

"You think you don't want me, Matt." Her voice was husky. "The truth is that you want me more than your next breath; you must have me."

"You're not the real Beth," I said. "You're someone pretending to be her. Get away from me."

The smile left her face. She reached into the top of her black teddy and pulled out a switchblade. I could see it gleaming in the moonlight. She licked her index finger and ran it across the razor-like blade.

"Oh, poor Beth cut herself," she said in that little-girl voice I hated. "You'll have to kiss it and make it well."

"What are you going to do with that thing?"

"That depends on you, Matt," she said, thrusting her bloody finger toward me.

I didn't know how or when she had done it, but she had handcuffed me to the chaise.

"Kiss Beth's finger," she said.

I had to obey her; she was holding a knife, and I was cuffed and helpless. I kissed the finger and tasted blood.

"Now, kiss me on the mouth."

My lips didn't feel like they belonged to me, but I tried to kiss her.

"Do you call that a kiss? Kiss me like you mean it, or I'll make you very sorry."

She pulled away from me and stood next to the chaise. From my perspective she looked like a giant. She held the knife between her teeth, then leaned down and tugged off my boxers.

"Now, where were we?" she said.

She laid the switchblade on a low table close to my head, and sank down beside me.

"Oh, yes, I remember," she said. "You desperately wanted to kiss me, and I refused."

She bit her lower lip, then smiled.

"I won't tease you anymore, you poor darling," she said.

She kissed me long and hard, cutting off my air.

"That was ever so much better," she said. "Are you ready, darling?"

"For what?"

"To make love, of course."

Her eyes roamed my nude body, and my muscles tensed.

"What's the matter with you?" she said. "Don't I turn you on anymore?"

"No!" I shouted, waking myself.

I pushed myself up on the chaise lounge. My right arm whipped to the side involuntarily, knocking the wine goblet off the table, and I realized that I wasn't cuffed to the chair. I had on my underwear. Cold sweat was slick on my arms and legs, and I felt it on the back of my neck. The wine glass hadn't broken. I retrieved it and went into the house, feeling foolish.

Sleep didn't come easily after the crazy dream, and my mind began filling with the unfortunate circumstances I couldn't control. I figured I had dozed off and on for about four hours when the alarm sounded, and I smacked the snooze button a couple of times before I could make myself get out of bed.

Trudy was in the kitchen when I came downstairs. She had on an apron over her Sunday-go-to-meetin' dress.

"Don't you look lovely this morning," I said.

"Is that what you're wearin' to church?" she said.

"I'm not going to church; I'm playing golf."

Just then the rest of the family trailed into the kitchen. They were all dressed in their Sunday best.

"Good morning," I said.

"Nice outfit," Sam said.

"Thank you. I think it'll pass muster at the country club."

My sister shook her head derisively, seated herself at the table, and took great pains to place her napkin just so across her lap. She was finished with the conversation.

Uncle Stuart sat at the table, sipping coffee. I took a seat beside him.

"I was going to invite you to play, too," I said.

My uncle brightened and loosened his tie.

"Well, that would be most enjoyable," he said.

"Stuart, you're already dressed for church," Aunt Lela Maude said.

"I never get to spend time with my nephew. I accept your invitation, Matt. It won't take but a minute for me to change."

I hadn't considered inviting Ron to join us. He didn't seem like the athletic type, and even if he was, my sister would have seen to it that he didn't accept the invitation.

Joe Bob rolled up in front of Mother's house at 8:30 sharp. He got out of his truck and started up the walk as Uncle Stuart and I came out onto the porch. My friend was dressed in high-end golf attire, and had the demeanor of a pro on tour. Uncle Stuart and I gave one another the onceover, then started down the steps. Our khaki shorts and plain-looking golf shirts would have to do.

"Good morning, Joe Bob," my uncle said. "Thank you for the invitation."

"Oh, I'm glad you can join us, Judge," Joe Bob said.

Nobody mentioned the accident on the drive to the country

club, and I wondered if it would stay buried all day. If I had an opportunity to bring it up, I was definitely going to do it.

Bernie was getting clubs out of his trunk when we drove into the parking lot. We all went into the pro shop together.

"It's nice to see you, Mister Kincaid," said the assistant pro behind the counter.

"Good to see you, Brandon. Uh, we're gonna need a coupla sets of clubs."

"I'll fix you right up," Brandon said.

"Put everthing on my tab," Joe Bob said, handing his club card to the young man.

"No, Joe Bob," I said. "I'm paying for Uncle Stuart and myself."

"No, you're not. You're my guests."

I tried to argue with him, but he wouldn't budge.

"Come on," he said. "We don't have but a coupla minutes to warm up."

We lined up on the driving range. Everyone teed up and began practicing shots except Bernie. He looked like a contortionist, going through a series of stretches.

Joe Bob stopped working on his swing to watch Bernie.

"Damn, Bernard, you look a whole lot like a pretzel. I'll bet you can git a job in a circus if you ever git tired of the dry cleanin' business."

"Very funny. Stretching is important. Ask any sports doctor."

"Well, I hope you're stretched all you want to be, because we're up."

I had assumed Uncle Stuart and I would share a cart, but Joe Bob had other ideas.

"Judge, why don't you ride with me," he said.

Bernie said he would drive our cart since he was familiar with the course. He was a terrible golfer, and seemed to seek out trouble on every hole. His prescription sunglasses were new, and he put the onus on them for every bad shot.

I had never played golf with Uncle Stuart, and I was surprised at how good he was at the game. He approached each tee box with deliberation. His khaki shorts came nearly down to his bony knees, and his calves were skinny and hairless. I thought he looked so fragile that a strong gust of wind might blow him over. His drives didn't go very far, but they were all straight, and he was able to stay out of trouble. We all admired his short game. He chipped so close to the hole that he rarely had more than one putt.

If my game was sporadic, Joe Bob's was more so. He would birdie a hole, then take his maximum strokes on the next one. His ball might go a mile down the middle of the fairway, or it could go so far out of bounds we couldn't find it, but he never seemed to get rattled and stayed in good humor.

Bernie was in a snit before we began playing, and his attitude didn't improve during the round.

"Hey, Bernie, you're driving this cart like a hacked-off kid," I said.

"Sorry. I'm a little out of sorts."

"Hey, it's a beautiful day, and we're on a golf course," I said.

"Yeah, yeah, yeah. It's a beautiful day, and I'm playing a round with my friends. My golf game stinks, and my wife's mad at me. What could be more fun?"

"Why is your wife mad at you?"

"Well, if you must know, she's upset about last night."

"What about last night?"

"You know, but it's no big deal."

"How would I know? She seemed happy enough when I left."

"That's just it; you left. She's bent out of shape; thought you were rude."

I had to take a minute before speaking. It was hard for me to believe a grown man was letting something so trivial get under his skin when we were faced with a life-altering situation he seemed to have forgotten.

"You know why I had to leave, Bernie. I couldn't sit there and smile any longer while Beth relived our entire marriage. If I had known she would be there, I never would have accepted your invitation. I plan to do everything I can to avoid her until I leave town. End of conversation."

Bernie puffed up like a wet hen, and we finished the round in uncomfortable silence. I didn't think either of us could play worse than we had been playing, but I was wrong.

Joe Bob wanted to show us the club and spring for lunch. I thought Bernie would decline, but he didn't. We had admired the pool and tennis courts, and were washing up in the locker room. Bernie reached for a towel in a basket to my right side and mumbled something. His expression told me he was sorry he had been such an ass. I nodded.

The grill was on the second floor overlooking a practice green. Three of the walls were nothing but glass, and a hostess seated us at a large, round table with a great view.

"How 'bout a drink before we order," Joe Bob said. "What'll it be, Judge?"

Uncle Stuart ordered his usual bourbon neat, and the rest of us asked for beers.

"I must say that was an enjoyable round," my uncle said. "And the company was superb. I can't recall when I've had such a good time."

"I'm right glad to hear that, Judge," Joe Bob said.

We talked about the game of golf, then ordered more drinks and lunch. Bernie seemed to have brightened considerably, and I was glad. We were nearly finished eating when someone mentioned our fishing trip. Uncle Stuart listened with rapt attention to each of the tales.

When the table was cleared, we ordered more drinks. Uncle Stuart wasn't one to sit on the sidelines, listening to other people's adventures. He began spinning a few yarns of his own, and the more he drank, the more exaggerated they became. I laughed with everyone else, but the laughter sounded hollow to me, even my own.

The grill had emptied except for us, and I watched Joe Bob's expression change.

"Judge," he said, "there's somethin' I've wanted to talk to you about all mornin', but I couldn't git up the nerve to do it."

"What's that, Joe Bob?"

"'Bout what happened the other night."

"I don't think this is the time, or the place to discuss that," Bernie said.

"That might be true, but I got to talk about it," Joe Bob said. "Will you guys come by my place for a few minutes when we leave here?"

I knew Bernie would balk. He was a lot more interested in patching things up with his wife than discussing the forbidden topic.

"I need to get home," he said.

"Come just for a few minutes, Bernard," Joe Bob said.

"All right, but I can't stay long."

The afternoon sun was bright when we drove into the trailer park. It showcased the ugliness of the place. Low makeshift porches sported cheap indoor/outdoor carpet, and the plastic grass glistened in the white light. Gravel dust clung to the trailers like dirty glue.

Uncle Stuart stepped inside Joe Bob's double-wide and stood in the middle of the living room, admiring the TV.

"My, my," he said, "I don't believe I've ever seen such a large screen outside a theatre."

"'Scuse me for sayin' so, Judge," Joe Bob said, "but we ain't here to talk about TVs."

"No, 'course not. What was it about the other night you wanted to discuss?" Uncle Stuart said.

We all sat down but Bernie. He stood by the door with his arms crossed.

"Well, here's the thing," Joe Bob said. "What happened the other night haunts me; rules my mind. I can't sleep, and it's all I can think about."

"I'd say that's fairly natural," Uncle Stuart said. "It's still fresh in your memory. It takes time to get over something that strikes you as being traumatic."

"That's what Matt and I have tried to tell him," Bernie said, sensing an ally in my uncle.

"Here's what none of you can git through your heads," Joe Bob said, "I killed a man, and I'm not the kind of man who does things like that. It's destroyin' me."

He slumped down on the end of the couch and put his face in his hands.

"What do you think you should do?" Uncle Stuart said.

Joe Bob straightened up and looked at my uncle.

"Well, sir, I think I ought to go to the police and tell 'em I'm guilty. That's what I feel like I've gotta do. It would make me rest a little easier if I had everbody's approval."

"I don't think I would do anything like that without giving considerable thought to the matter," Uncle Stuart said.

"I know what you're thinkin', Judge. It could screw up all of your lives, too, but what I'd do would be to tell the cops I was by myself when it happened. That way y'all wouldn't be involved, you see."

Uncle Stuart tugged at his mustache the way he does when he is pondering something.

"I don't think that's such a good idea," he finally said. "It's admirable that you don't want to involve the rest of us, but we certainly wouldn't want you to perjure yourself if you were questioned about it under oath."

Joe Bob's eyes glistened, and he threaded his fingers through his hair.

"I just don't know what to do," he said.

"Why can't you listen to reason?" Bernie said. "All you want to do is salve your conscience."

Something snapped inside me. I was off the couch and across the room so fast I don't think I could have stopped if I had wanted to. My fist crashed into Bernie's face with all the force I owned. This was totally out of character for me, but I stood in front of my stunned, bleeding friend with my feet apart and fists doubled up to do it again. Uncle Stuart and Joe Bob rushed to restrain me.

Bernie's nose was dripping blood all over the front of his shirt. He looked at me in disbelief.

"You hit me," he said. "You actually hit me. How could you do that?"

I didn't have an answer.

Bernie's wire rims sat askew on his quickly swelling nose, and all I could do was stare at him. I felt stupid, like I had just done something my brain hadn't told me to do.

"I'm outta here," Bernie said, reaching for the door. "It seems we don't always know who our friends are. Get this straight: the past few days have been nothing but hell for me. Nothing has gone right during the time I have spent with my two old high school pals. Don't call me whining again. I'm through with this whole mess."

Uncle Stuart traded my arm for Bernie's.

"No, no, son," he said. "You can't leave in such a state of mind. Come sit down. Let's take care of that nose. Things sometimes just get out of hand, and tempers flare. It happens all the time."

Bernie reluctantly let my uncle lead him to a chair. Uncle Stuart wet a kitchen towel and cleaned up Bernie's face, then placed the towel on the back of his neck. He found a matchbook on a counter and folded part of the cardboard to put under Bernie's upper lip to staunch his nosebleed.

"He had no right to hit me," Bernie said. "No right at all." The cardboard under his lip made him sound like he had a speech impediment.

"Joe Bob, do you suppose you might make us a pot of coffee?" Uncle Stuart said.

"Sure thing, Judge."

"Bernie, I don't know what got into me," I said. "I can't tell you how sorry I am."

He didn't acknowledge my apology.

"I caused it," Joe Bob said. "It's all my fault."

"Let's not spend the rest of the afternoon placing blame," Uncle Stuart said.

"What am I gonna do?" Joe Bob said. His hand shook as he poured coffee.

"I'm afraid you'll have to make that decision by yourself," Uncle Stuart said. "We've all given you our opinions. Know everything that has happened is history, and nothing can change it. Your decision, however, can change many things. For you as an individual, it means you'll be a free man, or you won't."

Joe Bob sighed. "Thank y'all for comin' by here. I'll let you know what I decide."

The four of us shook hands. It wasn't until we had left the

double-wide that I realized Uncle Stuart and I needed a lift back to the house.

I had turned to go back inside when Bernie called to me, "Come on. I'll drive you guys home."

It was a quiet ride. I thought it was really decent of Bernie to take us home, and couldn't imagine what he thought of me. If I'd had to make an educated guess, I would bet that our friendship was kaput.

Chapter Eighteen

There was a car I didn't recognize parked in front of the house when Uncle Stuart and I got home. I hoped it was one of Sam's old friends so I could just say hello and head for the shower, but that wasn't the case. We entered the living room to find Aunt Lela Maude serving tea to Beth and an elderly gentleman who looked vaguely familiar. He stood, and Beth put on her sweetest smile.

"Hello, Matt; Uncle Stuart," she said. "Matt, you remember my Uncle Clyde."

The uncle extended his hand, so I shook it. "How do you do, sir," I said.

"And Uncle Stuart Maxwell," Beth said, "I'd like you to meet Clyde Baxter."

"This is a surprise, Beth," I said.

"We do apologize for dropping in unannounced," she said. "Uncle Clyde and I went to church. Then, he insisted on taking me to brunch. We've been out all day."

She paused to sip her tea, and I waited for a further explanation.

I assumed she had wanted to act fast, before she was served with the restraining order I promised.

"You see, over brunch I told Uncle Clyde about the little talk you and I had the other night, and he thinks the three of us should discuss things," she said.

"What things?" My tone was as rude as I had meant for it to be.

Aunt Lela Maude and Uncle Stuart excused themselves and went to their room.

"Well, Matt, since I'm a retired minister and have done my share of counseling over the past forty years, I thought I might be able to give you kids some guidance in this matter," Beth's uncle said.

"You'll have to forgive me, Reverend Baxter," I said. "I'm afraid I'm totally in the dark. What matter do you have in mind?"

He looked at his niece, then back at me.

"Well, your plans, my boy."

"What plans?"

"Why, your plans to get back together like the good Lord intends for you to do, of course."

"I'm afraid you've been misinformed. We have no plans to get back together. I'm flying to Denver tomorrow, and won't be coming back to Martinsville."

"You see," Beth said, "I told you how confused he is."

"I'm not one bit confused, Beth. Why are you telling everyone we're getting back together when you know it's not true?"

She threw up her hands in mock despair.

"That's not what you said when you made love to me two short nights ago," she said. Tears welled in her green eyes.

"I'm confident the Lord will forgive that indiscretion, son," Uncle Clyde said. "After all, neither of you has been married to anyone else."

"There's nothing to forgive! I don't know what lies your niece has been telling you, but I most certainly have not been intimate with her since we divorced. I will tell you that she has suggested it more than once during the week I've been here."

Beth took that as her cue to turn on the tears.

"He's in denial for some reason, Uncle Clyde."

"Why don't we join hands and pray about it," the minister said.

"Forgive me, Reverend," I said, "but I don't want to pray about it."

Something caused me to look up, and my eyes focused on Sam at the top of the stairs, leaning on the banister. I didn't know how long she had been standing there, or how much of the conversation she had overheard, but there was no mistaking the hatred in her eyes.

"You don't know when to give up, do you, Beth?" she said.

My ex looked up, surprised.

"Samantha," she said.

"You've done too much damage to this family already," Sam said. "Get out of this house, and leave my brother alone!"

Sam started toward the stairs.

"Forgive me, dear, but this conversation doesn't concern you," Beth said.

"Don't call me dear."

Sam rushed down the first few steps.

"Get out of my mother's house!"

Sam's foot slipped, and she tumbled forward and rolled down the stairs, bumping like a rubber ball.

"Call an ambulance!" I yelled.

Sam lay curled up at the bottom of the stairs, hugging her still-flat abdomen.

Then, I was kneeling beside her.

"Lie still, Sam," I said. "An ambulance will be here in a few minutes."

Beth and her uncle were standing over us as Ron came running down the stairs.

"What happened?" he said, dropping to his knees.

"She missed a step," I said.

Aunt Lela Maude and Uncle Stuart stood in their bedroom doorway quiet as mice.

"The ambulance is on its way," Trudy said.

Sam was making little moaning noises, and Ron slid his arms under her.

Aunt Lela Maude snapped out of her trance.

"Don't move her, Ron," she said.

"My baby," Sam whimpered.

I looked up at Beth.

"You need to leave," I said.

Without a word of protest, the minister and his niece walked out the front door just as the ambulance attendants were hurrying up the front steps.

I held the door open for the EMTs, and they rolled in a gurney. Ron was hovering over Sam, and I had to pull him away from her so they could get close enough to get her on the stretcher.

"My wife's pregnant," he said.

The love and pride in his voice were palpable.

I told Ron to ride in the ambulance with his wife. The rest of us would follow in Uncle Stuart's car and meet him at the hospital.

"Elizabeth has overstepped her bounds," Aunt Lela Maude said.

"Yes, she has, but Sam's temper didn't help matters," I said.

We didn't have to wait but a few minutes before the doctor joined us in the waiting room. His facial expression told us the bad news before he spoke.

"I'm very sorry," he said. "I'm afraid she's lost the baby. She's young and healthy, and she's going to be fine, but I want to keep her overnight."

"May we see her?" Ron asked.

"She said she'd like to see her brother," the doctor said.

"But I'm her husband."

The doctor looked embarrassed. "She specifically said that she wants to see only her brother right now."

Sam was sniffling when I entered the room.

"I blew it," she said.

"I'm so sorry, Sam."

"Me, too. I never could do anything right."

"Stop talking foolishness. You missed a step; it could have happened to anybody."

"Only to a hothead."

"You're not the only hothead in the family. I punched Bernie in the nose this afternoon."

"Why?"

"I'm not sure. I guess I've been spending too much time with him."

"Is Ron angry at me?"

"Of course not. He's disappointed like the rest of us, but I think he's hurt that you don't want to see him."

"I can't right now, Matt. I wish Mama were here. I miss her so much; Daddy, too."

"You can call Dad."

"No, I can't." She started crying. "He called the day before Mama's funeral and said he wanted to come to be here for you and me, but I told him to stay away. I told him I never wanted to see him again."

"Why did you tell him that?"

"At the time, I meant it. I felt so alone knowing I'd never see Mama again, and you and I were bickering. Truthfully, I think I wanted to hurt Daddy the way he hurt us when he left home."

"I'm sure he'll forgive you. Dad was never one to hold a grudge."

"Maybe I'll call him tomorrow. I think I'd like to go to sleep now. I'm awfully tired."

"Are you sure you don't want to see Ron for just a minute?"

"I can't, because I feel like such a hypocrite. I don't love Ron, Matt. When I married him, I thought did. I've tried to make myself love him, because he's such a good person, but I just can't."

"You're just upset," I said.

"That's true, but I know how I feel, and I don't love my husband. I loved our baby, though. Now it doesn't exist."

"Maybe you'll feel differently about Ron after some time passes."

"No, I won't. I kept my eyes closed on the way to the hospital so I wouldn't have to see him staring at me."

"I'll tell him you're very tired."

"Tell him not to hate me. He wanted this baby more than anything in the world."

"I'll tell him."

I didn't want to tell my brother-in-law an out-and-out lie. He worshiped Sam, and I knew it stung that she didn't want to see him. I ended up soft-pedaling the blow by telling him she was heavily sedated and couldn't keep her eyes open.

"I'm staying here at the hospital," Ron said. "I want to be here when she wakes up."

"Sam wants us all to go home and get a good night's rest," I said. "And Ron, she said for me to tell you that she knows how this has hurt you. Oh, and for you to please not hate her," I trailed off.

"Hate her? I absolutely adore her."

"I know."

Chapter Nineteen

I asked Uncle Stuart if I could borrow the car. Sleep wasn't my top priority; Joe Bob was. I wanted to see if he had been able to make a final decision. He had said the guilt was killing him, and I assumed he was going to turn himself in to the police. But if Uncle Stuart's straight talk had hit its mark, my friend might be back to weighing the pros and cons. Freedom was a precious commodity, and the thought of throwing it away had to feel like a kick in the gut.

At this very moment I knew that nothing could make me let it go. If I were in Joe Bob's shoes, I would make myself live with the guilt and do my best to bury it. Being behind bars with real criminals was the worst thing I could imagine. I felt fairly confident at bending people to my will, and I was about to try my luck with Joe Bob.

There was an old motorcycle parked outside Joe Bob's trailer. He hadn't mentioned owning a bike, so I assumed it belonged to a friend. Maybe I should forget trying to talk some sense into him and go back to the house. If he had company, my mission would have to be scrubbed. I would just tell him I stopped by to say hello.

I was walking toward the door, but stopped short at the sight I glimpsed through the open wood blind in a living room window. Lucy Combs stood in the middle of the room with both arms wrapped around Joe Bob. He was kneeling on an ottoman, and his face was buried between Lucy's breasts.

I didn't know what to think. When we were at Morgan's the other night, I saw a look Lucy shot at Joe Bob. It told me that they were, or had been in a relationship—at least a casual one. I took a few steps backward. If Lucy happened to look through the blind, I was pretty sure she could see me.

Joe Bob was making muffled noises and sounded like he might be crying. Surely, Lucy wasn't his confidant. If he had told her about the accident, things could really get sticky.

"Joe Bob, you got to pull yourself together, baby," she said.

I thought Lucy had a nice voice. It was sort of soft with a soothing timbre. She sounded as though she were talking to a child who had spun out on his bike in loose gravel and scraped all the skin off his arm.

Joe Bob let go of a loud sob.

"I'm just bad luck," he said. "It's wrote all over me."

"That's crazy talk, baby. You know it was an accident. Nobody would do a thing like that on purpose. I don't know anybody who'd be that mean."

"He never hurt nobody; just stuck to what he knew and didn't cause no trouble."

"I know, but what's done is done. Nobody can undo it."

"You think I'm crazy, don't you, Lucy?"

"Joe Bob, you know me better than that. I've got feelings, too."

This was definitely not a conversation I wanted to interrupt. I went back to the car and drove to the house. If Joe Bob had spilled his guts to Lucy, everybody concerned could be in trouble up to their necks. Lucy might be tight with Joe Bob, but what about the rest of us? Uncle Stuart and I would more than likely be making a trip to the law library first thing in the morning.

Ron was in the kitchen, loading the dishwasher when I got home. He looked up as I came into the room, wearing an embarrassed grin.

"I'm pretty good at this," he said. "I do a lot of things around our house."

His revelation didn't surprise me.

"That's nice," I said. "Chauvinism should be a thing of the past."

He pushed dishwasher buttons and wiped down the counter while I watched.

"It's a nice night," I said. "I think I'll go out on the patio for a while. You're welcome to join me."

"Sure."

Ron and I were barely acquainted. I doubted we would have much in common to discuss, but I felt sorry for the guy.

We reclined on a couple of chaises and looked up at the stars.

"I don't know what will happen now," he said.

"Excuse me?"

"I said I don't know what will happen now that Samantha has lost the baby."

"I don't understand."

"I worship the ground your sister walks on, Matt, but she doesn't love me; she never has."

Why was he baring his soul to someone who was powerless to do anything about it?

"You're upset about the baby," I said.

"No. Well, yes I am, but that has nothing to do with the fact that your sister doesn't love me. Well, that's not true, either. When she was going to have our baby, I thought I might have a fighting chance."

"Are you sure you're not overreacting, Ron?"

I felt like a hypocrite, asking such an inane question, but I couldn't let him know I was already privy to what he was telling me.

"We've been married for nearly two years," he said, "and I've known it the whole time. I've bent over backward to try to please her. I work hard to give her the things she wants, but the fact is that she doesn't want me."

I didn't know what to say to him.

"I'm real sorry to hear that, Ron."

"I know I'm a fool," he said, "but I don't think I can live without her. Sometimes I wake up in the middle of the night and just look at her, watch her sleep. She's so beautiful."

"She's a very pretty girl."

"I have a feeling she'll hand me my walking papers now that she's lost the baby. I think she was on the verge of doing it just before she discovered she was pregnant."

"Had the two of you discussed your marriage before you knew she was pregnant?

I wasn't sure why I didn't cut this conversation short. It might be helping him get his painful secret out in the open, but there was nothing I could do to help.

"Oh, no," he said. "We never discussed it. We both just tried to pretend everything was fine. We tried so hard to be happy."

Uncle Stuart came outside, wearing a long-sleeved shirt and a pair of khakis.

"By George, it's still hotter than Hades," he said.

"Why didn't you throw on a pair of shorts and a golf shirt?" I said.

"Mosquitoes. The little shits have a proclivity for wanting to snack on me."

"Pull up a chair," Ron said.

I was glad Uncle Stuart showed up. Surely, Ron would change the subject now that he was here. Uncle Stuart sat down and took a cigar from his shirt pocket.

"Would either of you fellows care to join me in a smoke?" he said.

We both declined.

"Helps deter the mosquitoes," he said, puffing furiously to get the thing lit.

I felt my cell phone vibrate.

"Excuse me, guys. I'll be right back."

I went into the half-bath off the kitchen to answer it. I figured Joe Bob was the only person who would be calling me on my cell phone. If the hospital staff had been calling, they would have called the landline.

Joe Bob sounded like he had lost his best friend. I assumed Lucy had left and he was home alone in his pitiful state.

"I can't understand you, Joe Bob. Try to get control of yourself before you tell me what the trouble is."

It took a couple of minutes for him to compose himself.

"I know all I've done is use you as my soundin' board since you got here," he said.

"That's not so, Joe Bob."

"Yes, it is, but this week has just about done me in. If I drove over to your house, could you come outside for a few minutes?"

"Sure."

"On my way."

Ten minutes later, I was sitting with Joe Bob in his truck in front of my mother's house.

"Okay, spill it," I said.

Joe Bob heaved a deep sigh.

"Okay, here goes. I just can't go by myself. Yes, it's crazy, but I can't help it. I couldn't think of anybody else to call but you, because I know you won't laugh at me."

"You're not making any sense, buddy. What are you talking about?"

"I'm afraid he's dead."

"Joe Bob, we know he's dead."

"Well, we don't know it. There's a fifty-fifty chance he's not."

"He's dead. You took flowers to his grave. Remember?"

Joe Bob rubbed his face with both hands.

"I'm not talkin' about Jimmy Banks."

"Who, then?"

"My old cat. Somebody drivin' like a maniac hit him and left him for dead, layin' in the gravel dust. My neighbor seen it happen. She could tell he was still alive, so she loaded him up and took him to the vet."

"You've been talking about your cat." I hoped I didn't sound too relieved.

"I called Lucy, but she was gittin' ready to go to work."

"I have a confession to make," I said.

Joe Bob raised his eyebrows.

"I accidentally saw Lucy at your place a while ago. You two got a thing going on?"

"What'd you do, spy on me through a window?"

"I came to talk to you and happened to see you and Lucy embrace as I passed the window. I couldn't actually tell what was going on between you two, but I decided it wouldn't be a good idea to knock on your door."

"Me and Lucy, it's not what you think. Yeah, we did git it on a couple of times a few years back, but we're just good friends—best friends. Lucy's a real good person. Me and her talk a lot, because we git lonesome. She stopped by on her way to work to make sure I was okay."

"So, you want me to go with you to the vet?"

"Would you? I can't help myself. I'm just stupid over my old cat no matter how crazy that makes me sound."

"Of course, I'll go with you."

Chapter Twenty

"Doc Green retired several months ago," Joe Bob said. "I don't know nothin' about the guy who took his place."

"I'm sure he's capable," I said. "Anyone who suffered through all the schooling it takes to become a vet has to be a big animal lover."

"I never thought about that, but I guess it's probably true."

"Let's go inside and find out how your cat's doing."

Joe Bob opened the door of his pickup, but hesitated.

"Do you think the guy would have called me if my cat hadn't made it?"

"Yes, I'd think so. Let's go."

I took a seat while Joe Bob spoke with a receptionist.

"Hello, ma'am. Name's Joe Bob Kincaid. A neighbor brought my cat in late this afternoon. He'd been hit by a car."

Joe Bob acted as nervous as he had the night of the accident. His mouth was dry, and he couldn't seem to keep his hands still.

"What is the cat's name?" the receptionist said.

"Tiger, but I just call him cat mostly."

"What breed?"

"I don't know. Somebody moved off and left him. He was just a little kitten, and he was half starved. Doc Green checked him over and give him all his shots. He's been takin' care of him for seven years. You've got all his records."

"Please have a seat. I'll check with the doctor."

"Thank you."

Joe Bob sat down beside me and cracked his knuckles.

"I can tell you're thinking the worst, Joe Bob," I said. "When did you become so pessimistic?"

"I don't know. Probably after Mama and Daddy got killed. My daddy was a mean son-of-a-bitch when he was drunk, but he was still my daddy. That don't make sense, does it? I mean I felt like he protected me from everthing—but him."

"I guess I can understand that."

"That wreck changed my life. My family was gone, and I was afraid of my shadow. There wasn't one single person I trusted. I kinda turned into a hermit."

"What about your uncle?"

"Uncle Jake's the one who saved me. He didn't bother knockin' on the door; just kicked it in and hauled me up off the couch; made me look him in the eye. I'd cried so much my eyes looked like two slits. He told me I had no choice but to git off my pity pot, stand up, and be a man."

"And that worked?"

"Yeah. I was scared and alone, and I needed somebody to tell me what to do. Uncle Jake took me to live with him while we got things worked out. He helped me git the house sold and shop for my double-wide. I couldn't have got a loan to start my business without him. He co-signed for me."

"I'm glad he was there for you."

A petite woman in scrubs came into the waiting room, pulling a paper hat off her dark hair. She held out her hand as she approached Joe Bob and me.

"Mr. Kincaid?"

"Yes, ma'am. That's me." Joe Bob stood to shake her hand.

"I'm Sydney Edelman," she said. "I'm taking care of your cat."

"Uh, this is my friend, Matt Stevenson," Joe Bob said.

I assumed he introduced me in case his cat was in terrible shape, or dead. He would need my support.

I stood. "I'm glad to meet you, doctor."

"Mr. Kincaid, your cat was a pitiful sight when he was brought in this afternoon. He's a sweet-natured animal. I could tell he was in a great deal of pain, but he didn't attempt to bite or scratch me when I gave him an injection to ease it. I wasn't sure he could be saved until X-rays showed how fortunate he had been."

"Do you mean he's gonna be okay?"

"I certainly think so. He did have some internal bleeding due to perforations from broken ribs, but I sutured those and stopped it. His left back leg was pretty mangled, but I was able to put it back together. It will have to be in a splint for a while, but I think it'll be fine."

"Is that all?" Joe Bob said.

"No. His tail was broken in two places, but I've splinted it, too. It should heal quickly."

"When can I take him home?"

"I want to keep him for a couple of days to make sure there's no more bleeding."

"Can we see him for a minute?" Joe Bob asked.

"You may, but his appearance might upset you. He's still asleep. I'm keeping him very lightly sedated for a while, because I don't want him to move."

"I just have to see him for a second," Joe Bob said. "Come on, Matt."

The doctor led the way to a door marked RECOVERY ROOM and took us to a cage with a padded floor. I couldn't tell that the thing in the cage was an animal. It looked more like a mummy.

Joe Bob bit his lip and turned away. "Let's go," he said.

Sydney Edelman walked us back to the waiting room.

"He'll be awake tomorrow," she said. "I promise he'll look better minus some of the bandages." She smiled.

I thought she had kindness written all over her, and there was something else she seemed to exude. Whatever it was beckoned to me. I hoped I would be able to make time to go with Joe Bob to check up on his cat before my flight.

"The doctor was encouraging," I said. "You should feel much better."

"Yeah. Yeah, I do. Now, there's somethin' else I need to tell you."

I was beginning to feel like a shrink.

"Can you tell me on the way to the house? I sort of walked out on Ron and Uncle Stuart without telling them I was leaving."

"Tell you the truth, I'd like the judge to be in on this, too. I'll drop you off, and go git a quick shower. Then, I'll come over here."

"I have a better idea. You get cleaned up, and we'll meet you at Morgan's for a drink. Uncle Stuart would like that."

Ron and Uncle Stuart were discussing the accounting business when I got back.

"I've always enjoyed working with figures," Ron said.

"That's good. If a person doesn't like what he does to earn his bread and butter, he won't do a very good job," Uncle Stuart said. "And that, my dear boy, translates to his not going far in today's world."

I knew Uncle Stuart would jump at the chance to get away from the house and enjoy a whiskey, and I assumed that Ron would want to be there to answer the phone in case someone from the hospital called.

"Sorry I was gone so long," I said. "My friend needed to discuss something with me before I leave town."

"We've been so busy getting acquainted we hardly missed you." Uncle Stuart laughed.

"Uncle Stuart, Joe Bob thoroughly enjoyed your company," I said. "He's going to Morgan's for a drink and invited us to join him there. Are you interested?"

"Well, of course I'm interested. I like your friend."

"Mind if I tag along?" Ron said. "I could use a drink."

"We'll be glad to have you, Ron," I said, knowing that his presence would throw a monkey wrench into Joe Bob's plan to speak candidly.

Joe Bob was sitting at the bar, nursing a beer when we arrived. I could tell he had cleaned himself up, but he still looked awful. He wore a doleful expression, and his eyes were just as red and puffy as they had been earlier.

I headed for the bar to try to explain Ron's presence to him, but that didn't work out. Uncle Stuart and Ron were right on my heels. All I could do was introduce the two men and hope for the best.

Joe Bob climbed off the bar stool, and he and Ron shook hands. Then, with Joe Bob, our host leading the way, we moved to a table. It was Lucy's shift. She came over to take our orders, dragging her crippled foot.

"How's the world treating you, Lucy?" I said.

"Okay for a Sunday night, I guess. You gonna be here in Martinsville for a while?"

"As a matter of fact, I'm supposed to leave sometime tomorrow."

"That's too bad," she said.

I couldn't tell whether she meant it or not. Maybe she thought I was a jerk for leaving town when Joe Bob was in such a state. After all, I was supposed to be one of his dearest friends. Friends didn't desert friends in times of need.

Ron surprised me by ordering a Gibson; he impressed me as the Diet Pepsi type. I wasn't sure why I was so quick to judge the guy. All I knew about him was that he was married to a woman who treated him like dirt, and he seemed willing to put up with it.

"Ron's an accountant," Uncle Stuart said.

"Is that so?" Joe Bob said. "You like it?"

"Yes, I do."

I had never witnessed such a pained conversation. Poor Joe Bob had wanted to have a serious conversation with Uncle Stuart and me. Instead, he was being forced to engage in small talk with an unwelcome stranger. I had botched his plan big time, but there was nothing I could do but play along.

"You should have played golf with us this morning, Ron," I said, breaking the silence. "The course was in great condition."

"Maybe some other time," he said. "Golf's an interesting sport."

"Do you play often?" Uncle Stuart asked, determined to keep up the chatter.

"I try to squeeze in a couple of rounds a week."

"What's your handicap?" Joe Bob asked.

"Six."

"On second thought, you might not have enjoyed playing with us," I said. "We're pretty high handicappers."

"That doesn't bother me," Ron said. "When I'm on a golf course, I'm not interested in what the people I'm playing with do, or how they play; it's just me against the course."

"And that's as it should be," Uncle Stuart said.

Joe Bob nudged me under the table. Surely, he knew I'd been cornered into bringing Ron along.

"Would you guys 'scuse me for a minute?" he said.

I couldn't miss the piercing look he gave me as he pushed back from the table. It was clear he expected me to meet him in the men's room.

I pulled my phone out of my pocket. It was pretty amazing how many times that little convenience had provided me with a reason to excuse myself from a conversation since I had been in Martinsville. It was a handy tool, even if it necessitated my telling a white lie each time I used it.

"Sorry, guys," I said. "I'm getting a call from Denver. I won't be but a minute."

I hurried around the side of the bar to the men's room where Joe Bob was bent over a sink, splashing cold water on his face.

"Ron invited himself to come with us," I said. "What was I going to tell him, that he wasn't welcome?"

Joe Bob dried his face with a fistful of paper towels.

"That's okay. I understand, but I got a problem."

"A new one?"

"Yeah, you could call it that. I called a lawyer to meet us here. He used to be a friend of my dad's, older guy. Now what am I gonna do?"

"I don't know. Do you want us to leave?"

"No. Actually, I kinda wanted you and the judge to meet him."

"What have you told him?"

"Nothin' yet. I just asked him to meet me for a drink. Told him I had somethin' to discuss with him."

"You can't discuss anything about the accident with Ron here. You'll have to reschedule your meeting with the lawyer. I'll go back to the table while you call him."

"Okay."

My old friend looked like a beaten man. He was willing to go to jail for something he would never have intended to do, and I was afraid he would go so far as to perjure himself to save the rest of our hides.

My relatives had ordered another round of drinks. The Gibson appeared to have revived Ron's spirits. He didn't look like the same person I'd been talking with an hour earlier. Smiling broadly, he was telling my uncle about a birdie putt he had made at the Harbourtown course on Hilton Head Island.

"It was so sweet." He grinned. "The ball broke just the way I thought it would and rolled into the cup."

Joe Bob was walking toward us, and I could tell by his expression that something was amiss. I had a bad feeling he hadn't been able to reach his lawyer friend. He pulled out his chair to sit down, but seemed to change his mind at the last second.

"'scuse me again," he said, looking both miserable and embarrassed. He hurried toward the front of the restaurant.

A man came inside and panned the room. Joe Bob rushed to meet him, and the two shook hands. This had to be the attorney Joe Bob had been expecting. They had a brief conversation. Then, Joe Bob escorted his friend to our table and made introductions. He didn't burden us with the fact that the newcomer was a lawyer.

Arnold Marcum looked to be in his early sixties. I guessed he was about six feet tall and not overweight, but he had a paunch which appeared to prevent him from buttoning his suit coat. He had greasy salt-and-pepper hair that grew down to his dingy shirt collar, making it stick out in sporadic little tufts. His dark tanned skin matched his worn suit. And his handshake was a bit too friendly for my taste. His demeanor struck me more as that of a high-pressure salesman than an attorney. I wished that

Joe Bob had sought counsel elsewhere, but that was none of my business.

Mr. Marcum ordered Dewars on-the-rocks and tossed it back as though he wanted to hurry and get rid of it. He picked up on the golf tales and told a couple of his own. I was more than certain that he had a wealth of hunting and fishing one-upmanship stories he could have substituted if the conversation had lent itself to either of them. No, I didn't like this man.

So there we were: five men of various ages and backgrounds, sitting around a table in an establishment which could only be described as a dump, chewing the fat. What a charade. Why were we doing this? Joe Bob was here for a failed purpose. Uncle Stuart and I were here because Joe Bob had asked us to come. I knew my uncle well enough, though, to believe he was here, because he wanted to enjoy his whiskey and to indulge in a bit of male camaraderie. Ron probably didn't know why he had wanted to come along. His miserable world had suddenly become even more miserable because his wife, whom he was aware didn't love him, had lost their baby whom they both had loved. He was simply tapped out, and wanted to experience normalcy for a couple of hours. Arnold Marcum, of course, had smelled money. He was unaware of the circumstance, but he believed this meeting would somehow turn a profit.

The tall tales weren't getting us anywhere. Joe Bob was miserable, and trying hard to conceal it. He couldn't get rid of Ron, and he couldn't explain to Arnold Marcum why he had summoned him. I was certain the greasy lawyer was confused but playing the game admirably. Ron and Uncle Stuart were both three sheets to the wind, and they genuinely seemed to be having a wonderful time. I wanted nothing more than to skip the rest of the act and go home, but just as I was about to suggest that, the conversation turned to the town of Martinsville.

Arnold Marcum began holding forth on the population growth and the plethora of business opportunities that were new to the small town.

"It all happened within the last five years," he said. "It seemed that all of a sudden, Martinsville was the place to be. All kinds of new businesses have sprung up."

"That's right," Joe Bob said. "I thought I was gonna starve to death gittin' my business off the ground, but now I have more work than I can handle."

I must have gone around town blindfolded for the past week. If Martinsville had become a new-born metropolis, I had missed it. It still looked like the same lazy little southern town where I grew up except for a couple of new housing developments.

I knew Joe Bob and Bernie were both doing well; especially Bernie. But they were special cases. As far as I knew, Joe Bob owned the only real garage in town, and Bernie owned the only one-hour dry cleaning business.

Beth had told me about the hospital expansion and bragged about her salary as its business administrator, but she had told so many lies that I couldn't tell her fact from fiction.

Maybe the town had changed more than met the eye, but I had a feeling that it held more appeal for those who found themselves stuck here. If Arnold Marcum was raking it in faster than he could spend it, why didn't he invest in a new suit?

"Gentlemen, I hate to interrupt this stimulating conversation," I said, "but I'm about ready to call it a night. I'm supposed to leave town tomorrow, and I have several loose ends to tie up before I go."

My uncle and brother-in-law looked at me like two disappointed children, but they pushed back their chairs. I signaled for Lucy to bring the check.

"I've got this," Uncle Stuart said. He eyed the total and laid several bills on the table.

As far as I knew, he hadn't sprung for a single thing all week, so I was glad to see him shell out for the drinks. He had money to burn, but he was tighter than the bark on a tree.

Arnold Marcum scrounged in his wallet and came up with one of his business cards for each of us, and Joe Bob said he would call the house before I left town.

I hoped Joe Bob wouldn't unload on the lawyer after we left. Arnold Marcum wouldn't be the person I would want to represent me. Maybe Joe Bob had picked up on my vibes. If he had, he would put the guy off until he had a chance to hear my opinion of him.

I persuaded Uncle Stuart to let me drive back to the house. He and Ron were both walking on rubber legs, and getting them into the car was no easy feat. Both of them claimed to be wide awake when we got home, and Ron informed Uncle Stuart that he was now ready to take him up on the previously offered smoke. So the two of them retired to the patio, and I went up to bed. My last thought before falling asleep was that I was certain Arnold Marcum was a sleazebag ambulance chaser, or worse. I wouldn't wait to hear from Joe Bob. He'd be getting a call from me first thing in the morning.

Chapter Twenty-one

Monday—it was the day I would escape Martinsville, Tennessee and return to civilization. I had set an alarm, but was so anxious for the day to begin that I awoke before it made a sound. This was the last time I would have to face a pink room the second my eyes opened.

I showered and shaved, then went to the closet to retrieve the suit I had worn to my mother's funeral. The inevitable wrinkles which were always present after having worn the suit were nowhere to be seen. Trudy had taken it upon herself to make sure I looked presentable when I went to the attorney's office.

I dressed and packed my bag. There were only a couple of things on my agenda for the day besides listening to what I already knew would be in my mother's will. I wanted to talk to Joe Bob about Arnold Marcum. There were bound to be better qualified lawyers than that sleazebag, even in this small town.

I also wanted to make another quick visit to the cemetery just to have a private moment at my mother's grave. If I had been asked why I wanted to do that, I wouldn't have had an answer.

It simply felt important to me. Maybe I would be able to shed a few tears.

On a less somber note, I wouldn't mind accompanying Joe Bob to the animal hospital to see how his cat was progressing. Doctor Sydney Edelman had made a very favorable impression on me during the short time I had been in her company yesterday. I wasn't sure why I wanted to see her since I was about to leave town.

Trudy was taking a pan of biscuits from the oven. Just smelling her biscuits could get me out of bed and down the stairs when I was a kid. They were always the same—big, fluffy, golden brown, and delicious. I wondered if this batch would be the last one she would make in my mother's kitchen.

"Thanks for pressing my suit," I said. "You didn't have to go to all that trouble."

She grinned. "You didn't think I'd let you leave this house lookin' like a ragamuffin, did you?"

"Not for a minute."

Trudy took off her oven mitts and looked out the window above the sink.

"Come here," she said. "Now I've seen everything."

I crossed the room to take a look at the sight she found so hard to believe. Ron and Uncle Stuart were sprawled on a couple of chaise lounges fast asleep.

"I'd better go out there and wake them before my aunt sees them," I said.

They were both snoring. Their clothes were rumpled, and they could have easily passed for a couple of winos, sleeping it off in an alley. I couldn't resist whipping out my cell phone to take a picture of them.

"Rise and shine, gentlemen," I said. "If Aunt Lela Maude finds you like this, you'll have the devil to pay."

They squinted up at me simultaneously, shielding their eyes from the early morning sun. Ron automatically felt around on the table for his glasses, and dragged his hand through a dirty ashtray. He appeared not to know where he was. I wondered if he had told my uncle all of his deep dark secrets.

"What time is it?" he asked.

"Nearly eight."

Uncle Stuart was slow to come alive. He flopped an arm over his eyes and told me to go away, but I managed to shake him awake and herded both men into the house.

I could hear Aunt Lela Maude dressing down Uncle Stuart.

"You old fool! You're a disgrace!"

Trudy chuckled as she fried bacon. "Ain't love grand?" she said.

I laughed. "Those two have pretended to fight ever since I can remember," I said. "I think I'll call the hospital to find out when Sam will be released."

"I just called her. She's already had her breakfast, but the doctor hasn't been in to see her yet. She said she'd call as soon as he discharges her."

"How did she sound?"

"That child sounded fine. If I didn't know better, I'd think she wasn't upset about tumblin' down the stairs and losin' her baby. She was always good at movin' on and leavin' things that she found bothersome behind. I envy that."

"I'm glad she's in a better frame of mind. She was pretty down when I left her last night. I think she might call Dad today. She felt pretty bad since she told him to stay away from Mom's funeral. Did you know she did that?"

Trudy shook her head. "Didn't know it, but I'm not surprised. Sam's been messed up in the head about her daddy since he walked out the door. I don't think she's ever understood why he left." She paused. "But you did."

"Yes, I understood why he left. I think I would have done the same thing if I'd been in his shoes."

"Don't feel guilty about feeling that way. Your mama wasn't an easy woman, but I loved her, and I miss her somethin' fierce."

"What are you going to do, Trudy? I guess I mean how are you going to fill your days now that you don't have Mom to make up household chores for you to do so the two of you can have lunch together and share the town gossip?"

"The Lord only knows," she said, and shook her head sadly.

I wished I hadn't asked her that question. I thought it had probably made her feel more lost and lonely, but I seemed to have been wrong; she suddenly brightened.

"When He made your mama, He threw away the mold," she said, laughing. "Don't you remember how she'd put on those skimpy, little bikini swimsuits and that big, floppy hat to work in her flower garden?"

"Sure, I remember."

"Then, she'd be in the front row of the choir on Sunday mornin', singin' her heart out and darin' anybody to question her weekday wardrobe, let alone her morals. Your mama was famous for her cocktail parties, too. I'll bet she'd have made a good bartender."

"Just hang onto the good memories, Trudy, and know that you'll always have my phone number and any support you need from me. There are these modern inventions called airplanes, and I can be on one and on my way here in a flash."

I hugged her, and went to find Uncle Stuart to ask him if I could use the rental car to go to the cemetery for a few minutes. Aunt Lela Maude opened the bedroom door when I knocked. She appeared to have gotten over her mad spell; she smiled and kissed me on the cheek.

"We're packin' a few things before breakfast, dear," she said.

"I thought it would be a good idea to get a head start on it this mornin'. I'm not sure what time we'll be leavin'. Stuart will want to miss the afternoon traffic. You know how he hates that."

I was about to request the use of the car when the phone rang. It was Sam, and she was steaming. She was talking so fast I couldn't understand what she was saying.

"Sam, stop talking and take a deep breath," I said. "You're going to have to back up and slow down, so I can understand what you're telling me."

"You've got to come and get me out of this place right now!"

"Has the doctor released you?"

"No. He said I was too emotionally upset to leave, but I want you to come and get me. I will not stay here under the same roof as that brazen bitch another minute."

"The brazen bitch being my ex?"

"Good guess."

"What's she done now?"

"You won't believe it. She showed up right after I spoke to Gertrude on the phone this morning, carrying a huge flower arrangement and apologized for upsetting me yesterday."

"Forgive me if I missed something. That sounds like a step in the right direction."

"You don't know what you're talking about, big brother. I'll explain it all when you get here."

"Sam, be reasonable. I can't get you out of the hospital until the doctor releases you."

"Just come over here now," she said, and hung up.

I didn't care whether Sam wanted to see her husband or not. I was taking him with me to the hospital.

When Ron and I arrived at the hospital, Sam was dressed and sitting in a chair. Her eyes were spitting fire. The flower arrangement that must have been Beth's peace offering was smashed on the floor, and we had to walk around the mess. I looked at my sister and grinned. She seemed perfectly normal to me.

"Hello, sweetheart," Ron said.

"Hey. Thanks for understanding and giving me some time by myself last night, Ron."

"Sure." He smiled.

"All right, guys, we're going down to the administration office and checking me out," Sam said, all business.

"Are you sure?" Ron said. "Why did you say the doctor wouldn't release you?"

"Because I was mad, and he didn't understand me. Let's go."

"Shouldn't we get a wheelchair to take you down there?" Ron said. "Patients always leave hospitals in wheelchairs."

"I don't need a wheelchair, Ron. Let's go."

The three of us stepped around the dying flowers, broken vase, and the puddle of water, and went to the administration office. We checked Sam out without much of a hassle. Luckily, we didn't see Beth.

"That nutcase had the nerve to come to my room last night," Sam said. "She woke me up and nearly scared the life out of me."

"What did she want?" Ron said.

"She said we needed to talk. I told her we had nothing to talk about, and she said I was wrong. I wanted her out of my sight, so I pushed the call button and had her removed from my room. Then, I tried calling the house, but nobody answered. I guess you were all asleep."

I was perfectly willing to let her live with that erroneous assumption. She must have called before we got home from Morgan's. Trudy would have already gone home, and Aunt Lela Maude couldn't hear thunder once she went to sleep.

Ron, on the other hand, must have surely gone nuts. I wondered how well he knew his wife as he confessed to his whereabouts and what he had been doing. He sounded almost proud of his uncharacteristic behavior.

"You did what?" Sam said.

Ron repeated his indiscretion, embellishing it with insignificant details. He finished by adding that he had a great time.

"What's gotten into you, Ron?" Sam said.

"Nothing's gotten into me."

I thought he was going to break down and beg my sister's forgiveness, but I was wrong. He swallowed, then took a deep breath.

"Samantha, I love you, but I want you to understand that some changes are about to take place in our relationship," he blurted.

"What kinds of changes?" Sam said.

I assumed my brother-in-law was about to shoot himself in the foot.

"Well, for starters, I'm going to play golf more often. If you'd like to learn to play, I'll arrange for you to take lessons. I don't think it would be a good idea for me to teach you."

"Why can't you teach me?"

"Spouses should never try to teach one another anything. You'll need to work with a pro."

I expected my sister to bite back. Her meek attitude was something I had never witnessed.

"What other changes do you have in mind?" she said.

"I've been pampering you way too much. I was doing it even more because of the baby, but I've always spoiled you."

Sam looked like she was about to turn on the waterworks.

"Look, I wanted our baby as much as you did, maybe more," Ron said, "but we can have other babies. The doctor says you're healthy, and I know I've got the bullets. Right now, we need to work on our marriage."

I watched my sister's facial expression in the rear-view mirror. She looked thoughtful as though her husband's suggestion was something she hadn't considered until that very moment.

"You're right, Ron. That's exactly what we need to do," she said.

Sam seemed to have had some sort of transformation. I wondered if she had been given a high-powered medication which could have temporarily altered her personality.

"Good," Ron said. "I'm glad you agree. I want our marriage to work and for us to be happy together, but you need to know that I'll be calling most of the shots. If I'm going to be a good husband, I'll need to regain my self-respect."

If Sam had a problem with that, she kept it to herself. We were climbing the porch steps when she turned to me.

"I didn't finish my story about the witch," she said.

"Well?"

"When she apologized for upsetting me, she said she was sorry if the truth hurt, but that the two of you were definitely going to remarry. She said that she and I were going to be sisters again. That's when I threw the flowers at her."

Chapter Twenty-two

Everyone noticed how the atmosphere had changed when Trudy called the family to lunch. There wasn't a frown or a snide remark. I didn't think any of us knew what to make of the change. The tension which had been ever present during the past week had simply disappeared.

Trudy hummed as she set a platter of stuffed crabs and a big bowl of salad greens on the table. I hadn't heard her hum since I arrived.

Uncle Stuart and Aunt Lela Maude appeared a little awestruck, and I assumed they were trying to make sense of what they were experiencing.

I relaxed and enjoyed the company, realizing that Sam and Ron were the agents of the dramatic change. Sam exhibited an almost sweet nature, and Ron monopolized the conversation, apparently having overcome his shy disposition overnight.

We migrated to the living room after lunch where my brother-in-law proceeded to surprise us even more. He took a seat at the piano and began playing "Autumn Leaves", and I realized the guy had real talent.

"Why, Ronald, that was truly lovely," Aunt Lela Maude drawled. "I had no idea you played."

"I don't anymore," he said. "We don't own a piano. Maybe we'll buy one someday."

My mother was the only person in our family who played. If she hadn't specified who she wanted to have her piano, I would suggest we give it to Sam and Ron.

"I played at a piano bar a couple of nights a week when I was in college," Ron said. "It didn't pay much, but I was always broke, and the tips weren't bad."

I thought I heard the doorbell ring and went to see who it was. Bernie Zuckerman stood on the porch, looking like a naughty child who had just suffered a severe reprimand. I opened the door to admit him, but he stood where he was, looking down at his feet.

"Got a minute?" he said.

"Sure." I opened the door wider.

"Out here," he said.

I stepped outside, and we went to the far end of the porch to sit in the swing. We had engaged in many heart-to-hearts and solved a ton of problems in this very spot when we were teenagers. The trellis that screened the end of the porch was covered with honeysuckle, swarming with bees and hummingbirds. We watched the activity for a minute before either of us spoke.

I figured my old pal had come to put a formal end to our relationship. That was what I deserved. My behavior had been deplorable. I trained my gaze on Bernie's swollen nose.

"Listen, man, I'm really sorry," I said.

Bernie waved it off.

"You know I don't go around hitting my friends," I said. "I don't know what came over me."

"Forget it, Matt. I do know what came over you. I was way

out of line, and you were defending a friend. We both know I was wrong. That's what I came to tell you."

So he was letting me off the hook, and I was relieved. I would have hated to leave Martinsville with the guilt of ruining our long friendship.

"Joe Bob's hiring an attorney," I said.

"That's good; he's going to need one."

"I agree, but I have qualms about the guy he has in mind. I met him last night."

"You met him?"

"Yes. Uncle Stuart, my brother-in-law, and I met Joe Bob for a drink, and the lawyer joined us for a while."

"Who is he?"

"Name's Arnold Marcum. I've never heard of him. He has the look of a guy who's down on his luck—cheap suit, needed a haircut, just kind of smarmy. I don't think I'd want him representing me if I were in Joe Bob's shoes."

"You're damned right, you wouldn't. The guy's bad news."

"How do you know him?"

"I don't know him, but a guy who works for me hired him to settle an insurance claim several months ago. My guy told me he wished he'd never laid eyes on the son-of-a-bitch. Said Marcum didn't do his homework and lost the suit. He's still paying the good-for-nothing lawyer off for nothing."

"So I didn't misjudge him."

"He leases office space in one of those old houses on York Street. From what I hear, he doesn't have much business; advertises cheap divorces and wills, that sort of thing. And, I understand he's Johnny-on-the-spot before an ambulance can get anywhere near the scene of an accident."

"That's what I figured."

"Do you know how much Joe Bob told Marcum?"

"He didn't tell him anything when I was there, but I don't know how long they talked, or what was said after I left. I thought about calling Joe Bob today to encourage him to check out some other lawyers, but I haven't gotten around to it. He might think I'm overstepping my bounds."

"Want to ride over to the garage with me now? I need to make peace with him. He's bound to think I'm a real horse's ass."

"You and I both know Joe Bob's not like that. He's very forgiving. I'd like to go with you. Maybe we can nudge him in the right direction about the lawyer, but we have to be careful. Joe Bob's dad and this guy were good friends, and Joe Bob said he'd like to throw some business Marcum's way. I don't think I've ever known anyone who always pulls for the underdog as much as Joe Bob."

We found our friend under a late-model Oldsmobile. Only his feet were sticking out. An old radio on a workbench blasted country music loud and proud, and he didn't hear us calling his name.

I had on the suit I planned to wear to the reading of Mother's will, but I hunkered down beside the car, careful not to touch anything greasy.

"Joe Bob!"

More of his body appeared as he snaked himself out from under the car on a wooden platform with wheels. Then, he rolled himself all the way out. He remained on the dolly, looking up at us without speaking. Finally, he let the wrench he was holding clatter to the concrete floor. He rubbed a greasy hand over the stubble on his chin and stood up.

"I guess this means you two musta shook hands and made up," he said.

"Yeah, we're fine," Bernie said.

Joe Bob stretched his tall body toward the ceiling, then to each side.

"I'm stiffer'n a board," he said.

"You got a few minutes?" Bernie said.

"I got all the time in the world for you, Bernard."

That was another of Joe Bob's qualities I admired. I would have bet anything he thought Bernie had come to convince him to change his mind, but he would listen regardless.

Joe Bob's place of business was no less messy than his home. Tools and wrenches were lying around all over the place in no particular order, but I was certain he could locate the one he needed without having to search for it. I'd read that Einstein was messy that way, but I had no idea whether or not it was true.

Joe Bob opened the two doors on the passenger side of the Oldsmobile to offer us seats, and perched his rear on a stack of tires.

"Shoot," he said, lighting a cigarette.

Bernie launched into a long-winded apology for his mulish attitude and childish behavior, and I could tell Joe Bob was relishing Bernie's discomfort. I also knew he was glad to finally have his old friend's support.

I hadn't said a word since I yelled for Joe Bob to come out from under the car, figuring Bernie would broach the subject of the lawyer, but he seemed reluctant to bring it up.

"Joe Bob," I said, "I told Bernie about last night; and to tell you the truth, we're a little concerned about your choice of attorneys."

"Why's that?" he said, expelling a cloud of smoke.

When Joe Bob looked at you, it was clear there wasn't a speck of guile in him. His eyes held naked truth, honest questioning, with no hidden agenda. He wasn't being argumentative when he asked for clarification.

"Well, Mister Marcum didn't strike me as someone who's very successful, and I have a feeling he's not the type to bend over backward for a client."

"I know the man's not rich," Joe Bob said. "That's one reason I called him. I'd like to give him some business. He and my dad was friends. I told you that. How can you know how hard he works for his clients, Matt? You said you didn't know nothin' about him—you'd never met him."

Bernie answered for me. "Matt doesn't know him, but I'm familiar with the way he works."

"How's that, Bernard?"

Bernie reiterated what he had shared with me earlier, but left out the bit about ambulance chasing.

"Well, that's just one case, and I'm guessin' you only heard one side of that story."

"Have you already hired the guy?" I asked.

"Not exactly."

"What does that mean?" Bernie said. "Either you hired him, or you didn't."

"What it means, Bernard, is that I told him I'd stop by his office later."

"But you haven't actually made an appointment with him, right?" Bernie asked.

"No."

"Have you discussed the accident with him?" I asked.

"No. I'd had a few beers by the time I was alone with him last night. I didn't trust myself not to tell him more'n I meant to."

Bernie sighed his relief. "That's good," he said. "We can talk to some other lawyers before you make a final decision. How much time do we have before your appointment, Matt?"

"A couple of hours, but the family's expecting me to come

home and go with them to the lawyer's office. I'll call and tell them I'll meet them there."

I went into Joe Bob's office and closed the door to block out the street noise to call the house.

"Stevenson residence," my aunt drawled.

"Aunt Lela Maude, this is Matt."

"Hello, dear."

"I'm calling to let you know I won't be coming back to the house before you leave for the attorney's office. I'll meet you there."

"Mathoo, have I ever told you what a wonderful telephone voice you have?" she said. "I declare, you have missed your callin'. You ought to be on the radio. People would never guess you grew up in the south. I think I'd put you somewhere in the midwest."

"Thanks, Aunt Lela Maude, I guess. Listen, I'm kind of in a hurry. Please just let the family know that I'll meet them there."

"Oh, no, dear. Don't do that. I'm afraid we won't be meetin' with the attorney today after all. We've had to reschedule."

"What?"

This guy was really beginning to piss me off.

"Your little sister has taken a turn for the worse, I'm afraid. She's been crying nonstop since you left the house."

"She seemed fine at lunch. What happened?"

"Yes, I know, but that was before Elizabeth called her. Samantha worked herself into such a terrible state. She threw a regular tantrum just the way your mother used to do, rest her soul. The poor child ran around the house, demolishin' everything in her path. To make a long story short, she started bleedin', so Ron had to take her back to the hospital. He told me he's not goin' to leave her side this time. Poor man. I feel as sorry for him as I do for her."

"Do you know how Sam is now?"

"Ron called a little while ago. He said the doctor says she'll be fine after she rests for a couple of days."

"Does she want to see me?"

"I'm afraid not, dear. She said she doesn't want any company except her husband."

"All right. By the way, did you book another appointment with the attorney?"

"Yes, I did. You're not goin' to like this, dear, but it was the best I could do. He was booked solid until Thursday, so I made the appointment for ten o'clock that mornin'."

"I'll see you later this afternoon," I said, thinking I was never going to make it back to Denver.

It seemed that Murphy's Law was totally in effect. Everything that could possibly go wrong had done so. I'd have to call Jack again, and I wouldn't blame him if he told me he was looking for a new partner. He had been covered up with his work and mine for a week, and he was going to be in for more of the same.

It would be ridiculous for me to fly to Denver just to turn around and come back to Martinsville. There was no reason for me to be present for the reading of my mother's will except that my family wasn't only expecting it—they demanded it. Good southern families always followed protocol in these matters.

Chapter Twenty-three

I started recapping my phone conversation with Aunt Lela Maude for Bernie and Joe Bob. Nearly everything I said was a revelation to Bernie. He didn't know that Sam had lost the baby. I had failed to tell him in all the excitement. He was also unaware of all the crazy stunts Beth had pulled except what he had seen firsthand at his dinner party.

"Well, that's it," he said, throwing his arms into the air. "She's turned into a real nutcase."

"You got that right," Joe Bob said. "She's one evil woman with more than her share of guts."

"I can't imagine what happened to the sweet young thing I married."

"You've got to admit she's still a looker, but she needs to put the brakes on that mean shit," Joe Bob said.

"You're right, and I'm just the guy to help her with that," I said.

"What are you going to do?" Bernie said.

"We're going to pay my ex a little visit."

"Who's we?" Joe Bob said.

"The three of us. I want witnesses to what I'm going to say to her."

"Now, wait a minute, buddy," Bernie said. "She's a friend of Lee Ann's. I'm not so sure I want to be in on this."

"You said she was just an acquaintance."

"I told you they were friends, just not good friends."

"Bernard, I swear you're the biggest coward I ever seen," Joe Bob said. "Are you afraid of that little girl you're married to?"

"Of course not. What kind of question is that?"

"Looks like it was one that got you all riled up. Tell you what; I'm gonna make you a deal. I'll cross Marcum off my lawyer list right now if you'll go with me to support Matt here."

"I don't know," Bernie said.

Joe Bob and I looked at him like he was pond scum.

"Oh, all right, but I'm not going to say anything to her," Bernie said.

"I don't expect either of you to do any of the talking," I said. "I'm going to threaten her with a restraining order for harassment if she dares to contact my sister or any other member of my family again. That's all."

Joe Bob scratched his head. "I ain't ever gonna get through workin' on this car, but first things first. I reckon I'd better call Arnold Marcum. What'll I tell him?"

"You haven't told him anything at all, right?" Bernie said.

"That's right."

"You don't need to tell him you're checking out other attorneys. Just tell him you've decided you can handle the problem without his help."

Joe Bob made his phone call while Bernie and I started going through the yellow pages. We found a couple of established attorneys whose names we both recognized, and Joe Bob made appointments with both of them. He could retain the best one and write the other one off.

Joe Bob locked up the garage, and we went to his place so he could clean up to go to the hospital.

I considered myself lucky to have two old friends who were willing to have my back, especially since neither of them had anything to gain from it.

We were men on a mission as we presented ourselves at the administration office. A dishwater blond sat at a reception desk, chewing her thumbnail as we approached.

"Hi there," I said.

I must have startled her. She sat up straight, cleared her throat, and produced a tentative smile.

"We're here to see Beth Stevenson," I said.

"What did you say your name was, sir?"

"I didn't, but it's Matt Stevenson." I smiled at her.

The young woman looked at her computer screen. She turned to me, blinking.

"I don't seem to have you scheduled for an appointment, Mr. Stevenson."

"That's because I don't have one, but I need to see Beth Stevenson," I said. "I only need a few minutes of her time."

"I'm terribly sorry, sir, but Ms. Stevenson doesn't see anyone without an appointment. Would you like to make one?"

"Does Ms. Stevenson have anyone in her office right now?"

"Well, no."

"Is she in her office?"

"Yes, she is, but I'm sure she's quite busy."

"Please tell her I'm here and would like to speak with her." My tone was as pleasant as I could make it.

The birdlike receptionist looked miserable. "Ms. Stevenson doesn't like to be disturbed," she said. It was no more than a whisper.

"Please just let her know I'm here."

I was afraid I was going to have to barge past the young woman and force my way into Beth's office just as she opened the door. She was clearly taken by surprise at seeing me.

"Matt, what brings you slumming?" she asked.

"Hello, Beth. Do you have a couple of minutes?"

"Of course. Hold my calls, Joann."

Beth stepped into her office, and the three of us followed.

"I don't know if you remember Joe Bob Kincaid, but, of course, you know Bernie."

"Of course." She smiled.

Neither of my companions could seem to manage more than a nod. I wasn't certain, but I was pretty sure neither of them looked Beth in the eye.

"Please, sit down," she said as she stepped behind a dark cherry desk to seat herself.

Joe Bob took a seat quickly and seemed to be studying the Oriental rug beneath his feet, and Bernie was making a production of unbuttoning his coat and lifting the legs of his pants before sitting.

Beth clasped her slender hands under her chin, and I couldn't help wondering how such a beautiful creature could be as conniving and cruel as she had become.

"What can I do for you gentlemen?" she said.

Her question seemed to draw Joe Bob's attention away from the rug toward the scenery across the desk. I assumed he had developed a new appreciation for my ex after having seen her au naturel. He watched her with interest.

"I'll get to the point," I said. "I'm sure you know you've put my sister back in the hospital."

"That's ridiculous."

"No, it's the truth. Your coming to the house with the tale that you and I were getting remarried, along with Sam's temper, caused her to lose her baby. Then, your visit to her in the hospital made matters worse. And as if that weren't enough, you called her at home and taunted her, causing her to have a relapse. What's the matter with you, Beth?"

Her features hardened. She opened her mouth to say something, but I cut her off before she had a chance to speak. I was out of my seat, leaning across her desk and in her face. She gripped the arms of her chair and leaned back.

"My friends are here for only one reason," I said. "I want them here to witness what I'm about to say."

Beth geared herself up to bite back. She stood, pulled herself up to her full height, and looked as if she had no intention of backing off.

"Stop raising your voice in my office this instant," she said. "This is a hospital, in case you've forgotten where you are."

"I'll raise my voice as much as I like. The whole building can hear me for all I care. I'm having you placed under a restraining order the second I leave this room. You are through harassing my family. Stay away from us. Don't write; don't call. I won't warn you but once."

Beth's eyes blazed, and I could tell she was clenching her jaw from the way her chin jutted up and out. It was reminiscent of the way Franklin Delano Roosevelt lifted his chin, but without his winning smile. Her five-inch heels clicked across the polished oak floor, and she held the door for us to leave.

I knew Bernie was glad to be out of there. Beth would more than likely tell Lee Ann about the scene and make it sound like Bernie played a big part in it. Then, he would be back in the doghouse. I probably shouldn't have dragged him into it.

"Well, I guess you told her which side her bread's buttered on." Joe Bob grinned. "I kinda wish you'd made it last a little longer, though. That feisty woman's even better lookin' when she gets mad."

"She'd better heed the warning," I said.

"I certainly would," Bernie said. "I'd like to see you in a courtroom sometime."

"No, you wouldn't," I said. "I haven't had an exciting case yet. Everything's pretty much cut and dried. I don't mind telling you, things need to pick up soon."

We were driving down Main Street—the same route we had taken dozens of times as teenagers, going from one end of town to the other with our eyes peeled for pretty girls or somebody to challenge to a drag race.

"Where do we get the restraining order, the courthouse?" Bernie said.

"I don't think it'll actually be necessary to get one," I said. "Beth will be expecting it, and that's all that matters. Ron won't let her near Sam while she's in the hospital, and I'll stick close when she's released. Besides, my entire family will be long gone in a few days."

"So, where to now?" Bernie said.

"You name it," I said. "Since my meeting has been postponed, I don't have any plans."

"How about going to my house?" he said. "I told my manager I didn't know what time I'd get back. He'll close up for me if I don't show."

"Fine with me," Joe Bob said. "I'm done for the day once I git cleaned up."

I was thinking about Sam. I should have stopped by to see her while I was at the hospital. She'd said Ron was the only visitor she wanted, but I wasn't at all sure she had meant it. I wondered if she and Ron were working on their plans for the future, or if he was back to mollycoddling her. If he had gone back to letting her push him around, she would dump him for sure.

Lee Ann was teaching ballet lessons, and the baby was at the sitter's, so we had Bernie's place to ourselves. The house was immaculate. None of Claire's toys were strewn around, and there were no dirty dishes in the sink. I didn't think it looked lived in.

Bernie went to the fridge and brought out three light beers. We took them out to the patio so Joe Bob could smoke. Bernie scrounged up an ashtray.

It was there in Bernie's backyard that the three of us came face-to-face with a moment of truth: we had time on our hands and nothing to talk about. We had, during the time we had spent together, exhausted all the memories of our youth. The three of us had rehashed the details of the unfortunate accident to the point that there was nothing more to say about it. Besides, it was settled. Joe Bob was about to turn the heavy lifting over to his lawyer.

"Bernard, this is a great backyard," Joe Bob said. "You got some shade, but not so much it kills the grass, and that limb over there is the perfect spot for a hummin' bird feeder."

I had to hand it to him for trying to keep the conversation from dying, but I knew it was wasted effort.

"You know, this could have been time well spent talking with one of the attorneys," I said. "Here we sit, drinking beer when we should be working on Joe Bob's defense."

"Now, Matt, you guys have done enough," Joe Bob said. "You found me two good lawyers, and I'm gonna talk to 'em tomorrow and pick one."

The sound of a sliding glass door drew our attention to the back of the house. Lee Ann came out wearing sandals and a mini skirt, showing off her gorgeous legs.

"Hello," she said, unsmiling.

We got to our feet. Bernie air-kissed his wife on the cheek and introduced her to Joe Bob. Lee Ann barely acknowledged Joe Bob, and didn't even nod in my direction. I assumed I hadn't been returned to her good graces.

"You're home early, sweetheart," Bernie said.

Joe Bob was so far away from Lee Ann that his smoke couldn't possibly have bothered her, but she fanned the air.

"I had a cancellation," she said. "It's such a nice day I thought I might sunbathe for a while."

"Well, sweetheart, it's nearly too late in the day for that," Bernie said.

"A bit crowded, too," she said, turning to go back inside.

Red crept from Bernie's collar to the top of his shiny head. There was nothing Joe Bob or I could do to ease our friend's pain, except leave.

"I need to be getting back to the house," I said. "The family will be wondering where I am."

"I ought to git on down the road, too," Joe Bob said.

Bernie's wife had gone inside and left him to make excuses for her rude behavior. I felt sorry for him.

He shook his head as if he couldn't believe what his wife had done. "Guys, I'm sorry," he said. "Lee Ann's not really like this. I don't know what got into her. She must be tired. The baby's been cross lately."

"No big deal, Bernard," Joe Bob said.

"Thanks for the beer, Bernie," I said. "It was real good seeing you again."

Joe Bob and I were halfway down the front walk when we realized we didn't have any transportation. I didn't want to do it, but I walked back to the porch to ring the bell. Bernie opened the door, grinning before I had a chance.

"I forgot, too," he said.

I pretended not to hear Lee Ann yelling at her husband from some remote part of the house, and Bernie stepped outside as quickly as he could and closed the door to keep me from hearing any more.

"You can take us to my place," Joe Bob said. "It's closer and you prob'ly want to get back since your wife's home."

"Okay. I still have to go by the sitter's to pick up Claire."

Joe Bob invited Bernie to come inside, but he declined.

"Matt, until next time." Bernie smiled. "And Joe Bob, give me a shout if you need me."

He drove down the gravel road, the tires of his Cadillac kicking up a cloud of dust that would soon settle on the rows of trailers in its wake.

"Come in for a while," Joe Bob said.

"I've spent more time here than I have at the house," I said, and followed him into the trailer.

"Can you imagine bein' married to that woman?" Joe Bob said.

I shook my head. "I'm afraid I wouldn't handle that very well, but I guess it must work for Bernie."

"She is one mean-spirited, cold woman."

"Martinsville seems to have more than its share of those," I said.

"Bernard's got a nice place, don't he?"

"Yes, very nice. Bernie's done real well for himself," I said.

"Yeah, he has, and I gotta tell you it kinda surprises me. He never was much of a go-getter back when we hung out in school; always waited for one of us to take the lead. I reckon it was because he was such a nerd, and nobody much liked him."

I laughed. "He's still kind of a nerd, in case you haven't noticed, but he's our friend."

"Today's the first time he's ever invited me to his house. I figured he prob'ly thought his wife wouldn't approve of him havin' a grease monkey for a friend."

"Hmm."

Joe Bob lit a Marlboro and sucked in the smoke.

"It's true we don't have much in common anymore," he said, allowing the smoke to escape through his nostrils as he spoke.

"That just happens," I said. "One day we're suddenly adults. We get jobs and go our separate ways, and then we drift apart and our worlds change."

"I reckon so, but it don't seem that way with you. I mean it's been a lotta years since we've seen each other, but we just kinda picked up where we left off last time. I like that."

What he said had an element of truth in it.

"I've always admired you, Joe Bob," I said, not knowing why I had waited until that very moment to tell him.

"Git outta here."

"I mean it. You've been your own man since the day I met you. That shows a lot of strength of character."

"Well, thanks, but I'm not so sure everbody around here feels like you do."

"Maybe they don't really know you."

"They might not know me, but they know the kind of lifestyle I have. At least, they think they know. Take Bernard's wife. I'll guarantee you that woman thinks I'm pure white trash, because I work on cars and live in this trailer park. I'm not too dumb to know that's why Bernard don't have time for me."

"You know better than that. Bernie's henpecked; that's all. If he doesn't spend much time with you, I don't think it has anything to do with your friendship. I have a feeling he spends most of his time taking orders from his wife."

Joe Bob shrugged, and I had the impression that meant he wasn't up to arguing the point. I wasn't sure why I was trying to convince him he was misinterpreting Bernie's behavior, because I knew he was right on the mark.

"Well, so much for philosophizin'," he said, stubbing out his cigarette. "I reckon I'd better git you home before they come lookin' for you."

Joe Bob was dismissing me. He knew I was still his friend, but he thought he had lost Bernie, and nothing I could say would change his mind.

Chapter Twenty-four

My aunt and uncle were in the living room so engrossed in conversation that neither of them seemed to notice when I came into the room. They were sitting in the Queen Anne chairs, separated by an occasional table that was always home to a lamp and a crystal candy dish. I noticed the addition of a bottle of sherry this afternoon.

"Am I interrupting?" I said.

"Hello, dear. Of course you're not," Aunt Lela Maude said. "Won't you join us in an aperitif?"

"No, thanks."

Uncle Stuart took it upon himself to justify their imbibing in my mother's living room since Mom had never allowed liquor in the house.

"I purchased this sherry to calm your aunt's nerves," he said. "This week has been quite a strain on the old girl. Learning that the attorney has postponed our departure has seemed to exacerbate her stress. I'm having a glass with her, because I've always been of the opinion that nobody should drink alone."

He had to be explaining their unusual behavior for his wife's benefit, because I had witnessed his soaking up alcohol like a sponge every chance he had since he hit town.

"Enjoy," I said. "I understand it also aids digestion."

"That it does," Uncle Stuart said, finishing the small amount in his glass and refilling it.

"Trudy's makin' chicken and dumplin's," Aunt Lela Maude said. "Dinner should be ready in a little while."

"She works way too hard," I said.

"Yes, she does," my aunt agreed. "It just seems to be her way. Oh, how I wish I could take that lovely woman home with me, but she won't go. I've already made her a handsome offer, but she refuses to budge. She told me she could never bring herself to leave Martinsville. Such a shame."

My aunt held her empty glass toward Uncle Stuart for a refill, and sighed.

"We were just reminiscing about your mother," Uncle Stuart said.

"She had a good life, you know, despite the fact that her marriage was always stormy," my aunt said.

"Do you really think so?" I asked.

"Oh, my, yes. Your mother did exactly as she pleased. Why, I recall the time she was playin' the piano at that fancy supper club. Your father referred to it as a common bar. He thought it was beneath her to play in such a place."

"I didn't know she played at a supper club," I said.

"Well, she did. I think she did it simply to spite your father. There was nothin' Eloise enjoyed more than pushin' him to the limit."

"I never heard them argue, even once," I said.

"Neither of your parents would have permitted their children to witness such a thing," Uncle Stuart said. "They were extremely civilized."

"Humph! You call it civilized," my aunt said. "I call it what it was—sneaky. I knew my sister well, and I could tell by the gleam in her eye when she was gettin' ready to torment Howard."

"You always did take his side," Uncle Stuart said, "but I'm telling you there are always two sides to every story. You were partial to Howard, because he was such a charmer. You might as well admit it."

Aunt Lela Maude smiled. "He most certainly was," she said. "I'm sure he's still charmin' the women folk and leavin' a few broken hearts along the way."

I was learning a great deal about my parents from my aunt and uncle—things I had never imagined.

"Did you and my dad get along, Uncle Stuart?"

"Oh, sure. I haven't seen him in years, but I liked Howard. It's true that he had a way with the ladies, and I'll admit I was a little jealous of him, especially when he practiced his talent on my wife."

"How ridiculous." Aunt Lela Maude laughed, and I couldn't help but notice that a flush crept into her cheeks.

"Did it bother Mom that Dad was something of a ladies' man?"

"Oh, no. She enjoyed watchin' him flirt," my aunt said. "Eloise knew he was hers alone for as long as she wanted him."

I was trying to absorb what my aunt and uncle were telling me about my parents, but it all sounded incredible to me. How could I have missed noticing such things, especially by the time I was a teenager? I couldn't have been so wrapped up in myself during my raging hormone years that I totally ignored my parents' unusual behavior. Maybe they hid their true personalities from Sam and me. Now, I assumed I would never know.

"Dinner's ready," Trudy called.

Uncle Stuart helped his wife up, and they started toward the kitchen. I noticed that the two continued holding hands as they walked down the narrow hallway.

"I thought it might be nice to have dinner in the dining room," Trudy said, steering us in the opposite direction.

The table was set with Mother's fine china and crystal, and Trudy had arranged a pretty centerpiece with flowers from the garden. Candles glowed, bathing the room in a soft intimate ambience.

"So this is the dining room," I said, unable to resist teasing my dear old friend.

"Yes," Trudy said. "I decided you were probably old enough to get through a meal without breaking the dishes."

"Gertrude, the table looks absolutely lovely," Aunt Lela Maude said.

"I couldn't agree more," Uncle Stuart said.

He seated his wife, and kissed her on the forehead.

"You're still the fairest of them all, my dear," he said.

Aunt Lela Maude gave him a playful swat with her napkin.

"And you're still an old fool," she said, lowering her lashes.

It seemed a glass or two of sherry must have had a powerful effect on my relatives.

"Has anyone heard from Sam?" I asked.

"Yes," Trudy said. "She'll be coming home tomorrow afternoon."

"That's good news," I said. "I hope she's in a better mood this time."

"I do wish that child wouldn't get so overwrought," Aunt Lela Maude said. "I declare, she's exactly like her mother."

I assumed my aunt had loved her sister, but it seemed that nearly everything she had said about her was derogatory. Aunt Lela Maude was never one to mince words, and I thought she was simply stating what she considered to be factual. Maybe I could have noticed a resemblance between Sam's behavior and that of our mother if I had ever seen Mom lose control of her temper. But that had never happened in my presence. My mother was a cool head.

I went to bed at a decent hour for the first time since I arrived in Martinsville. I was an adult; too old to wish for something that was impossible, but I had really looked forward to leaving my hometown today. Uncle Stuart and Aunt Lela Maude meant well, of course, but they were beginning to get on my nerves. I knew I shouldn't judge them too harshly, because they were of a different generation. So was Trudy, but she didn't get on my nerves. I loved Sam in an odd sort of way, even though she was liable to fly off the handle at the slightest provocation. And Ron—I didn't really know what I thought about him.

Stretching out on my sister's bed, I tried to make my mind go blank and relax, but I couldn't make that happen. Everything imaginable began marching through my head. I still hadn't made it to the cemetery, and that was something I felt was my duty. The pretty new vet crept into my thoughts, too. I had noticed she didn't wear a wedding ring, but that should have been a moot point since I was about to leave town. And I worried about Beth. She had turned into someone I didn't know, but I had been married to her for nine years. Forgetting her and all of her problems was not as easy as it should have been.

Last on the list was my old friend. I could imagine Joe Bob flopped on his couch, wishing for the company of that damnable cat while he drank beer and chain smoked in front of his big screen. He would be watching a sports channel, but he wouldn't be tuned in. Joe Bob would be thinking about Jimmy Banks and reliving the accident to keep it fresh in his memory. He would be turning himself in to be punished for taking the life of another human being.

Everyone appeared to be in good spirits at breakfast the next morning. My aunt and uncle were smiling at one another like newlyweds, and when Uncle Stuart got up to pour himself a cup of coffee, I noticed a definite spring in his step.

Aunt Lela Maude watched her husband with adoring eyes. And when he brought the coffeepot to the table to refill her half-empty cup, she giggled like a schoolgirl.

"You don't need to wait on me hand and foot, Stuart," she said. "I'm not an invalid, you know."

It was obvious she was enjoying my uncle's attentiveness. The more I observed the two of them, I didn't think there was any doubt that they had been making whoopee. How old did people have to be before they lost interest in sex? I tried to envision my aunt and uncle in the throes of passion, but I simply couldn't do it.

Aunt Lela Maude began staring back at me.

"Why are you grinnin' so, Mathoo?"

"Forgive me," I said, setting down my cup. "I was just thinking what a pleasure it is to see such sunny dispositions so early in the morning."

"Well, there's no reason for any of us to be a Gloomy Gus, is there?" Uncle Stuart said. "It's a beautiful day, your sister's being released from the hospital, and Mrs. Giles has prepared a bountiful feast for us. She must have gotten up at the crack of dawn."

Trudy had made eggs Benedict. She plated the food before bringing it to the table, serving my aunt first.

"I hope you enjoy it," she said. "I won't be here at lunchtime. There are cold cuts in the refrigerator. I have to take Fifi to the vet to get her shots."

"Fifi?"

"Your mother's French poodle," Trudy said. "Don't tell me you don't remember her."

I hadn't seen the dog since my arrival and had forgotten all about her, assuming she had died of old age.

"Where is she?"

"She's at my house. Miz Stevenson wanted me to have her. She made me promise that if anything ever happened to her, I'd take care of Fifi."

That spoiled dog had never liked me, and the feeling was mutual. Mom got her after Sam and I were both away at school. I came home for a weekend and met my mother's new pet for the first time. The dog bared her teeth at me, and a deep growl emanated from her throat. I remembered thinking how silly she looked, lowering her head, pretending to look ferocious with bow-bedecked ears, and trying to sound like a killer.

"That dog is ancient," I said. "I assumed she was already in dog hell."

"She's an old girl like me, but she's still in pretty good health. Her attitude hasn't changed," Trudy said.

After breakfast, I called Jack to check in and find out if he was still speaking to me. I was embarrassed to have to give him the news that I had been delayed again, but it didn't seem to upset him in the least.

"Matt, I'm really glad you called," he said.

"Oh? What's up?"

"You won't believe it," he said. I could hear excitement in his voice. "We've got a case to die for. You and I are about to make some serious money."

"So what is this manna from heaven case that's been dropped in our laps?"

"We're going to be defending a rape case."

"Rape?"

"That's right. Can you believe it?"

I couldn't. Neither of us had broken a sweat since we started our practice. We'd had lots of piddling cases, but those barely paid the rent.

"The guy's innocent, Matt," Jack said. "He has an iron-clad alibi."

"You're telling me that you and I are going to defend an alleged rapist. I certainly hope he's as squeaky clean as you seem to believe, and that he has a ton of money."

I never quite knew when I could trust Jack. He was a dreamer—the kind of guy who's always a little too quick to jump on a bandwagon blindfolded.

"He's innocent, I tell you," Jack said. "And you don't have to worry about his bank account. He comes from old money. This guy walks into the swankiest restaurant in town without a reservation and ends up with the best table in the place."

"Who is he?"

"His name is Reggie Fairchild. He's got money ain't never been spent."

The name sounded vaguely familiar. I must have run across it in the society section of the newspaper.

"Wonder why he would want a couple of nobodies like us to defend him?" I said.

"I met him at a party not long ago. Real nice, down-to-earth kind of guy. We hit it off right away."

"Tell me about the circumstances," I said.

"Circumstances?"

"Yeah. Concerning the rape."

"It's pretty detailed. I'd rather fill you in when you get back to Denver. When's that going to happen?"

"Thursday night. The reading of the will is that morning, but I couldn't get a flight out until eight o'clock."

"Okay. I'll see you soon. Dream about making it big, buddy. This case is going to put us in the headlines."

I called Joe Bob as soon as I hung up the phone. He must have picked up on the first ring. I knew he was nervous about meeting with a new attorney.

"Hey, Matt. How you doin'?"

"I'm fine. Listen, I was wondering if you might want some company when you go for your appointment."

"Thanks for the offer, but I'm a big boy. I think I can handle it."

"I'm free in case you change your mind."

"I'll call you after I talk to the guy."

He obviously wanted to do this thing solo. I hoped he wouldn't be asked some of the questions I would ask if I were going to represent him.

I had gotten all fired up at Bernie because he didn't want to be involved, but I was equally guilty. If the lawyer asked the right questions, and Joe Bob answered truthfully, as Uncle Stuart had instructed him to do, we could all end up in the soup. Then, I could kiss making it big goodbye. My partner would be enjoying his newfound fame and fortune while I spent time behind bars.

Chapter Twenty-five

I was on my way to the cemetery in Uncle Stuart's rental car, unsure of the reason I felt the need to visit my mother's grave one last time. It seemed a morbid thing to do. The visitation at the funeral home had seemed like an uncomfortable duty. I had felt compelled to attend, and the funeral was even worse. This seemed like a duty, too; one I couldn't ignore.

The iron gates of the cemetery were open, so I assumed there was another Martinsville citizen who would come here in a hearse to this final resting place later in the day. I drove slowly along the graveled path with its green strip of grass and weeds down its middle. The strip had been mowed short and neat, and I could hear the pebbles of rock crunch under my tires.

I parked the car and started walking toward my mother's headstone, careful to avoid stepping on the graves of strangers. We had put a rush order on Mother's headstone to ensure that it was exactly what we had ordered before any of the family left Martinsville. It stood out from the others that were similar in shape and size, because Mother's name was chiseled in script. Of course, my mother's headstone would be special. Eloise Stevenson: a beautiful name for a beautiful woman, a pillar of the community. My mother had died too young, I thought. She was only sixty-three. Many people lived well into their nineties; some with the aid of modern medicine, some with good genes, or good luck.

I could smell the fresh earth under its blanket of new sod. The mound was high compared to the graves nearby, and it was covered with baskets of flowers. Easels with expensive sprays held sentry at the headstone. I wondered how long the cemetery maintenance crew would leave those expressions of sympathy—probably until the flowers all shriveled and curled into rotting vegetation.

There was a large wreath of snow white roses at the foot of the grave, a little apart from the others. The roses looked fresh. I didn't remember seeing them at the funeral home, but I knew I hadn't paid attention to much of anything when I was there, let alone flowers.

I stood, looking at the heap of wilting blooms, knowing that the woman who had made it possible for me to be here was gone. I tried to feel something—anything, for her. If my aunt had been truthful with me, my mother had been proud of me; loved me. Why had she never told me? How could she have let me think she didn't care?

I turned to leave, and I saw him, standing several yards away, seeming to meditate while looking off in the distance. His height and build were familiar, and I knew it had to be him. I started toward him just as he turned to go, swiping a knuckle across his cheek.

"Dad?"

He turned in my direction, and I went to meet him.

"Hello, son."

We didn't embrace, and neither of us offered his hand. It was clear to me that he felt as awkward as I did.

"Dad, I apologize for not calling you. I knew Sam had talked with you."

"Yes, your sister and I did have a short phone conversation. She told me to keep my distance. Did she tell you that?"

I had never heard my father's voice sound tremulous before. It had always been strong, and suited a man of his stature. Today, it sounded sad and very unlike that of someone who was sure of himself.

"Yes, she did tell me, after the fact. She regrets what she said to you. I know she planned to call you again, but she's been having a pretty tough time the past few days."

"Oh?"

"She had a miscarriage, and since then, a relapse, compliments of Beth."

"I didn't know Samantha was pregnant. I'm sure you're aware she doesn't stay in touch with me. And I don't understand. How was Elizabeth involved?"

"It's a long story, and I'll explain it after we leave the cemetery if you have the time."

"I'll make the time."

"Another thing, Dad: I realize it's a lame excuse, but I've been real busy since Jack and I hung out our shingle. That's no reason for my negligence. I should get in touch with you more often."

"I know you've been busy. There's no need for apologies."

"Did you bring the white roses?"

My father nodded, and tried to smile.

"They were your mother's favorite. How could I ever forget that? I didn't come by the house, because my daughter didn't want me there, but I had to come here to say goodbye to Eloise. I've always loved her. It was simply too hard for me to live with her. Don't ask me for details, because I won't give them to you. She was your mother, and she loved you. Eloise loved her entire family, even me."

"Sam's been back in the hospital, but she's being released today. She's probably back at the house by now. I know she wants to see you, Dad. Will you go to the house with me?"

"Are you sure she wants to see me, Matt? She certainly gave no indication of that on the phone. I sure would love to see my baby girl, though. It's been a long time since I saw that pretty face. I've never met her husband. What's he like?"

"Follow me back to the house and see for yourself. Everybody will be glad to see you."

I pulled into the driveway behind the Lincoln, and my father parked on the street in front of the house. We climbed the front porch steps together, and Dad was taking his time to check out the familiar surroundings.

"Your mother's rose garden is still thriving, I see."

"Aunt Lela Maude has been tending it since last week."

"Oh, are she and Stuart here now?"

"Yes. They'll stay until after the reading of the will on Thursday."

"I haven't been in touch with them in ages. It'll be good to see them, too."

My mother's house didn't lend itself to a shy introduction. As soon as you walked through the front door and took a few steps forward, you were in the living room. That was where the family had congregated. Everyone had been hovering around Sam, who lay on the sofa in a Scarlet O'Hara pose with her pink robe spread out like a spring flower. I half expected to see a box of bonbons at her fingertips, but she looked awfully pale, I thought.

Ron was the one who noticed Dad's and my entrance. He pulled his eyes away from his wife, and looked up.

"Hello, everybody," I said. "Look who's come to see us."

Dad stayed where he was, looking apprehensive.

Sam looked at our father, standing at the door and tears brimmed in her blue eyes, then spilled onto her white cheeks.

"Daddy," she said, sobbing the word.

Dad rushed across the room and knelt beside his daughter. He placed his hands on her frail shoulders, and held her at arm's length, taking in her features while she cried. Then, he took her in his arms and held her for a very long time.

Sam began whispering her regrets close to our father's ear.

"Shhh. Shhh. It's all right, sweetheart. All of that's in the past. I love you, Sammy."

"I love you, too. I didn't know how much I had missed you until now."

When Dad finally got off his knee and pulled his six-foot frame off the floor, I introduced him to Ron. I knew it was an awkward moment for both men, because my sister hadn't invited Dad to her wedding.

"I'm glad to meet you, sir," Ron said.

"The pleasure's all mine," Dad said. "I know you've been taking good care of my daughter."

My aunt and uncle had taken their seats in the Queen Anne chairs, waiting their turns to greet my father.

Dad turned to face them and smiled. I had to admit that he was, indeed, a charming, handsome gentleman.

"Lela Maude, you're as beautiful as ever," he said, taking her hand and gracing it with a kiss.

My aunt smiled and blushed like a timid girl as Uncle Stuart stood to shake hands with Dad.

"Good to see you, Howard. It's been a long time," my uncle said. "I'd say this calls for a celebration, and I happen to have a delightful bottle of sherry. Matt, would you bring in some glasses."

I didn't think a celebration was appropriate, but I went to the china cabinet and came back to the living room with a tray of small glasses. It seemed that I was the only one who considered this an odd thing to do after the death of a family member.

My uncle poured the sherry and played host, passing around the tray.

"No, thanks, Uncle Stuart," Sam said. "I probably shouldn't."

"Nonsense. You're pale as a ghost. A taste of sherry will be good for you."

My sister wasn't used to having anyone tell her what to do, and I wouldn't have been surprised if she had told Uncle Stuart what he could do with his bottle of sherry. But that didn't happen. She lifted the glass from the tray, and held it in her delicate hand.

"Here's to a family reunited," said Uncle Stuart, raising his glass.

"And to Eloise," my father said. "May she rest in peace."

We all drank the toast, and as I looked around the room, I didn't see a dry eye.

Aunt Lela Maude excused herself to go to the kitchen to make sandwiches and coffee. Ron offered to help her. I assumed he felt uncomfortable having just met his father-in-law, knowing that his wife and her father had been estranged. He brought a chair from across the room and placed it close to Sam so she and Dad could talk privately.

Uncle Stuart and I were alone with what was left of the sherry, and he refilled our glasses.

"Bernie and I helped Joe Bob find a decent attorney," I said.

"That's good. He'll need one."

"Uncle Stuart, there's something I don't understand. I've never seen you back down from anything, but it seems to me you've turned your back on this accident. Is there some reason you want to distance yourself from it?"

"There's nothing I can do to help. You keep referring to what happened as an accident, and that's exactly what it was. There was no premeditation. As far as I'm concerned, Joe Bob's innocent. Any one of us could have been driving when the accident occurred. I don't see that there's a punishable offense. If your friend goes to prison, it's for naught. He can't re-live that evening, but he should be able to allow it to dim in his memory. That's what I intend to do. Does that answer your question?"

My uncle and I had both been keeping our voices quiet, and every time I glanced at my sister and father, they appeared engrossed in conversation. I watched them smile, then wipe away a tear, and every now and then, they embraced.

"Uncle Stuart, if you were Joe Bob's lawyer, wouldn't you keep digging until you got the whole truth out of him?"

"Sure. I'd ask questions he couldn't skate by, and he'd end up telling me who was with him and how it all happened."

"Same here. I don't mind telling you it makes me uneasy. Joe Bob doesn't want to involve us, but he might not have a choice. If he chooses to waste the rest of his life, or at least several years of it, I can't stop him. But I'm in my thirties, and I still have a shot at a good life. This could ruin me."

"It could wreck Bernie's life, too, as well as mine. I think it would probably do my darling wife in if she had to visit me behind bars. We're too old to be involved in such messes. Neither of us has the energy to fight battles this late in life."

Aunt Lela Maude brought in a tray loaded with tea sandwiches, followed by Ron with Mother's silver service.

Dad didn't stay long after lunch. He told us he was staying at The Greystone for a couple of days, and to feel free to impose on his time as much as we liked. He knew we were busy, and he didn't want to interfere with any of our plans.

The house was quiet after my father left. Sam and Ron went to their room to take a nap. It was time for Aunt Lela Maude's soap opera, so she turned on the TV to watch it while Uncle Stuart settled himself on the sofa with a *Time Magazine*.

I was sitting in the room that had been my dad's study. Mom had converted it into a sitting room, and I thought it gave the impression of never being used. The bookshelves which had been filled with literary fiction now were home to framed photographs and knickknacks. Dad's leather couch had been replaced by an overstuffed floral print loveseat and matching chair.

I sat staring out the window, thinking about my conversation with Jack, hoping his enthusiasm for the alleged rape case was well-founded. I'd be a fool to get too excited, knowing Jack as well as I did. He could get high on a prospect that might never happen. But what I wouldn't give to make some real money.

Chapter Twenty-six

"Stevenson residence."

"Hello, Mr. Stevenson. This is Sydney Edelman. I hope I have the number for the correct Stevenson. Were you the gentleman with Mr. Kincaid at my animal hospital yesterday?"

"Yes. That was me, Dr. Edelman."

How could an obvious business call cause me to feel something resembling a thrill?

"The reason for my call, Mr. Stevenson, is that I've been unable to reach Mr. Kincaid on the phone. He listed this as an alternative number."

"I see. Is there a problem with my friend's cat?"

"On the contrary. The cat is doing exceptionally well. In fact, he's well enough to go home. Of course, I'll need to check him over in about a week."

"That's good news. I'll track down my friend and give him your message."

"Thank you for your help. I'll be expecting to hear from Mr. Kincaid."

I couldn't imagine why Joe Bob wasn't answering his phone. He wasn't one to dodge calls, even if he was expecting an unpleasant one.

I scribbled a note to my uncle, telling him I was borrowing his car. Joe Bob's garage was only a ten minute drive from the house. I would probably find him working on a car with his shop radio turned up full-blast.

Sure enough, there he was under an old Chevy that looked like it had seen better days. Joe Bob had on what, at one time, had been light colored coveralls. His long legs stuck out from under the car, and the toes of his shoes tipped out like they belonged to someone who was asleep. I turned off the radio.

"Joe Bob, come out from under there for a minute."

He bent his knees, and wheeled himself out to look up at me with a raised brow.

"Hey, Matt. What's up?"

"The vet called. She said you can come and get your cat. He's well enough to go home."

Joe Bob got to his feet, and started wiping grease off his hands. He turned away from me with his head down.

"Joe Bob, aren't you relieved?"

"I am, for a fact. If he hadn't made it, I felt like I just couldn't have stood it." He spit out a strange little laugh that didn't sound like a laugh at all.

"The vet is expecting you to come get the cat."

"I guess I'd better let her know I'll come git him in just a little while."

"Want some company when you go?"

"Well, sure. I'll come pick you up as soon as I git cleaned up."

"Good idea. I need to get Uncle Stuart's car back to the house. I doubt he knows I took it."

I didn't know anybody who could get clean in as little time as Joe Bob. He showed up in less than a half hour, and that included driving time.

"I see you brought his bed," I said.

"Yeah. It's soft, but he don't sleep in it at home. He likes that old armchair and his blanket. I reckon Lucy'll take turns with me lookin' after him. One of us is most always free when the other one's workin'. Then, if I end up goin' to jail, she'll keep him. She's got a good heart."

Sydney Edelman brought the cat from a back room in what looked like a padded sling. She was kneading behind his ears, and he was purring.

"Here's your handsome boy, Mr. Kincaid," she said, handing the sling to Joe Bob.

"He still sure looks awful bunged up," Joe Bob said.

"He's in much better condition than he appears. Most of these bandages will come off in about a week. He'll still have a splint on his leg, but he'll look much better. When his hair grows back, he'll look like nothing ever happened to him."

Joe Bob handed me the sling so he could get out his wallet, and that old cat stuck his head out for me to scratch his ears. I declined.

Sydney Edelman smiled. "I think he likes you, Mr. Stevenson."

The receptionist handed Joe Bob a receipt. He pocketed it and took the sling from me.

"I can't thank you enough, doc. I was afraid he was a goner."

"You're quite welcome. Bring him back to see me in a week. In the meantime, call me if he has a problem."

I had let my chance go by. We were leaving the animal hospital, and I hadn't said a word to Sydney Edelman.

"She sure is a good vet," Joe Bob said.

"I wouldn't mind getting to know her," I said. "It's too bad I'm leaving town so soon."

"You ever plan on comin' back here after you leave?"

"I'm sure Sam and I will end up selling the house. I might have reason to come back then."

"Git yourself back in there and leave one of your lawyer cards for her. It's worth a shot. I'm not in a hurry. All I plan to do tonight is play nursemaid to my cat and hang out with him and my big screen."

I felt like a kid, but I was ready to grab at any straw there was, so I started back into the building. Dr. Edelman was on her way out. She was adjusting the strap on her purse. When she looked up, we were face to face, nearly colliding.

"Oh, Mr. Stevenson, I'm so sorry. I'm afraid I wasn't looking where I was going. Is something the matter?"

I felt tongue-tied, so I just stared into her hazel eyes, feeling like an idiot. She stared back. It must have been a full minute before I found my voice.

"No. No. Nothing's the matter." My card case slipped out of my hand, and my knee popped when I stooped to retrieve it. "I just wanted to leave one of my cards with you."

The good doctor looked confused, but she accepted the card.

"Well, I see you're probably leaving for the day. I won't hold you up."

"How perceptive of you. I'm doing just that. Skipping lunch is one of my bad habits."

I couldn't just let her get away like that, having her think I was some clumsy dolt with a cracking knee.

"So, are you one of those professional women who work all day, then go home to cook dinner for your family?"

"No. I don't cook very much. But as I said, I did skip lunch, so I'm a little hungry."

She wanted me to get the hell out of her way. That was plain to see, so I turned to leave. She fell into step with me. I was sure it was unintentional. Then, she smiled at me as if she knew there was something more I wanted to say, the way one might encourage a shy child.

I didn't know what had come over me. I was a professional, an attorney. How many times had I spoken in public—to juries and judges? Why couldn't I muster the courage to approach this woman in an adult fashion?

"Dr. Edelman, I'm leaving Martinsville in a couple of days and returning to my law practice in Denver. Might you consider letting me take you to dinner at the restaurant of your choice this evening? That is, unless you have plans."

A smile flirted with the corner of her mouth, and I noticed she had a dimple in her right cheek.

"I'm being presumptuous. Please forgive me. I didn't see a ring on your finger, so I assumed you weren't married. Normally, I'm not this forward."

"As a matter of fact, I don't have plans." She smiled openly. "But I am hungry."

"May I take that as a yes?"

"You may." There was that smile again.

"Great. I grew up here, so I'm familiar with the town. What's your address?"

"I'm having a house built in Sweetgrass Estates, but I'm staying in an apartment until it's finished. My address is 311 Ashland Street, #205. I'm directly across from the elevators. Shall I expect you in about an hour?"

"I'll be there. Do you have a favorite restaurant?"

"No, I don't. I've only been here for a couple of months, and I haven't had much time to scout out the restaurants."

"All right. I'll surprise you."

As I climbed into Joe Bob's pickup, I watched Sydney Edelman slide behind the wheel of a BMW convertible and drive away.

"So, kinda looks like that went fairly well," Joe Bob said.

"It sure did. I'm taking her to dinner tonight."

Since I didn't have a car, and I didn't want to show up at Sydney Edelman's place in a cab, I asked Uncle Stuart to borrow his rental car again. None of the family seemed to have an interest in my plans for the evening, and that worked for me. I was getting tired of explaining my every move.

I perused the restaurant guide, having in mind an establishment touted for excellent cuisine, an outstanding wine list, and an intimate atmosphere. It didn't take long to find what looked like the perfect one. I made a reservation, hoping my credit card wouldn't be denied.

Sydney Edelman had changed into a crisp, white sleeveless blouse, pencil skirt, and sandals when I rang her doorbell. Her hair was tucked behind her small ears, displaying diamond studs. If she was wearing makeup, it wasn't apparent, and I thought she looked like a pretty fresh-faced teenager.

"Hi, there," she said, opening the door wide. "Won't you come in?"

I had just met Sydney Edelman, but her apartment expressed her taste perfectly, I thought. The living room could have been featured in decorator magazines: snowy white loveseats, glass-topped tables holding fresh flowers in crystal vases. The light oak hardwood floor was scattered with thick oriental rugs.

"This is a lovely apartment," I said.

"Thanks. I decided to rent this particular one for its view of the river," she said, nodding toward a large bay window. "It's too bad I don't have a chance to spend more time at home."

I had never been a fan of small talk, even when it was appropriate, so I decided to dive right in.

"Sydney. May I call you Sydney?"

She laughed. "I think that could be arranged. I see no reason to be formal. And you are?"

"Matt."

"Thank you for inviting me to dinner, Matt. I haven't met too many people since I've been here. How about a glass of wine?"

"I'm not sure we have time. I made our reservation for seven o'clock."

"In that case, just let me grab my purse."

I stood by the window, looking out at the lovely pastoral scene on the edge of my hometown, wondering why I had asked a perfect stranger to dinner. Nothing could possibly come of this. Maybe I had done it simply because I realized I was lonely. I hadn't admitted that to myself until now.

Chapter Twenty-seven

The maitre d' led us to a window table with a view of an exotic landscape. It looked like manicured nature at its best with an array of shrubbery, flowers, and ornamental trees.

"What a lovely place this is," Sydney said.

"I agree. This is the first time I've been here. Martinsville seems to have blossomed quite a bit since I lived here."

"Look!" Sydney was pointing to something she had spied through the window. "It's a peacock; he's gorgeous."

I had to admit that watching a peacock strut its stuff while sitting in a restaurant, waiting for drinks to arrive was a bit unusual, and the delight in Sydney Edelman's eyes was something akin to uplifting.

"He certainly is a proud one," I said.

I wanted to get to know the woman sitting across from me. Her every move, or remark held charm for me. Although I would be leaving town soon, I knew that I would not soon forget Sydney Edelman.

Our drinks arrived.

"Here's to a new friendship," I said, lifting my glass in a toast. Sydney smiled and touched her glass to mine.

"Tell me a little about yourself, Matt. I know you grew up here, and that you practice law in Denver now. What brings you back to your hometown, maybe a class reunion?"

"I'm afraid I didn't come here for pleasure. My mother passed away a little over a week ago, and I came home for her funeral and to be with my family."

"I'm so sorry. Please accept my condolences. I shouldn't have asked such a pointed question."

I tried to smile. It was an innocent question—one that anyone might ask in casual conversation. I wasn't sure why it had struck such a tender chord in me.

"Don't apologize. You had no way of knowing. My mother's death was sudden. She hadn't been ill. Her heart just stopped while she was grocery shopping. It was a terrible shock to the entire family. My sister and her husband are here, and so are my aunt and uncle. We're all staying at mother's house until the reading of the will."

The kindness I had seen in Sydney Edelman's face the first time I saw her shone in her eyes. I didn't think I had ever seen such feeling exhibited in another person's facial expression.

"I'm glad you have your family here. That must mean a lot when you're feeling fragile."

I nodded. "It does."

She seemed to brighten, and took a sip of her drink.

"I suppose you're wondering how I came to be in Martinsville," she said.

"I guess you could say I'm a little curious." I smiled.

"Dr. Green and my father were good friends. They went to school together. My father was also a veterinarian. I suppose a love of animals runs in our family. Dad and I were attending a conference a few years ago, and Dr. Green was there. Dad introduced us, and Dr. Green told me that if I ever wanted to leave Cincinnati and head south, he could use a young partner in his practice."

"Did you work with your father in Cincinnati?"

"Yes, I did, but Dad's health began failing, and he wanted to retire. I took over his practice for a while, but I had a lot going on at the time and decided to give it up."

"I see."

"No, you don't, and you're too polite to ask questions."

She was right, but I didn't want to acknowledge it.

"I can tell you're a stand-up guy. Besides, you're leaving town, so I can use you for a sounding board." She smiled.

"Shoot."

"I was in a marriage that wasn't happy."

"I'm sorry."

"That's only part of it."

I took a drink of my bourbon.

"I discovered I was pregnant a few weeks after I filed for divorce."

"That's a tough predicament."

"I didn't tell anyone about the pregnancy. My husband moved out, telling me he planned to make sure our divorce wasn't going to be a walk in the park."

There was nothing I could say, so I waited for her to choose the words to tell me about the experience that brought her to my hometown.

"I have always been an advocate for women's rights. Women should have the right to choose. But when I was preaching that, I hadn't been pregnant. My marriage was over, and that was my choice, but I didn't think I could bring myself to end my child's life before it began. As fate would have it, I didn't have to make that decision."

Sydney took a deep breath, then downed a healthy drink of her martini.

"I was crossing the street at a busy intersection, and I was in a hurry. Pedestrians had a green light, but someone who was in a bigger hurry ran a red light and hit me. I was lucky he didn't hit me head-on. I landed on my side, but I hit the pavement hard. The doctor in the emergency room didn't have to tell me the bad news. I knew I had lost my baby."

"I'm sorry. I can't imagine how that must hurt."

"It did, but I have finally gotten over the hurt. Shortly after the accident I called Dr. Green and accepted his offer. I thought my parents would try to make me change my mind, but they didn't. They thought that moving to a new environment would help me forget the unhappiness I had suffered."

"I hope they're right."

"Martinsville seems to be a very friendly town. I've met some lovely people since I came here."

"I think most small towns are friendly. Martinsville was a great town for kids. It was safe, everybody knew everyone else, and there was very little crime. As soon as I was old enough to ride a bike, I was allowed to ride all over town and play with my friends until dinnertime."

"I'd heard about those kinds of towns, but this is the first time I've had a firsthand experience. I think I like it."

"I'm afraid it's not for me anymore."

"I see. Do you work for a large firm?"

"No. My partner and I have a small practice. We're what you might call a work in progress."

"So you simply prefer city life and all of its amenities?"

"That's right. I like being able to hop into my car and have my choice of a dozen fantastic restaurants within just a few minutes. It's nice to see a play, or go to the symphony without having to drive to the closest city. Also, Denver has every kind of medical specialist imaginable, and shopping galore. The laid-back lifestyle there is a big plus, too. What's not to like?"

"Well, it certainly sounds like you're hooked on the Mile-High City. I suppose you're something of a ski bum, too."

I laughed. "I might be if I didn't have to work. The Rockies are gorgeous all year. In the fall, the aspen trees don't look real. Their leaves quake at the slightest breeze; they look like gold half-dollars. In the wintertime, all the evergreens are covered in snow. It's a beautiful sight."

"The mountains sound lovely. Maybe I'll put them on my bucket list."

I looked at my watch and realized we had been at the restaurant for quite a while.

"I apologize, Sydney. You must be famished. I didn't realize how long we had been here. Shall we take a look at the menus?"

"I lost track of the time, too. That's a good idea."

Sydney's head was bent over her menu, and I was about to open mine when I saw a woman who looked exactly like Lee Ann Zuckerman from the back. She was walking toward the restroom area. I scanned the restaurant to see if I could spot Bernie. Not sure what motivated me to do it, I excused myself and made my way toward the restrooms. I could see the entire dining area from where I stood, and Bernie wasn't there. His wife could have been having dinner with a girlfriend, but for some reason, I had a feeling that wasn't the case.

I stepped behind a free-standing pillar when I saw Lee Ann leave the restroom area and head for the entrance of the restaurant. She was talking on her cell phone, but I was too far away to hear what she was saying. I didn't know why I felt the way I did, but she didn't strike me as being trustworthy. She dropped the phone into her purse, and walked out the door to stand on the steps like she was waiting for someone. I walked toward the entrance to see her get into a late model Cadillac with a man I didn't recognize.

Sydney had polished off the rest of her drink when I returned to the table.

"What looks good to you?" I asked.

"Everything, but I've decided on the trout."

I grabbed my menu, and gave it the once-over as our waiter hurried to take our order.

"The lady will have the trout, and I'll try the salmon. We'd also like a bottle of the Macon Lugny les Charmes."

Sydney grinned. "That's one of my favorites."

"Mine, too. I think it's great with seafood."

The meal was excellent, and I was finding Sydney to be the perfect dinner companion. She talked easily about her childhood, growing up in Cincinnati, and even went so far as to brag about her hometown's chili.

The waiter brought dessert menus, and Sydney waved hers away. My appetite was sated, too, but I wasn't ready to leave the restaurant. I was afraid that if I took this lovely lady home now, she would tell me goodnight at her door, saying she had an early day tomorrow.

"How about coffee, or an after-dinner drink?"

Sydney thought about that for a minute, wrinkling her nose, and I found that truly endearing. It seemed that everything she did impressed me favorably.

"I'll have a cognac," she said.

"That sounds good. I'll have the same."

My alcohol intake this evening was reminiscent of the evening

Beth had treated me to dinner. Unfortunately, I knew the rest of the evening would bear no resemblance to the one I had spent with my ex.

I was listening to Sydney tell me her plans for revamping her clinic. She thought the filing system was antiquated.

"I guess that's to be expected in a small town," she said, "but it's going to be short-lived. Everything is going to be handled electronically as fast as I can make it happen."

A look of recognition appeared on Sydney's face, and she smiled at someone over my shoulder.

"Liz," she said.

"Hello, Sydney."

The voice was unquestionably that of my ex-wife. What were the odds that I would run into the two women in this town I wanted to avoid?

Beth's heels clicked to a halt as she reached our table. She peered down at me with an evil gleam in her eyes, the one that was always present just before she delivered a vicious blow. Shaking her head as though she couldn't believe what she was seeing, she uttered a quiet laugh.

"Wow, Matt, you're just like Santa Claus and the Easter Bunny. Everywhere I go, there you are."

Sydney looked confused.

"I was about to make introductions, but I see you two know one another," she said.

"Yes. Matt and I know one another quite well. We were married once upon a time," Beth said.

"We've been divorced for several years," I said. "Give your mother my best, Beth."

Any sane person would have taken the hint and been on her way, but I was well aware that Beth wasn't sane, and assumed she would do her best to ruin not only my evening, but my chances with Sydney Edelman.

"I'll do that, Matt. You have a safe flight back to Denver."

Beth touched Sydney's shoulder and said, "It was good to see you, Sydney. Let's do lunch soon."

I waited until Beth's footsteps disappeared before saying a word. Sydney was rubbing her cognac snifter between her palms, and looking embarrassed.

"I see you've met my ex-wife. She does have a way of getting around."

"Yes. We met at a newcomers' luncheon. She seemed very friendly."

"I'm sure she did. She's the face of the new hospital; it's her job to be friendly."

Sydney cleared her throat.

"This has been lovely, Matt. Thank you for dinner and the stimulating conversation."

I asked for the check, and we sipped at our drinks. It seemed that Beth had, once again, accomplished her objective.

Chapter Twenty-eight

The delightful Sydney Edelman had politely let me know that she considered our new friendship a bad idea. She had a key in the lock, and one foot into her apartment before I had a chance to explain what I considered important things regarding my ex. I wanted her to know that I hadn't attempted to contact Beth while I was here; that it had been all her doing.

It was still early, and I was thoroughly out of sorts. I was driving down Main Street. Lights in the lobby of The Greystone looked welcoming from the street, and I wondered if Dad was still up. I decided to find out, and found a parking space about a half-block down the street. It was quiet in town. There was hardly any traffic. All of the new businesses were on the outskirts—some as much as fifteen, or twenty miles out of town, including the restaurant I had just left.

I walked past the library, breathing in the perfume of the honeysuckle I knew inhabited the brick wall behind the old building. The clay had shifted under sections of the concrete sidewalk, and by the time I reached the hotel, I knew I had scuffed the polish off the toes of both my shoes.

I was walking through the lobby to the front desk, and glanced toward the open bar to my left. There sat Dad on a stool at the end of the bar, nursing a drink. He was talking with another gentleman wearing a business suit. I assumed they were engaged in nothing more than casual conversation, since Dad was only in town for a few days and hadn't come here on business.

As I reached the entrance of the bar, I recognized the other man. He was one of Dad's closest friends, Hamilton Brock, vice president of The Peoples Bank and Trust Company. Mr. Brock saw me, and his face creased into a familiar smile.

"Well, if it isn't young Matt Stevenson." He extended his hand.

"Hello, Mr. Brock."

"I'm very sorry to have missed your mother's funeral, Matt. I've been in Jacksonville on personal business, and didn't know that Eloise had passed until I got back into town. How are you bearing up, son?"

"I'm all right, Mr. Brock. Thank you."

"I'm glad to see you, Matt," Dad said. "I was afraid you and I weren't going to see one another again before I leave town."

Mr. Brock laid some bills on the bar and slid off his stool.

"I have to be going," he said. "It was good seeing you both. Take good care."

"Let's go to a booth where we can talk," Dad said. "What are you drinking?"

"Cognac."

Dad placed the order, and told the bartender where we were headed.

"I assume it was just luck that you ran into your old friend," I said.

"Actually, it had nothing to do with luck. I called and asked him to meet me here for a drink."

"Oh."

"I would never come to Martinsville without giving Ham a call, but I had business to discuss with him."

I didn't understand why my father was telling me anything about his personal business.

"I have something to tell you that I should have told you long ago. When your mother and I split up, I opened trust funds for you and your sister. I'm not sure why I waited until now to tell you about them. Ham was supposed to contact you and Samantha upon my instruction. If either of you had ever been in dire straits, I would have found out, and you would have been given access to the funds. Samantha has accepted me at last, and we're all here together for a couple of more days, so I decided to tell you myself. The trusts are revocable, but I'm not a young man. You're both old enough to be responsible, and there's no reason you shouldn't have your money now. Each of you is about to have over a million dollars you weren't aware of."

It never occurred to me that my father had seen to Sam's and my future when he and Mother divorced, but I had assumed he would remember us in his will.

"Dad, you've just thrown me for a loop. I can't tell you how much I appreciate this. I know Sam will, too. And you were correct in assuming that neither of us is starving, but realizing we've just been given large sums of money is enough to make me giddy. I don't know how to thank you."

"You don't have to thank me; you're my son, and I love you."

I had a lump in my throat and found it difficult to speak, but I managed to express my love for him.

"I plan to call the house first thing in the morning and set up a time to meet with Samantha," he said.

"I'm sure she'll be surprised and delighted."

"I hope so. It would make me very happy to be close to both of my children again."

"I don't think you'll have to worry about that, Dad."

"Did you need to talk to me about something, Matt? It's not like you to drop by for no reason."

"I guess you're right about that, but there's nothing pressing I needed to discuss with you. I just wondered if you might still be up. I wanted to tell you how glad I am that you came to Martinsville."

My father smiled. "Hopefully, we'll see one another again before I leave town. And, Matt, if there's anything you'd ever like to talk about with your old man, let me know."

"Sure. Good night, Dad."

I left the hotel, feeling unsettled. Sydney Edelman's light perfume lingered in the car, and I could hear her laughter as though she were sitting right beside me. It felt terribly unfair for me to have found such a jewel to lose her just as I was getting to know her. I would do my best to somehow resuscitate our relationship.

I drove to Joe Bob's, feeling not one bit guilty. He had bent my ear for over a week. It was my turn to bend his. I knocked on his door and waited, listening to a bullfrog croak from somewhere behind the double-wide. A light was on in the living room, so I knew he hadn't gone to bed, but it took him a long time to answer the door.

"Hey, Matt, what brings you to the trailer park?"

"Early date."

"What happened? You two didn't hit it off, or what?"

"Are you going to invite me in?"

"Sure. Sure. You want a beer?"

"No, thanks. You're not going to believe what I'm about to tell you."

"I'm all ears."

"Guess who I saw at the restaurant."

"We're not ten anymore. Who'd you see?'

"Bernie's wife."

"What's she got to do with you and the vet?'

"Nothing, but she wasn't there with Bernie."

"No shit?"

"I saw her get into the car with a guy I've never seen."

"You're not one to jump to conclusions. It coulda been perfectly innocent, couldn't it?"

"Maybe, but I don't think it was. I think she's fooling around on Bernie."

"You gonna tell him?"

"I don't know. Would you?"

"I don't think I'm in a position to mess around in Bernard's litter box right now. It don't take much for me to slip outta his good graces."

"Well, it's none of my business, but I think he should know. When Beth had an affair, I was the last one to find out about it. I didn't actually know it until she laid it on me last week."

"But you don't really know anything. All you saw was her gittin' in the car with a man. He coulda been a relative for all you know."

"You're right. I guess I'll have to sleep on it."

"What happened between you and the vet?"

"Beth."

"You might want to explain that."

"I swear, I think the woman's stalking me. She seems to be everywhere I go."

"No lie? Your two favorite women in the same night."

"Things were going so well. Sydney and I were having a great time. We seemed to be a perfect match."

"What happened?"

"We were having after-dinner drinks when Beth showed up. Actually, she snuck up behind me. She and Sydney had met at some sort of luncheon not long ago. Sydney was ignorant of the fact that Beth was my ex. She was about to introduce us when Beth let her know that wouldn't be necessary."

"Bummer."

"That ended the dinner date. Sydney thanked me for a lovely evening. She left me standing at her door like some sort of pariah, and closed the door before I even had a chance to tell her goodnight."

"Well, I don't reckon that's really so awful. I mean, you're about to go back to Denver, and the relationship couldn't be much more than it is now, unless you plan to do a lot of flyin'."

"I guess you're right. It's just that this is the first time I've had much feeling about anything since my divorce. Sydney Edelman made me feel alive again. I realize it's a moot point since I don't live here, especially since she just moved to Martinsville and seems to like everything about it."

"She's a good animal doctor; no doubt about it. That little lady saved my cat. I feel like I owe her a lot."

Joe Bob's old cat was sleeping on his side in the cat bed, snoring contentedly.

"She'll be a welcome addition to the town. I'm glad you have her."

Chapter Twenty-nine

I crawled into bed in my boxers and tee shirt, and stared at the dark ceiling, thinking about how everything sucks. It seemed to me the ups and downs life hands out ought to be more balanced. My parents shouldn't have split up. Beth shouldn't have been unfaithful to me; she should have trusted me. We should be happily married instead of divorced and bitter. And just as I had begun to see a glimmer of hope because of Sydney Edelman, it disappeared, and I was once again in a state of ennui. I wasn't excited about getting back to Denver anymore, even with the possibility of making a ton of money in the rape case.

I almost wished I hadn't seen Bernie's wife with another man. Then, I wouldn't have to decide whether or not I should tell him about it. I remembered exactly how I had felt when Beth told me she wanted a divorce. Nothing had ever hurt me that much. I'd felt like I had been kicked in the gut by the woman I loved more than my life, and I hadn't cared whether I lived or died.

Lee Ann was a poor excuse for a wife in my opinion, but I didn't get to vote on that. If she loved her husband, she certainly had a strange way of showing it. She impressed me as a real control freak, telling Bernie what he could, and couldn't do. I couldn't imagine allowing my wife to scream at me the way she yelled at Bernie. She sounded like she hated him, and wanted to hurt him. If she was having an affair, Bernie deserved to know the truth. I didn't want him to be in the dark until Lee Ann surprised him by asking for a divorce. That would just about kill him. He might not like hearing it from me, but I felt compelled to tell him what I had seen. He could take it from there. It was clear to me that he came close to worshipping his cold wife. He might just want to pretend I hadn't told him.

Resolving to be Bernie's friend and deliver what I thought was most certainly bad news, I got up to go to the bathroom. I could almost feel the pinkness of the fluffy rug under my feet. Padding down the hall, I went into the small room. I flipped on the light switch and looked at my reflection in the mirror. Unhappiness was the only thing present in my face, and I didn't know how to remedy it.

Back in Sam's room, I mentally planned my schedule for the next day. Bernie was first on my list. I would call him as soon as I thought he was away from his house and his potentially unfaithful wife, and ask him to meet me for coffee. Then, I would tell him what I had seen. If Lee Ann had been innocent, and I had jumped to the wrong conclusion, Bernie would have known her whereabouts and whom she had been with. That being the case, I could be minus a good friend.

I had no idea how to approach Sydney Edelman, but I knew I would somehow manage to see her before I flew to Denver. There was no way I could leave Martinsville with her thinking I had any involvement with my ex-wife. I should have told her about my failed marriage during our dinner conversation. She had pretty much bared her soul to me, but I had been far from forthcoming about my personal life. If I could find an opportunity to explain things to her, she might not consider me such a loser.

I got up early and ran before anyone else was awake. Trudy's car was there when I got back to the house. I found her in the kitchen, making biscuits.

"Good morning, sunshine," I said.

"Good mornin', my sweet boy."

I smiled. "You used to call me that even when I was being a brat."

"I never knew you to be a brat. You just wanted some attention, and I tried to make sure you got it."

"I stopped by The Greystone last night."

Trudy looked at me with a nudge in her expression, telling me to get on with what I had to say.

"Hamilton Brock was there, having a nightcap with Dad."

"Mr. Brock's a nice man. He's still at the bank. I don't think he'll ever retire."

"He and Dad were discussing personal business when I arrived."

Trudy gave me the look again.

"Mr. Brock said goodnight shortly after I arrived, and Dad ushered me to a booth so we could talk in private. He told me that he had set up trust funds for Sam and me back when he and Mom divorced. Did you know he did that?"

"No, but then it was none of my business."

"I thought maybe Mom told you."

"I doubt she knew anything about it. When your parents divorced, that was the end of their communication. Your daddy probably didn't tell Miz Eloise anything about it."

"I just learned that I have over a million dollars. Sam does, too."

"My goodness! What a surprise."

"It certainly was. Dad's going to call Sam this morning and see when it's convenient for him to come over to give her the good news."

"That'll put a big smile on our little sourpuss's face."

I showered, then called Bernie at work. He sounded busy and maybe a little out of sorts, but he agreed to meet me for coffee. I felt kind of apprehensive because of his tone of voice, but my mind was made up.

I had borrowed Uncle Stuart's rental car so many times he had gotten used to it. He always left the keys in the tray on the end of the kitchen counter, and if they were missing, he knew who had taken them.

I parked on the street and fed a meter under a hanging basket of purple and white petunias, and walked a half-block to The Friendly Café. A smiling middle-aged woman with salt-and-pepper hair harnessed into a hairnet told me to sit wherever I wanted. I walked to a booth in a back corner of the room and waited for Bernie.

Twenty minutes later, a little bell over the door tinkled, and Bernie came in. I half-stood and waved to him. He walked toward me wearing an *all business* look.

"Glad you could make it," I said, pouring coffee from the pot I had ordered. I pushed the coffee toward him, and he dosed it with half-and-half and a packet of Splenda.

"What's up?" he asked.

I could feel myself losing nerve from the moment my friend entered the café. If I intended to tell him what I had seen the previous night, I was going to have to man up and get the job done. I looked directly into his dark, bespectacled eyes and swallowed.

"I saw Lee Ann at Christman House Restaurant last night," I said.

"Yeah?"

"Well, I didn't actually see her face, but it sure looked like her."

When he didn't say anything, I knew I'd been right; Bernie's wife was cheating on him. His hand shook when he picked up his cup, and he put it back on the saucer without taking a drink.

"Were you there, Bernie? I didn't see you."

"Stop playing cat and mouse with me, Matt. You know I wasn't there. If I had been, we wouldn't be having this conversation."

It was hard for me to look at the hurt and anger in my friend's eyes.

"See who she was with?" he asked.

"I saw her get into a late model black Cadillac when she left the restaurant."

Bernie looked down at his coffee and shook his head as if he were trying to convince himself this couldn't be happening.

"I didn't recognize the guy," I said. "Could he have been a relative, or friend, maybe somebody connected with the dance studio?"

Bernie knew I was grabbing at straws for his sake. I had told him what I saw, and that was all I knew to do.

"None of the above. The guy's name is Stan Mitchell. He's the father of one of the kids Lee Ann teaches dance lessons to."

I felt a ray of hope.

"Well, I guess Lee Ann could have a perfectly legitimate reason for being with him."

Bernie took off his glasses and massaged his broad forehead with a thumb and forefinger.

"I've come home after picking up Claire from nursery school to find him leaving my house a couple of times. Lee Ann passed it off, saying the visit had something to do with his kid. I'm not the jealous type. It never occurred to me to think my wife was having an affair. She takes her job at the studio seriously and works individually with the students, so I believed her."

"Maybe she was telling you the truth. You should ask her point-blank what's going on between them."

"No, I won't do that. I've seen the signs and ignored them, hoping I was wrong. Just been in denial because I couldn't stand for it to be true. I've known all along."

"I'm sorry, man. Maybe I shouldn't have said anything to you, but I'm your friend. I had to tell you."

"You did the right thing. I would have done the same if I'd been in your shoes."

"What are you going to do?"

"I'll have to hire the best attorney I can find. He, or she, will have to be good enough to make sure I get sole custody of my child. No slut is going to raise my baby girl. I swear it."

"When do you plan to approach Lee Ann?"

"Not yet. I'm going to make sure she's actually caught in the act so I can prove she's an unfit mother."

There's something that happens to a man when he realizes the love of his life doesn't love him. It's not a feeling that can be described, or explained, even to oneself. I knew Bernie was experiencing that hell after hearing me confirm the thing he had feared, and I didn't have the faintest notion how to ease his pain. He did have something left worth fighting for—his daughter. I had seen how he worshiped the child, so I was sure he would ignore his hurt and do everything humanly possible to gain sole custody of her.

"I'd better get back to work," he said, sliding out of the booth. "You're a good friend, Matt. I know how hard it must have been for you to tell me."

He turned and walked out of the café, making the bell over the door tinkle as he left. It didn't sound the least bit cheerful.

Chapter Thirty

I drove to Joe Bob's garage and found it locked with a *closed* sign on the door. Wondering why he wasn't at work, I cruised over to his place. The Buick wasn't there, but I knew he had kept it in a bay at the garage since the night of the accident. His truck was parked on the gravel patch that passed for a driveway.

Music seeped out through the seams of the double-wide's paneled walls, and as I reached the door, I recognized strains of Ravel's "Bolero". There wasn't a bell, so I knocked on the metal doorframe. I wasn't sure Joe Bob could hear me over the music, so I called to him as loudly as I dared so as not to attract the neighbors.

"Come on in. It's not locked," he called back. His voice sounded sort of calming—the way it had when he was talking to the pregnant gypsy girl.

I climbed into the trailer to see Joe Bob feeding his cat Fancy Feast from what looked like a baby's spoon. I deduced the cat was dining on tuna from the smell permeating the room.

"Looks like he's enjoying his brunch," I said, nodding at the cat.

"Yeah. He's eatin' pretty good this mornin'. Last night was a different story. He didn't have no appetite; wouldn't eat a bite."

"He seems okay now."

"Oh, he's better for sure, but you ought to see the poor old guy try to walk to his litter box. It's enough to make a grown man cry. I've been helpin' him, and I'm tellin' you, it embarrasses him."

"Who's the music for, him or you?"

"Both of us. We might live in a trailer, but we've got taste."

The cat had finished eating, and attempted to wash its face with a paw. Then, it curled up the best it could to take a nap.

I sat down on the ottoman I'd seen Lucy Combs use to comfort Joe Bob by stuffing his face between her breasts.

"You seen Bernard?"

"Yep. Just came from having coffee with him at the café."

"Tell him what you seen his wife doin'?"

"Yes, I told him. He already knew something was going on; just didn't want to believe it."

"What's he gonna do?"

"Hide and watch, I guess. At least that's what it sounded like to me. He said he isn't going to accuse her of anything right now. I assume he'll be patient until he can catch her in the act. He's going to fight her for the little girl."

"If she's been at this for a while, and he ain't caught her, wonder what makes him think he can catch her now?"

"Good question."

"Sounds like to me he's gonna have to set a trap for his quarry."

"That doesn't sound like something Bernie would do, but I don't think it's a bad idea."

"I know a guy might be willin' to help."

"Who?"

"Just a guy. He helped find out who was stealin' money from the Baptist Church. Turned out to be the church treasurer."

"Is this guy a private eye?"

"I don't think he's got a license, or nothin', but he's pretty good at sniffin' people out, and he's good with a camera. He took pictures of Ransom Wilhoit's wife with another man at the Wayside Motel."

"How'd that turn out?"

"The guy figured out the wife's pattern. Ransom was waitin' for her when she come out of the motel one afternoon, and showed her the pictures. Seemed like she was real sorry for goin' astray, and wanted to go back to bein' Ransom's sweet little wife."

"I doubt Bernie would hire someone other than a real professional. He might not even want to do that."

"Well, I can git the guy's number if Bernard wants it. I'd better git ready for work. Lucy'll be here in a few minutes to take over the cat-sittin'."

"I'll see you, or at least call you before I leave town."

"You bet you will. I'll catch up with you."

I drove out of the trailer park not knowing what to do next. Sydney Edelman was my top priority, but she had given me the impression that she wanted nothing more to do with me. I just couldn't leave Martinsville without seeing her again. Somehow, I would make that happen, even if it meant making a fool of myself.

It's strange how devious the human mind can be. I'd put it up there with the fight or flight instinct. It has nothing to do with real fear, but if a person wants something badly enough, his morals, along with common sense, go right out the window. It's simply what has to be done to achieve what he wants, so he does it.

That was how I felt, sitting in the parking lot of the animal clinic. I fished out my wallet and extracted Sydney Edelman's card—the one she had given me before Beth showed up at the restaurant. Although Sydney hadn't told me so, I knew the emergency number on the card was that of her cell phone. I remembered she had told me Wednesday was the one day of the week the office was closed two hours for lunch. It was nearly twelve o'clock. I would wait a few more minutes and call her on her cell phone, assuming she would be leaving the clinic for lunch. I screwed up my courage and typed in the number. It rang several times before going to voice mail.

"Sydney, this is Matt Stevenson. I apologize for calling you at this number, but I really need to talk with you. I'm sitting in the parking lot of your clinic, hoping you'll give me a few minutes of your time. There are things I need to explain. I hope you'll give me a chance. Thanks."

Ten minutes passed, and she hadn't returned my call or exited the clinic. I was about to give up hope when she came outside and looked around the parking lot. Subconsciously, I had expected her to ignore me. I wasn't sure what to do, or say, but I opened the car door and got out. Sydney looked in my direction, and I gave her a weak wave.

She started toward me, and I realized I hadn't rehearsed what I wanted to say to her. I wasn't sure where to start, and I didn't want to sound uncertain or sophomoric. My eyes searched her face as I attempted to put together an outline. Then, she was standing beside me, her expression unreadable. Her hazel eyes looked directly into mine.

"Thank you for seeing me," I said. "Will you please allow me to take you to lunch?"

"I can't be away from the clinic very long. There's a list of calls I need to make before two o'clock."

"We could go to The Friendly Café. The service is fast, and the food's good."

"All right," she said, and got into the car. "I can't imagine what's so important that you feel the need to tell me. We've barely met, and we'll probably never see one another again."

She was making me nervous. My hands were sweaty on the steering wheel, and I felt like a kid, not a responsible attorney.

"I'll explain it all when we get to the café. Hopefully, it'll make sense."

We rode the two blocks in silence. Sydney appeared to be taking in the scenery while I tried to plan my speech.

I parallel parked on the street, and attempted to play the gentleman, hurrying around the car to help her out, but she was already standing on the street by the time I made it to her side of the car. She looked like she would rather have been somewhere else, but she did allow me to escort her inside the café.

I asked to be seated in a booth in the back, and the waitress led us to the one Bernie and I had occupied earlier. We both ordered chef salads and iced tea. Then, time was up. I hoped I looked as sincere as I felt. It was important to me that Sydney believe what I told her, even if she still wanted me to disappear and let her get on with her life after she heard what I had to say.

I took a long drink of my tea, and then a deep breath.

"I want to apologize for keeping things from you at dinner. It didn't seem important at the time. You were telling me personal things about your past that I assumed you needed to tell someone, and I was there. I saw no reason to burden you with my forgettable past, that is, not until my ex-wife showed up."

"You don't owe me explanations or apologies, Matt. None of it matters. Our paths crossed while you were in Martinsville for a few days. We had a lovely dinner. The end."

"It matters to me. I want you to know that there is nothing, and never will be anything between my ex-wife and me. We're divorced, live far apart, and have nothing to do with one another. She has a mental problem. I don't know when, or why, it happened. She's been stalking me since I've been in town, and harassing my family. If you ask me why she's doing it, I can't tell you, because I have no idea. She's a devious woman, and I think she's dangerous."

"She didn't seem dangerous when I met her at the luncheon. I thought she was friendly and quite pleasant. She did impress me differently last night. I had the impression she was sweetly letting me know that you're not exactly fair game."

"You interpreted her message correctly. She's spreading a rumor all over town, saying that she and I are getting back together. Nothing could be further from the truth."

"That sounds more nasty than dangerous."

"She caused my sister to have a miscarriage."

"How in the world?"

"My sister's temper was partly to blame. She couldn't take anymore of Beth's harassment. My ex had the gall to bring her uncle, a would-be minister, to our family home. It seems he was there as a moral and religious counselor to reunite his niece and me. My sister overheard the conversation, and started down the steps to tell Beth she needed to take her uncle and leave our house. She tripped and rolled down the steps. The result was a miscarriage."

"That's terrible."

"There's a lot more I could tell you, but it's just more of the same: lying, conniving, laying traps. That pretty much covers it. The reason I'm telling you these things is that I hope you won't get involved with Beth. She seems to enjoy hurting good people. I don't want her to hurt you."

"I don't know what to say. Thank you, I suppose."

"I just wanted you to know. There are lots of kind people in

Martinsville. You're one of them. Don't be fooled by Beth. She's quite the actress."

"Thank you for lunch, but I need to get back," Sydney said.

I drove her back to the clinic, and she opened her door to get out of the car.

"Sydney," I said, leaning toward her.

She turned back and looked into my eyes. I took her face in my hands and delivered a brief kiss—not a passionate kiss, but one I hoped told her I cared about her.

"Take care, Sydney," I said.

She got out of the car and walked toward the clinic, and I memorized the way she walked until she went through the door.

Chapter Thirty-one

I'd had a good run, and was finished with my cool-down about a block from the house, so I slowed my step and looked at the scenery. Nothing seemed to have changed in all the years I had been gone. I assumed that some of the residents of this quiet street had either moved, or were deceased, but the overall appearance of the neighborhood remained the same, down to the landscaping. It struck a nostalgic chord in me that I didn't know existed. I had never considered myself the sentimental type.

Dad's rental car was parked at the curb by the front walk, and I assumed he was inside, making Sam's day. Laughter met me as I opened the door and went down the hall to the kitchen. My family sat around the table, sipping sweet tea and enjoying Trudy's rhubarb pie.

I stopped in the frame of the kitchen doorway unnoticed and took in the scene. Trudy came from the far side of the kitchen and began refilling glasses. The family was in such high spirits that nobody bothered to notice the tear tracks on the face of our loyal housekeeper.

"Daddy, this is just wonderful," Sam said. "I had no idea you had set up trusts for Matt and me."

"You're my children. Of course I wanted to provide for you."

"This is going to change our lifestyle," Sam said, turning to her husband. "Of course, there's not anything wrong with our current lifestyle."

Trudy squeezed past me and hurried down the hall on her rubber-soled shoes. She headed for the stairs, and I followed her. I knew she was going to the bathroom to cry herself dry and clean up the evidence.

I waited in the hall and looked at the array of family pictures that adorned the walls. My mother had dismantled Dad's study, but hadn't touched these photographs. I thought that was strange, but then, my mother was an anomaly.

Trudy came out after about five minutes, looking calm and collected. She smiled and patted me on the shoulder. As she turned to leave, I took both of her warm hands in mine. She had always had warm hands.

"Why do you do that?" I said.

"Do what?"

"Hide your feelings. You don't have to do that. Everyone has a right to cry. This has been your home just the same as it's been mine. You're like a mother to me, one who always let me know she loved me."

Trudy's brown eyes filled again as they looked directly into mine.

"I've lost a dear friend of many years, and I miss her somethin' fierce," she said.

"Everybody knows how close you and my mother were. It's understandable that you're sad."

"Yes, I miss your mama as much as I'd miss my right arm, but

I'm also a sentimental old fool. A person's got to be crazy to miss a house. It's just a building."

I hugged her close.

"You're not crazy; you're the most levelheaded person I know."

Trudy pulled away from me, and gave my arm a soft smack that told me she'd had enough of this indulgent conversation. Then, she turned and descended the stairs with her head held high.

As I stood in the shower, letting the hot needles sting my skin, an idea began to structure itself in my mind. Trudy had lived in her little clapboard house on the edge of town all her adult life, but she had spent most of her waking hours here in this house on Mulberry Street. Her house had been nothing more than a place to change her clothes and sleep. I had just come into a large sum of money, enough to buy Sam out and still have plenty. Trudy could live in this house rent free for the rest of her life as far as I was concerned. It would be small payback for the love and care she had given me since I was a toddler. I wouldn't tell her just yet. Sam had suggested selling the house and splitting the profits, but I needed to make sure she hadn't changed her mind. She was unpredictable these days.

The family had finished their celebration, and it was quiet when I came downstairs. Dad's car and the Lincoln were both gone. Trudy was the only one I could find in the house. She was napping on the couch in the room that used to be my father's study, snoring like a kitten. I assumed Bernie and Joe Bob were both at work, and I had nothing to do but wait until Thursday when my family and I would go to the lawyer's office to hear him tell us what we already knew.

I decided to call Jack in Denver to find out how he was doing on the rape case. He hadn't been inclined to tell me much the last time we talked, but maybe he wouldn't be so close-mouthed this time. All he had done so far was whet my appetite. There was no reason for him to keep quiet about the case until I got back to Denver.

My partner sounded disgruntled when he answered the phone.

"Evans and Stevenson." He was brusque.

"Hey, Jack, you don't sound real happy. You covered up, or what?"

"Hi, Matt. No, I'm not covered up, but I have to tell you, I'll be glad when you get back into town."

"I'll get in late Thursday night."

"I've heard that one before; I'll believe it when I see it."

"Believe it. I'll be there, champing at the bit; ready to put in as many hours as it takes to clear our guy. I assume you've collected some positive evidence."

"Tell you the truth, things aren't as clear-cut as I thought they were."

"Oh?"

"Matt, it's too complicated to go into on the phone. I'll lay it all out for you when you get back. See you first thing Friday morning."

He hung up without saying goodbye, and I was beginning to have a bad feeling. I hoped he hadn't gone off half-cocked again. He had done that a few times in the past, but it hadn't amounted to much. This case was different; it sounded like it had the potential to give us real credence. We might even be able to hire a secretary.

I took my phone outside to check my email, and found Bernie Zuckerman sitting in my mother's porch swing, looking like a lost soul. His glasses were sitting on top of his bald head, and his eyes were red and puffy. He stared straight ahead with tears pouring down his face, and didn't look at me.

"Bernie, what's going on?"

"I don't know what to do. My wife's cheating on me, and I'm

not sure what to do about it. I hate this situation so much I don't want to believe it's true, but I know it is. My precious baby girl is going to be right in the middle of it all. How could Lee Ann do this? Tell me! She acts as innocent as a little child, and she's ruining our family—our perfect family."

I didn't know what to say. I had confirmed his wife's guilt, cemented what he already knew, but had chosen to ignore. There was nothing I could say, or do to make it go away. For the second time in one day I wondered if I should have kept my mouth shut. Now I had two old friends who were miserable, and I was about to leave them both to flounder in their uncertainty and go on my merry way.

"I left work to get myself under control," Bernie said. "Claire won't understand what's wrong with her daddy if he shows up at nursery school looking like something stepped on his face."

"You want a bottle of water?" I said.

Bernie shook his head.

"Let's go for a walk. You can talk it all out. It'll help get your head on straight."

Bernie nodded, blew his nose, and settled his glasses back on his nose. We started down Mulberry, neither of us talking. I figured he would open up as soon as he thought he could make sense. We were nearly downtown by the time he spoke, and what he said had nothing to do with his marital situation.

"That guy creeps me out," he said, nodding in the direction of Fred Peyton who was diligent in his pursuit of discarded soda pop containers. Fred glanced at us, hauled his gunny sack up over his shoulder, and took off. He appeared to be limping.

"He creeps everybody out. Why are we discussing the town weirdos?"

"No reason. I just looked over toward the tracks, and there he was in that filthy coat, picking up trash to put in his sack. Wonder why he does that?"

"I never thought about it. It's just what he does. Do you want to talk about your wife, or not?"

Bernie stopped walking, and looked toward the railroad tracks, then on past them into the distance.

"I don't know what to say. This is all like a bad dream. It doesn't seem real to me. I swear it never occurred to me that my wife might be having an affair when I saw that guy leaving my house. And it didn't just happen once—it was more like two, maybe three times. How blind can a man be?"

"Maybe it isn't what it looks like. Is it possible Lee Ann's innocent, and we're jumping to conclusions?"

"That would be a wonderful thing, but I think she's guilty. I never saw it coming. She never turned me down. Wouldn't you think she would be cold toward me if she was messing around with somebody else?"

"I don't know, Bernie. What are you going to do? I hate to go back to Denver and leave you and Joe Bob like this."

"I don't know what you could do to help either of us. Joe Bob's going to hire a good attorney, and you're not a detective, so you couldn't very well help me."

"So you're not going to confront Lee Ann?"

"No, I don't think so."

"Joe Bob told me he knows a guy who does some detective work around here. The guy doesn't have a license, and I don't know anything about him. Joe Bob said he can put you in touch with the guy if you're interested, but you and I know the kind of lawyer he was willing to let represent him. Using this person probably isn't a very good idea."

"I'm not going to do anything like that. I realize Joe Bob's trying to help, but I think I'll just play this by ear. From now on, I'll pay more attention to Lee Ann's behavior. I make my own hours at work. Maybe I'll come home for lunch sometime, or take off early every now and then. Sooner or later, she'll slip up."

"It sounds like a plan," I said.

Sometimes, like now, I was glad I was single. I didn't have anyone to answer to but myself, and that was a good feeling. On the other hand, if I thought I had a chance with Sydney Edelman, I would probably be willing to risk being in a close relationship. But that was a moot point.

Bernie and I walked back to the house, and he did seem in better spirits. We were standing beside his Cadillac, and he started to get behind the wheel. Then, he pulled out his wallet and opened it to show me his latest photograph of Claire. I had to admit she was a very pretty child.

"Look at that face, Matt. This little girl is my world. She's the only thing that matters when I think about the big picture. I love my wife, even after realizing she's cheating on me, but I'll be willing to give her up in a heartbeat to make a good life for my baby girl. I'll get proof of Lee Ann's infidelity, and I'll take my child away from her."

There was nothing for me to say, so I simply nodded. Bernie nodded back, and drove away.

Chapter Thirty-two

Sam and Ron were at the house. She and I had both been on the same page about selling the house, but since my unexpected windfall, I had changed my mind. I walked in to see my sister tagging furniture with different colored sticky notes. She appeared focused on the task.

"Sam, what are you doing?" I said.

"What does it look like, Matt? We have to do this sometime, so we might as well start now."

"Could we sit down and talk about this?"

"I thought we had already agreed to sell the house and turn most of the contents over to someone local to sell it on consignment."

"We did, but we didn't know about the trusts then."

"I don't see what the trusts have to do with this. Neither of us lives here, and I certainly have no intention of hanging onto the house for sentimental reasons and renting it to someone who'll probably let it get run down and not worth selling."

"I don't want to sell it, or rent it to strangers, Sam. I'd like to buy you out; I want to keep it."

"What on earth for?"

"I have my reasons. Mother most certainly left the house to us. After the reading of her will, we can have it appraised, and I'll take it off your hands."

"What about the contents?"

"I don't know yet, but we can have them appraised, too. If I decide to keep any of them, I'll pay you for half of what they're worth. I'll make sure you get your fair share no matter what."

"I trust you, big brother, but that doesn't mean I always understand you. Shall I leave the sticky notes in place, or not?"

"I don't care. Let's hear what's in the will, then look at the situation. I feel sure the house will be ours to do with as we please."

Ron had discreetly made himself scarce so Sam and I could talk privately. I thought he must have a sixth sense, because he showed up just as we finished our business. He stood beside the piano, saying nothing, with his hands in the pockets of his pleated pants and looked out the large bay window like a man of means, surveying his property.

"Hi, Ron," I said.

He turned, and without addressing his wife, or me, he announced that he was taking the family out to dinner.

"Gertrude's already made beef stew, Ron," Sam said.

"It'll keep," he said, and rattled the change in his pocket.

I could only assume my brother-in-law was practicing his king of the castle skills.

"Thanks, Ron. That's very nice of you," I said.

Fire flickered in my sister's eyes, then disappeared. "I'll tell Aunt Lela Maude and Uncle Stuart," she said.

Ron took a seat on the artist's bench and began playing my mother's piano. He didn't seem to care whether or not he might be disturbing someone's nap.

It was the middle of the afternoon, and I was bored. I went to the kitchen and picked up Uncle Stuart's car keys. There was nothing to do in this small town. I didn't want to go back to the cemetery. It had made me feel strange the last time I had been there. I drove to Joe Bob's garage. It was locked up tighter than a drum, and I was beginning to wonder if my friend had already given up on being a free man. He certainly wasn't doing anything to encourage business.

I drove to the trailer park. His truck was there on its patch of gravel. There were no other vehicles in front of the double-wide, not even Lucy's motorcycle. The trailer emitted muted country music as I approached the door. I knocked. No answer.

"Hey, Joe Bob, you in there?"

He still didn't answer, but I thought I heard muffled noise coming from inside the double-wide. I waited a minute, then called his name again.

"Matt? That you?"

"Yes. Are you okay?"

"Yeah. Just a minute. I'm comin'."

A few minutes later Joe Bob came to the door, pulling on a pair of jeans. He was shirtless and barefoot. His hair was tousled and he seemed a little flustered. His old cat was asleep in its bed close to a water dispenser by the couch. It still looked pretty much like a mummy. Joe Bob hadn't invited me in, and I had a feeling that might not happen.

"You busy?" I said.

Joe Bob stood with his hand on the doorknob and looked down the narrow hall behind him. I heard a door close from somewhere inside the double-wide.

"Uh, no, I'm not real busy," he said.

He still hadn't asked me inside.

"Maybe I'll come back later," I said.

"All through, Joe Bob." It was a woman's voice.

Arlene Watkins appeared behind Joe Bob. I didn't think she looked like her usual *put together* self. Her makeup was a bit smudged, and a little tail of her blouse wasn't completely tucked into her skirt. Arlene had been a neatnik since she was a little kid. She wasn't what one might consider pretty, but she wasn't homely by any means, and her figure was awfully easy on the eyes. She looked a bit disgruntled.

"Your accounts were pathetic, Joe Bob," she said, handing him a manila folder. "I've never seen such a mess. Don't wait so long to call me the next time you start falling behind."

Arlene hadn't looked at me. I had a feeling she didn't want to stand around and chat with me about old times. Joe Bob was still hanging onto the doorknob.

"Thanks, Arlene," he said, and held the door open for her to leave.

Arlene squeezed past him and stepped outside. She was almost face-to-face with me.

"Hey, Matt." She nodded once and started picking her way down the dusty road.

"Come on in," Joe Bob said. He laid the folder on the Formica table.

I took a seat in the living room as far away from the cat as I could, and waited for Joe Bob to speak. He didn't. Instead, he grabbed a rubber band off the counter and pulled his hair into a ponytail.

"Arlene's still looking good," I said.

"She is, indeed."

"Does she live here in the park? I noticed she left on foot."

"Yeah. She lives just down the road. Works out of her home. She runs a little bookkeepin' service."

"Oh."

"She wasn't here to clean up my messy bookkeepin'."

"Oh."

"I think you got that word mastered, so you don't need to say it again. Arlene was here to participate in a little afternoon delight with yours truly."

"I see."

"You don't see nothin'. I'm human; I've got needs just like anybody else, and in the very near future I can kiss the good life goodbye. I'm ninety-nine percent sure I'm about to go to the slammer. I made a appointment with one of the lawyers on your list. Tomorrow mornin' I'm gonna be truthful when I answer his questions, just like the judge told me to. If you was to be doin' the interviewin', I'll bet you'd git the whole truth out of me in no time. I'd think any good lawyer could do the same. What do you think?"

What he said was true, and we both knew it. It still wasn't too late for him to back out, and I almost wished he would, but I would never suggest it. I knew I should say something, but the words wouldn't come.

Joe Bob went to the refrigerator and pulled out a jug of orange juice. He unscrewed the top and slugged down about a quarter of the contents.

"Back to Arlene," he said. "Her husband's in the nursin' home here in town. He's got Alzheimer's. I'd rather check out. Poor man's about to die. Probably be a good thing when he does. Anyway, they haven't had any kind of marriage for several years. She goes to see him ever day, but she's human, too, you know."

"I didn't know she was married."

"She's got a sixteen-year-old son, kind of a badass kid. I don't think he's in a gang, or nothin', but he hangs out with a kinda rough crowd. He's givin' his mama gray hair; that's for sure. He refuses to go see his daddy in the nursin' home, stays out 'til all hours, misses a lot of school, and his mama don't know where he is half the time. That kinda thing. It's hard for Arlene to relax and have a little fun. She's a good woman, and she flat knows how to float my boat."

I wasn't about to judge my friend or Arlene Watkins, because I had no right to do so. I thought both of them deserved what little happiness they could find.

"What time is your appointment tomorrow?" I asked.

"Nine o'clock sharp."

"Give me a call after your meeting."

"Will do. I doubt I'll have anything surprisin' to tell you."

I left Joe Bob's place feeling like a heel. He'd been relishing the freedom he knew he had left with someone who was no doubt starved for love when I had showed up, because I'd been a little bored. I hoped I hadn't arrived in the middle of their afternoon delight, but I assumed I would never know whether I had, or not.

I drove through town feeling at loose ends. It seemed unbelievable that I was being pushed and pulled in so many different directions. I had been within a stone's throw from broke, but I had just come into a million dollars, plus I had a shot at making a bundle on the rape case. My ex had dumped me, but wanted me back. And then there was Sydney Edelman, the woman I couldn't dismiss from my mind. The unfortunate accident that took a man's life just days earlier would rule my life and that of everyone else who was involved. We were all in limbo.

Chapter Thirty-three

My phone told me I was getting a text message. I had just gotten back to the house, and was thinking about catching forty winks. Ron had left a note on the kitchen counter, saying our dinner reservation was for seven o'clock, so I had plenty of time to grab a nap. I read the text on my way up the stairs to the pink room. It was from Bernie Zuckerman.

Bernie had told his wife a bald-faced lie, and wanted me to help him do a bit of spying on his cheating wife. I was beginning to form a worse opinion of small towns than I'd had before I came back to Martinsville. There had always been local political corruption, thievery, infidelity, and the like here, as in most small towns, but I had never known the participants up close and personal.

I didn't want to send Bernie a text. For all I knew, he didn't keep a close watch on his phone while he was at work. I didn't know who might have access to it. The color pink was beginning to grate on my nerves. Something about it seemed stifling, but I sat down on the bed and punched in Bernie's number.

"Hey, Matt, did you get my text?"

"I did, Bernie. Listen, I'm going out to dinner with the family tonight. Besides, you and I are not private detectives. We don't know how to go about catching somebody in the act; one of us could blow it. Why did you tell Lee Ann you had to go out of town?"

"I told her that, because I want her to feel free to cheat on me when she thinks it's safe to do so. It would make me feel better just to have a good friend with me when I actually see my wife sneaking around like an alley cat. I'm not sure I could do this alone."

"Do you think she would actually have another man in your house with the baby there?"

"I don't know what she might be brazen enough to do, but I want to give her the opportunity to hang herself. The baby doesn't go to bed until after seven o'clock, so I'm sure she won't do anything until then. If I'm not in town to pick up Claire from nursery school, Lee Ann will have to do it. That means she won't have a chance for an afternoon rendezvous."

"When did you tell her you'd be coming home?"

"Sometime tomorrow. She'll know tonight will be her only safe chance. I tell you, Matt, it literally makes me sick to plan this, but I know it's something I have to do. There has to be proof, and I don't want to let the affair drag on and on. I have to think about my daughter."

I didn't want to be in on his scheme, but I also didn't want to turn him down. We were friends. I told him I would think about it and let him know, but that any help I might provide would have to take place after the family dinner. That seemed to satisfy him.

Aunt Lela Maude and Uncle Stuart had taken pains to dress appropriately for dinner in one of Martinsville's new upscale restaurants. I noticed that my aunt wore a pair of designer pumps with pointed toes and slender heels, not the sensible type shoes she normally preferred. She carried a clutch that matched her shoes rather than one of her matronly Queen Mother type bags that hung heavily on her arm. There was also something different about her face; I wasn't sure what it was. My uncle's eyes shone with pride in his spouse, and he walked with the gait of a much younger man.

My sister put forth her most sunny disposition, in spite of the fact that her husband had taken control of the dinner plans without her consent. She appeared almost subservient to him, and I couldn't help wondering how long this act would last. Sam had fashioned her hair into a French twist to show off a pair of pearl studs. Her skin was creamy, and her elegant neck was lovely without a hint of adornment. She stood at her husband's side in our mother's living room where we had gathered to embark on our night out as a family before leaving Martinsville the next day.

Ron's hand rested lightly at Sam's slim waist. He pushed the black plastic frames of his glasses up on his slender nose and cleared his throat. Then, he told the family how much he appreciated their warm acceptance of him as one of its members. This elicited a little sniffle from Aunt Lela Maude, and my brother-in-law swallowed hard, sending his protruding Adam's apple up and down above the knot of his crooked tie.

"Shouldn't we be leaving soon, Ron?" I said. "Isn't our reservation for seven o'clock?"

"Yes, it is. You're right. I hope all of you enjoy the restaurant I chose. There are quite a few new ones."

"I'm sure it'll be lovely, Ron," Aunt Lela Maude said. "You have such wonderful taste."

I was beginning to like my brother-in-law. He was nerdy; that couldn't be denied, but there was something about him that I found appealing. I was glad he loved my sister. She hadn't received much affection when she was growing up, so I figured she deserved it now.

I guess I admired Ron for being true to himself, even when he was letting Sam push him around. He was doing what he wanted to do, and that wasn't an act. I hadn't known him at all until this visit. None of us had known anything about him. He would never have impressed me as an accomplished pianist, or a great golfer, or a man who could throw back one Gibson after another. But the thing that boggled my mind was the fact that he had decided to take charge of his marriage and be a man.

Everyone talked about the many changes in Martinsville on the way to the restaurant—changes I must have ignored until someone else called them to my attention. The town had indeed changed, but it was still a small town.

Sophia's was the name of the restaurant. There was valet parking, but patrons still had quite a distance to traverse before reaching the restaurant. From the curb we took a vine-covered walkway that curved through a lush jungle of exotic plants and trees. On one side of the path was a rock structure with a waterfall, cascading down into a pool where what appeared to be tropical fish swam away from the rush of the water. The restaurant was dark-colored brick with vines growing up its side.

A tall, whippet-slim hostess with ebony hair down to her tiny waist greeted us as we stepped inside. She had on a short black dress which looked as if it must be mostly spandex and strappy heels that looked very difficult to walk in. The shoes didn't seem to bother her at all. She led us through a foyer to a small area with a tall desk where three young women wearing lots of makeup smiled at us.

"This is Rosemary," the hostess said. "She will take you to your table."

Rosemary ushered us to a round table dressed in a gold-colored cloth with deep purple napkins that were folded into an impossible-looking configuration, and we were seated.

Yet a different young woman appeared to pass out menus and take drink orders. Ron opened his mouth to ask for a wine list just as the waitperson handed him one. He took it upon himself to order glasses of a good chardonnay for the ladies without asking what they might like, and said he would hang onto the wine list until we made our dinner choices. Then, he nodded to Uncle Stuart who stuck to bourbon, neat. I asked for a Wild Turkey with club soda, and Ron once again, ordered a Gibson. I thought Sam might object to the hard liquor drinks, but she said nothing.

The cocktails arrived, and we toasted my mother for what would probably be the last time. Then, since we had exhausted our trove of family remembrances from times past, and had nothing in common with one another, we grasped at straws, pointing out interesting aspects of the restaurant like the light fixtures and the modern art on the walls by unknown artists. When our glasses were close to empty, we began perusing the eclectic menu. That exercise gave us another topic to discuss, and we all decided to order something different from the rest so we could play the tasting game Aunt Lela Maude had suggested.

Uncle Stuart and Ron ordered second drinks, but I declined. I didn't want to be in my cups in the event that Bernie and I actually did set a trap for his wife. Ron ordered red and white bottles of wine for the table, and I realized that he had some knowledge of the grape.

"I understand you might have an interest in keeping the house, Mathoo," Aunt Lela Maude said.

"Well, I don't know that it will be mine to keep," I said. "We won't know what Mother put in her will until tomorrow, so we probably shouldn't discuss it until we do."

"We're pretty sure we know what's in the will, Matt," Sam said. "You and I have already talked about that."

"I know, but we need to know exactly what's in the will before making decisions concerning the real estate. We'll know Mother's wishes soon enough."

My sister knew I was trying to politely cut her off, but she took a sip of wine and didn't argue.

The wine arrived. Ron tasted the red, and asked his wife to taste the white. Both were deemed very nice. Our meals were brought to the table by five waiters dressed in black and white. The waiters placed the food in front of us, and lifted a silver-plated dome from each on what seemed a silent count of three.

I had to admit my brother-in-law had outdone himself with the restaurant choice. It was definitely top-of-the-line. If he hadn't paid much attention to the prices on the menu, he would no doubt be staggered by the bill. It wouldn't be long before he could spend money like it was water if he so chose. I was pretty sure my sister would approve of such a lifestyle.

I kept glancing at my watch as the meal progressed. It was a little after eight when a desert tray was wheeled to our table. I would have bet the farm that at least one person would order desert, and I would have won the bet. I was the only one to decline, but I was stuck here until everyone was ready to leave, so I ordered an espresso.

It was 8:45 by the time Ron paid the check. His expression didn't change when he surveyed the bill, and I decided that he would have been a good poker player. He could add that to his list of unexpected talents.

Aunt Lela Maude was sandwiched between Uncle Stuart and me in the back seat of the Lincoln on the way back to the house. Every now and then she patted me on the knee. I assumed it was to let me know she loved me, and she was trying to make up for lost time.

"Ron, thank you so much for a delightful evenin'," she said. "The food and the service were superb, and the restaurant was beyond elegant. Can you imagine what the landscapin' alone must have cost?"

"It was great," I said. "That was very generous of you, Ron."

"What was that little tweet that sounded like a bird?" my aunt said.

"I'm getting a text on my phone. It can wait until we get home," I said.

"Honestly, there are so many new-fangled gadgets these days. I don't know how you young people keep up with them all. Someone my age is too old to learn how to take advantage of the new conveniences, but we get along just fine. Don't we, Stuart?"

"Huh? I'm sorry, dear. What did you say?"

"It doesn't matter. Go back to your catnap."

Back at the house, the troops scattered. I went to Sam's room to read my text, assuming it was from Bernie Zuckerman. I must have dreamed it was a text; it wasn't. And it wasn't from Bernie. Jack had sent me an email, and I figured he had something to tell me that couldn't wait until Friday morning.

> *Things aren't going exactly as planned, Matt, but I still think our guy is innocent. I just want to give you a heads up, so you won't walk into the office Friday morning, thinking you're a rich man. See you then.*
>
> *Jack*

I should have known. How many times was I going to let him get my hopes up for nothing? It was a good thing I would be coming into some money soon. Jack and I had worked hard to succeed at our practice, but it seemed we were spinning our wheels.

Bili Morrow Shelburne

My phone rang; it was Bernie.
"Well?" he said.
"I'll meet you in front of the house."

Chapter Thirty-four

The night sky was ablaze with stars; it was light enough to see without the streetlight that was close to the house. The air was hot and heavy with humidity, typical summer weather in the southeast. I had changed into jeans and a golf shirt, but I hadn't been standing outside more than five minutes when my shirt began to feel damp. Mulberry was a quiet street, and I was fairly sure the headlights coming my way belonged to Bernie's Cadillac.

The gray sedan pulled up to the curb and stopped. Frosty conditioned air spilled out when I opened the passenger door to climb into the car. Bernie looked nervous. Beads of perspiration covered his forehead and the front of his head. He was chewing his lower lip.

"Thanks for doing this, Matt," he said.

"Exactly what are we doing? Do you have some sort of plan, or are we just going to stake out close to your house and wait to see if a man comes to call?"

"Please don't make jokes at a time like this. I'm not sure how to go about it. We'll have to play it by ear. I know a little about what's going on now, but not nearly enough."

"Okay. What do you know?"

"I know Lee Ann hired a babysitter, because I was across the street in the park when the girl went into the house. I recognized the kid. We've used her before. She lives a few doors down the street."

"Did you see Lee Ann leave the house?"

"Yes. She left in her car, and I tried to follow at a distance, but I lost her in traffic."

"Bernie, if we don't know where she went, we're wasting our time. Even if we stake out the house until she decides to come home, what can we prove? She'll come home alone, pay the sitter, and go to bed."

"That's true. I guess this was a harebrained idea. How am I ever going to prove she's cheating? She could be anywhere."

It was hard for me to think with so many other things on my mind. The funeral was over, but my mother wasn't forgotten. I still hadn't come to terms with my relationship with her. The family would hear the will tomorrow, and hopefully, I would be on a plane to Denver by tomorrow night. For all I knew, Dad had already left town, and I wouldn't be spending any more time with him. Then, there was Joe Bob. I would probably find out tomorrow if he would be facing a prison sentence. And when I, at last, made it back to the Mile-High City and my law practice, my bubble might well burst when I walked in the door.

Bernie took out a handkerchief and rubbed the sweat from his head. He looked like a beaten man. I didn't like his wife, but it was clear to me that he had adored her until he discovered her true colors. I knew that knocked the wind out of his sails.

He sighed. "Any ideas?"

I wracked my brain for anything that might be useful, and finally I came up with something I thought was worth a shot.

"What kind of car does Lee Ann drive?" I said.

"Late model Buick Enclave. Why?"

"Does she have the same kind of GPS that you have?"

"Yes. Why?"

"We can track her car. There's an app for it: Remote Link. It'll tell us where the car is."

"I'm so rattled I don't think I would have ever thought of that."

We found Lee Ann's car parked in the lot of the same restaurant where I had seen her several nights earlier. All we had to do was wait until she and the guy came out of the restaurant. Lee Ann would either get into the car with him, or get into her car and follow him to their love nest.

"You sure you want to do this?" I said.

"No, but I have to. There's no way around it. I know she's cheating, and that's killing me, but I need to see it. Sure, I'll have to hire some hotshot to prove it, but there's no way in hell I'm going to let her have my baby girl. I'm not going to lose but one love in this deal."

We knew Lee Ann and her squeeze would still be in the restaurant, because Bernie knew what time she left the house. They wouldn't have had time to finish dinner yet, so we would wait. I knew Bernie was miserable, and the silence between us was making me uncomfortable, too. But there was nothing else to say. We had a plan, and at this point, that was all we had.

A few minutes passed. When I glanced over at Bernie, his head was bent over the steering wheel, and his body shook. He had laid his glasses on the dashboard. He muffled his sobs with a handkerchief, and I couldn't do anything to ease his pain.

A little while later Lee Ann came out of the restaurant. She didn't stop at the valet stand, but went straight to her car. We were positioned so we could see when she started backing out of the parking space. She drove to the front of the restaurant and stopped close to the valet stand, letting her engine idle. A couple of minutes passed. We kept our eyes peeled for her paramour. I didn't really know what the man looked like, but Bernie did. He was tall and slim, and moved down the three stone steps of the restaurant self-assured.

"That's him," Bernie said. He sounded like he had a bad taste in his mouth.

"Are you sure?"

"Yes."

The tall man swiveled his head both ways. His head movement stopped in the direction of Lee Ann's car, and he hurried into the parking lot. When he pulled up beside Lee Ann's car and paused for a second, I recognized his car from the last time I had seen it here. Then, he drove slowly out of the lot; Lee Ann followed.

"Son-of-a-bitch!" Bernie said.

"I'm sorry, Bernie."

"I know you are, and I appreciate that."

"Now what? Do you want to follow them?"

"Yes, I certainly do."

"We don't have to do that, you know. We can find them using the app."

"I need to see her with him while I'm pissed off just to cement what she's doing in my mind."

"I think I understand."

"Here's what I have to do: I have to stop loving her, so I can take care of business. That business involves taking away something she loves: our child. I can give Claire enough love for two parents."

Bernie pulled out of the parking lot and fell in a couple of cars back from his wife's Enclave.

"I guess we can assume they're going to a hotel. Are there any decent ones besides The Greystone?"

"Nope. All the others are cheapos. Lee Ann wouldn't be caught dead in any of them."

"Then, this should be easy."

I didn't want to be in on Bernie's scheme, but I felt I didn't have a choice. We'd been friends since our teens. I thought the better route would have been for him to hire a professional to prove Lee Ann's adulterous behavior instead of the two of us taking a chance on botching the job, but it wasn't my decision to make. It seemed to me that if Bernie actually saw his wife with another man that would hurt him more than hearing it from an outsider.

Bernie kept his eyes glued to the road. There was nothing for us to talk about, so we rode in silence. I assumed we were headed for The Greystone, since we had reached the Martinsville city limits and were driving down Main Street, but I was wrong. We followed the Enclave past The Greystone and made a right turn onto Maple Street. I had no idea where we were going, but I assumed Bernie did.

"I'm not believing this," he said.

"What?"

"There aren't any hotels or motels over this way."

"Maybe they're going to his place."

"Yeah, I guess they must be."

The caravan made a left turn onto Hickory, and drove past a new apartment complex. Bernie had to hang back, because the two vehicles between the Enclave and our car had left our route. I thought his breathing sounded kind of strange, and he mopped his forehead again.

"What's the matter, Bernie?"

He didn't answer. Then, I understood his anxiety. Lee Ann's car disappeared around a corner, and stopped at the end of Elm—the street where the Zuckerman's lived. The black Cadillac parked behind Lee Ann's car, and the driver got out and slid into the passenger seat of the Enclave. Bernie pulled over to the curb and let his engine idle. Neither of us spoke. The Enclave took off and made its way slowly down the street to Bernie's house.

Bernie turned off the ignition, and got out of the car.

"Come on," he said.

I followed him down Elm and into the park across the street from his house. The foliage blocked the moonlight, and it was dark in the park. We couldn't see where we were going, but we stumbled along until we were directly across from Bernie's house. We were both being bitten by a swarm of mosquitoes, but neither of us was willing to leave our bird's-eye view of the house to get away from them. Bernie slapped one just as the garage door opened. Lee Ann drove inside, but didn't close the door. We saw the man get out of the car. Then, Lee Ann backed out and closed the garage door. She left her car in the driveway, then went to the front door and used her key to let herself in. A few minutes later, she and the baby sitter came out and got into the car. It took less than three minutes for Lee Ann to drive the sitter home and return to her own home. The downstairs lights were turned off one by one, and somebody turned on one dim light upstairs.

"Well, she doesn't have a heart, but she has just a touch of class. She didn't take him to our bedroom. That light's in the guest room."

"I'm really sorry, man."

"You need to stop apologizing for my wife's infidelity. I know you're sorry. Let's get out of here."

Bernie led the way, and we stumbled out of the park and went back to his car. We got in and sat in the quiet for a few minutes.

"Now what?" I said.

"I could use a drink," Bernie said.

"You're supposed to be out of town."

"That's true, but I think I'll be safe having a drink at Morgan's. Lee Ann and her friends don't frequent such establishments."

"Want to call Joe Bob? This could be the last time we have a chance to hang out with him."

"Sure. He already knows about my cheating wife, doesn't he?"

"Yes."

We drove to Joe Bob's place, and saw Lucy's old bike parked beside the double-wide. I went to the door and knocked. Joe Bob was in the process of writing a note to let Lucy know where he was going, because she was asleep on the couch under an afghan. The cat was stretched out on his bed beside the couch, and there was an old movie playing on the big screen.

"I'll just leave the TV on. They both like to sleep with a little bit of noise. Lucy comes over here a lot now. She wants Tiger to feel comfortable with her in case I turn out to be a jailbird."

"Try to have a positive attitude, Joe Bob. Don't give up before you even talk to the lawyer. Let's go have a drink."

"Just bein' realistic, my friend. Let's go git that drink."

Chapter Thirty-five

Morgan's was busier than usual. Joe Bob was the first through the door. As we walked past the bar, he stepped up his pace and headed for the back of the room. He led us to a tall wooden booth and slid across the seat, leaving room for one of us to sit beside him.

"What's up, Joe Bob?" I said. "You hustled back here like you just stole something."

I sat down beside him.

"I guess you two didn't see who was sittin' at the end of the bar."

Bernie and I shook our heads.

"Arnold Marcum. I sure hope he didn't see me."

"What if he did?" Bernie said.

"I'm not in the mood to go into detail, tellin' him why I decided to handle my problem on my own, which is a big lie, by the way. Somebody else is gonna hear my account of what happened that night, but I don't want to hurt the man's feelin's, or insult him."

"If he had seen you, he wouldn't have mentioned business if he's professional," I said.

"You're right, I reckon. I'm just kind of nervous about the whole thing, you know."

"Well, don't be. If he comes over to our booth, just speak to him. He won't be pushy."

A waitress came to take our drink orders. We all ordered Wild Turkey neat, even Bernie: Shades of our evenings at Uncle Jake's cabin. That was the moment I knew how very low both of my old friends felt.

I watched Arnold Marcum get off his barstool and head for the men's room. He looked a little unsteady on his feet. A few minutes later he came back and paid his bar tab. As he started toward the door to leave, he glanced in our direction and spotted Joe Bob. I didn't know whether to alert my buddy, or just wait and see what happened. Marcum was making his way to our booth through a maze of tables. He had on the same seedy suit he'd worn the last time we saw him. I must have been watching him wobble toward us, because Joe Bob and Bernie turned to see what I found so interesting.

"Oh, shit," Joe Bob said. He sounded more defeated than mad.

"Stop worrying," Bernie said. "The man's just coming over to say hello."

Marcum stopped just short of our booth and grinned. He didn't appear to be focused on anyone in particular, but he grabbed a wooden chair from a nearby table and pulled it across the floor, making a loud noise. Until that moment, the three of us had been talking nonsense to appear deep in conversation. Marcum placed the back of the chair next to our booth and straddled it while maintaining his Cheshire cat grin.

"Hey, Mr. Marcum," Joe Bob said.

"Hey, yourself," the lawyer said. His words were slurred. "I was just leaving. Then, I happened to spot you and your friends.

You boys solvin' the world's problems over a few drinks, or what?"

"Oh, we're just havin' a farewell drink with Matt, here," Joe Bob said, nodding at me.

"Is that right?" Marcum said. "You're the attorney, aren't you?"

"Yes," I said. "I'll be going back to my practice in Denver."

"Oh, yes," he said, "I 'member now. Too bad you have to leave town right now."

"Oh?"

"There's about to be some pretty big excitement around here."

"Yeah?" Joe Bob said.

"I didn't know anything about it until yesterday," Marcum said. "People tell me it's been kinda hushed up for some reason. Seems there was a hit-and-run one night a little over a week ago; killed a man. Don't know why there wasn't anything in the *Martinsville Herald* until after the guy was buried. There wasn't much of an obit—just a name and dates of birth and death. The guy didn't have a family, and if there was a funeral, there were no details in the paper."

"That's real sad," Joe Bob said. He took a large gulp of his bourbon, and began moving his glass around on the table in a small circle.

Marcum looked like he had settled in for a while. He motioned the waitress over and ordered a drink. I noticed Bernie's ears had turned a bright shade of red, and he was pushing his glasses up on his nose more than usual. It seemed to me that Joe Bob was making a concentrated effort to avoid looking at Marcum, so I felt obliged to join in the conversation to find out what the man actually knew.

"You said there was about to be some excitement over the man's death," I said.

"Yes, indeed. Somebody is about to be in a heap of trouble," he said.

"Sorry," I said. "I'm not following you."

"Son, you're a lawyer. Didn't you hear me say *hit-and-run?*"

I nodded.

"Well, whoever hit and killed the guy didn't stick around. He didn't even stop to see if the man was dead, or alive; left him layin' in the middle of the street, and never called the police. What do you think of that?"

"Have the police found out who the driver was?" I asked.

Marcum took a healthy swallow of his drink, then rested his crossed arms on the back of the chair.

"Joe Bob," he said, "you probably know the deceased. I'll wager most everybody in Martinsville knows him."

Joe Bob stopped pushing his glass around, lifted it, and took a long pull of bourbon. I didn't know what he might blurt out, so I decided to fill the silence.

"What was the dead guy's name?" I asked.

"Banks was the poor bastard's name. He was crazy as hell, but perfectly harmless from what I hear. Considered himself a traffic cop."

"I might have heard something about such an accident," Bernie said. "I understood there were no witnesses."

Marcum grinned.

"Wrong," he said. "I'm sure the driver thought he'd gotten away without a trace, but he was mistaken. There was definitely a witness."

I heard Joe Bob begin to breathe in quick, short gasps, and I turned to face him.

"'scuse me," he said, and nudged me out of the booth.

"Sure," I said, sliding out of his way, so he could escape to the men's room.

"Who was the witness?" Bernie said.

"That's the big mystery," Marcum said.

"I don't understand," Bernie said. "If nobody knows who the witness is, how do you know there actually was one?"

"My eyes and ears are always open, son. Suffice it to say I know there was a witness. You just wait. You'll see."

"Why are you being so secretive, Mr. Marcum? Are you involved in the case?" I said.

"No, I'm not involved—just interested."

I saw Joe Bob coming toward our booth and got up to let him reclaim his seat. Marcum sucked down the rest of his drink and backed off his chair. He pushed the chair out of his way and looked down at the three of us. Then, he stretched his mouth into that goofy smile that seemed to be his trademark.

"I must be off," he said. "What I wouldn't give to be young again." He made a gesture with his right hand that spanned our thirty-something trio. "You have your whole lives ahead of you. Do something courageous for mankind." Then, the sleazy lawyer stumbled across the room and disappeared out the front door.

"What the hell is he talkin' about?" Joe Bob said. "What did he say while I was gone?"

"He might have just been running his mouth," I said. "He says there's a witness, but it seems nobody knows who that witness is."

"We know there wasn't a witness," Bernie said. "Nobody was there but Judge Maxwell and the three of us."

"I reckon somebody coulda been lookin' out a window and seen it," Joe Bob said.

"I'll tell you what I think," Bernie said. "That old has-been was just flapping his lips. He simply wanted to stir up a bit of exciting conversation. If he had actually known something, he would have told us what he knew."

"I don't know," Joe Bob said. "He might not be the stupid old fool you two think he is."

"I don't think he knows anything," I said.

"What do you think he meant by that speech just before he left? Why'd he tell us to do somethin' courageous for mankind? You think he knows I was the one hit Jimmy Banks?"

"No, I don't," I said. "I think the man was lonely and wanted to have a drink with someone he knew. He's probably gotten tired of talking about the weather and how progressive Martinsville has become."

Joe Bob sighed. I assumed he had decided there was no point in debating Marcum's rationale for insisting there had been a witness to the hit-and-run. Joe Bob was already planning to tell his attorney what happened that fateful night. He was prepared to take his punishment, witness, or no witness, so he changed the subject just as if Arnold Marcum hadn't shown up to interrupt our last drink together.

"So, Bernard," he said, "what's the plan with your wife?"

Bernie's expression reverted to one of despair, the way it looked when he and I forsook our mission of spying on Lee Ann. He drained his glass, motioned the waitress over, and ordered another round.

"My first plan is to get shit-faced this evening to keep from thinking about her. I want to be able to go to sleep one night without thinking about what a tramp she is and how she has wrecked my life."

"I think we can prob'ly help you with that, ol' buddy," Joe Bob said. "Matter of fact, I wouldn't mind gittin' a little shit-faced myself. How 'bout you, Matt?"

"Sure, but we can't do that until we work out some sleeping arrangements."

"What are you talking about?" Bernie said.

"I'm talking about the fact that you're supposed to be out of town, Lucy's at Joe Bob's place, and there aren't any empty beds at my mother's house."

"Oh, yeah," Joe Bob said.

"I forgot, too," Bernie said, "but I have a solution."

Joe Bob and I looked at him with raised eyebrows.

"We'll check in at The Greystone. Problem solved," Bernie said. "We can park in the lot behind the hotel."

Chapter Thirty-six

The parking lot behind The Greystone was poorly lighted. There was only one dim light to service the entire lot. Bernie pulled into a parking space at the very back of the lot, and we began walking toward the rear entrance of the old hotel.

"Guys," Joe Bob said, "I just thought of somethin' else we prob'ly want to do."

"What now?" Bernie said. "I'm ready to get drunk, and that's what I intend to do."

"Well, don't you think it might be a bad idea to do that in the hotel bar where somebody we know might stop by for a nightcap?" Joe Bob said. "I mean, you're not supposed to be in town."

"Let's go to a liquor store and buy a bottle to take to the room," I said.

"Room?" Bernie said. "Did you say the room? Don't you mean rooms, plural?"

"Bernie, you know what I meant," I said. "We'll each have our own room, but don't we want to get drunk together?"

"Sure, we do," Joe Bob said. "There's no way I'm gonna drink alone. Anybody does that, he's got hisself a drinkin' problem."

We went to a drive-through window at Snow's Liquors and bought a bottle of bourbon. Then, we staggered our checking into the hotel. Joe Bob and I hung out at the elevator until Bernie got his key. As it turned out, he was on the fourth floor, but Joe Bob and I were on the third in adjoining rooms. We decided to do our drinking in Bernie's room.

"Hard to believe this is the best place to stay in Martinsville," Bernie said, as he unlocked the door, "but it is."

The room had two double beds and a couple of chairs. Bernie told Joe Bob and me to take the chairs, and he'd make do with one of the beds, using the headboard as a backrest. He grabbed the ice bucket, and went down the hall to fill it at the ice machine.

Back in the room, he played the host, taking wrappers off plastic glasses.

"Neat or on-the-rocks?" he said.

"Rocks for me," Joe Bob said. "I might even add a little water. I'm not that much of a purist."

We settled in with drinks in hand, and I decided to make a toast.

"Here's to the three of us," I said, raising my plastic glass. "May our friendship be everlasting."

"Hear! Hear!" Bernie said.

"I'll drink to that," Joe Bob said.

We all drank together.

"I want you guys to know how much I appreciate your support," Joe Bob said.

"Sorry I waited so long, Joe Bob," Bernie said. "I can be pretty self-centered sometimes."

"Now, don't go there, Bernie," I said. "What matters is that we're all on the same page now. Nobody needs to have regrets."

"That's the truth," Joe Bob said. "Well, we all regret what happened that night, but it's done, and that's that."

"Things might turn out a lot better than you think," Bernie said. "A good lawyer can make all the difference. And there's another thing in your favor. No matter what Marcum says, we all know there wasn't a witness." He drained his glass. "Everybody ready for another?"

Joe Bob and I chugged our drinks, and Bernie poured refills, then climbed back into his seat on the bed.

"I know you guys would do whatever you could to help me," he said, "but there's nothing anyone can do."

"You bet we would, if we could," I said. "I empathize with you, Bernie. You know I've been there."

"Yes, you have," he said. "You sure as hell have."

"What are we talkin' about?" Joe Bob said.

"Haven't you been listening?" I said. "We're talking about Bernie's unfaithful wife."

"Oh, yeah. Tha's right. You two got somethin' in common: drop-dead gorgeous cheatin' wives."

"That was a harsh way to state it," I said.

"Well, Bernie said, "'strue. Might as well admit it. Yours cheated first, 'n mine played follow-the-leader."

"I think I'm glad I never got hitched," Joe Bob said. "Givin' my whole self to somebody'd be awful hard."

The room was still then. We drank in silence. I didn't know what the others were thinking, but I was recalling how happy I had been with Beth until she broke my heart.

"I loved Beth from the time I was old enough to date," I said.

"Yeah, I 'member," Joe Bob said. "She kinda messed up some of our three-man stuff in junior and senior years. You was one lovesick puppy."

"That's how I felt about Lee Ann," Bernie said. "I still do." He started crying.

"Oh, man, don't do that," Joe Bob said.

Bernie ramped it up into full-scale bawling. "What am I going to do?" he wailed.

"Bernard, me and Matt heard the way your wife yelled at you; talked to you like you was a dog," Joe Bob said. "How can you still love the woman? Tell me that."

"She didn't mean it!" Bernie yelled. "You don't understand her. Jewish women are high-strung. That's all."

"High-strung, my ass," I said. "Your wife is just plain mean-spirited."

Joe Bob got up and grabbed the bottle of booze. He didn't ask if anyone wanted another drink; he just refilled our glasses.

"Well, what're you gonna do about this cheatin' wife you love so much?" he said.

"That's' none of your damn business," Bernie said, and took a gulp of his drink.

"How 'bout you, Matt? You got the hots for the pretty new vet, but she ain't hot for you," Joe Bob said.

"At least, I'm not doing somebody's wife," I said.

"Now, that was mean," Joe Bob said. "Me and Arlene ain't doin' nothin' wrong, and you know it. Like I told you, her husband don't even know who she is. She's human. So am I."

"Arlene who?" Bernie said.

"Arlene Watkins," Joe Bob said.

"I know Arlene Watkins," Bernie said. "She went to school with us. You screwing her, Joe Bob?"

"Y'all are makin' it sound awful," Joe Bob said.

"Let me see," Bernie said, and took another swallow of his drink. "Tell me if I've got this right. You're screwing a woman who is cheating on her husband just like my wife is cheating on me."

"Well, tennicly, tha's right, but Arlene's husband is 'bout to die in a nursin' home. He's got the Alzheimer's, you see."

"You know the man?" Bernie said.

"What difference does that make?" Joe Bob said.

"Just does," Bernie said.

"Joe Bob's right," I said. "We shouldn't pick on him. After all, he's about to be living in the big house." I regretted it the second the words escaped my lips.

"I am. I know I am," Joe Bob said. "Y'all been lyin' to me, tellin' me a good lawyer could prob'ly save my ass, but I know tha's not gonna happen. I'm goin' up sure as the world."

He got up and stumbled to the table to get the nearly-empty bottle. Then, he picked it up and hugged it to his heart, falling back into his chair.

"Truth serum," he said, and began laughing.

It didn't take long for the laughing to turn into tears. I pushed myself up from my chair to walk the few feet to Joe Bob. I desperately wanted to apologize and try to comfort him, but I was so inebriated I was seeing double. I sat back down.

"Sorry, Joe Bob," I said. "You, too, Bernie. I don't think I've ever been this drunk. That's no excuse. I want you both to know I didn't mean a word I said all night. Don't know what got into me."

"I do," Bernie said. "Booze."

He wiggled himself to the edge of the bed and slid to the floor. I saw him attempt to get up, but felt no inclination to help him.

"A little help," he mumbled.

"Gimmie a hand, Matt," Joe Bob said.

He and I managed to get to our feet. We pulled on Bernie's arms until we had him upright. The three of us stood unsteadily beside the bed, swaying.

"Gotta take a trip," Bernie said.

He pushed me out of his way and began staggering toward the bathroom.

"Oh, no," he said, and fell to the floor, throwing up.

Chapter Thirty-seven

Sunshine poured into the room. The drapes were wide open, inviting the day. I must have been lying on my left arm, because it tingled like it was asleep. Nobody had made it out of this room the previous night. Joe Bob was spread-eagle on Bernie's bed, and I was lying crossways on the other one. Bernie was curled up on the floor in a corner. A pile of towels evidenced our attempt to clean up his unfortunate mess, and a foul odor permeated the room.

My head throbbed. I sat up on the side of the bed, and located my cell phone.

"Joe Bob! Bernie! Wake up! It's almost eleven o'clock. We've missed our appointments."

"Don't yell," Bernie said. He sat up in the corner and looked around the room, massaging his temples.

I listened to two missed messages in my voice mail. They were both from my sister, wanting to know where I was. She had called just before the family was leaving the house to go to the attorney's office. The second one was from his office, and Sam sounded furious. I was almost afraid to return her call, but I knew I had to.

"Where in the hell are you, Matt? I hope you're satisfied. You've embarrassed our entire family. I was able to persuade the attorney to allow us to come back to his office at one o'clock, Just so you know, the reading of Mother's will is going to take place then, whether you're there to hear it or not. I don't even want to know what you've been doing." She hung up.

"Come on, Joe Bob," I said, shaking him awake. "You have to wake up and call your lawyer."

"Why?"

"We've all overslept, and you and I have missed our appointments."

"I'm hearin' drums beatin' in my head, man," he said.

Bernie had gotten to his feet and leaned in the corner for support. He stepped into one of his loafers and scanned the room for the other one.

"Damnation!" he said. "This place smells like a dumpster."

"Yes, it does," I said. "Let's get out of here."

Joe Bob had a message on his phone from his attorney's secretary, wondering if he planned to make his appointment, or needed to reschedule.

"How am I gonna explain this situation?" he said.

"You'll just have to call and apologize. Ask to reschedule the appointment," I said.

"Can't do that 'til I have coffee," he said.

We went to a pharmacy. I seemed to be the most sober, so I went in and purchased a bottle of mouthwash. We drove to a deserted side street where we took turns with the mouthwash, Bernie being the last to participate. Then, we went to the diner and asked to be seated in a booth in the back where we drank black coffee.

Joe Bob made his phone call, then announced that we should all have some grease. We settled for scrambled eggs and dry toast.

I prayed that the family had stayed downtown for lunch, because I didn't want them to see me looking the way I did. Fortunately, they had done just that, but Trudy was there to give me the special look she had for me when I had done something disappointing. She didn't say a word; she knew she didn't have to.

"I'm sorry," I said, finding it as hard to look into those brown eyes as it was when I was ten.

"You had anything to eat?" she said.

"Yes."

I knew she wasn't going to ask where I had been, or what I had been doing.

"I was with Joe Bob and Bernie," I said. "We spent the night in a hotel room getting smashed."

"You don't smell like roses," she said. "Better go upstairs and clean yourself up."

When I came out of the bathroom, my other suit was pressed and laid out on Sam's bed.

Trudy was sitting at the kitchen table, having a cup of tea when I came downstairs.

"We're all ashamed," I said. "It was our last night together, and both of my old friends are having some problems right now. I know it's no excuse, but I'm not going to lie to you; never could."

"You've inconvenienced your family, and I'm not happy about what you did, but you're still my precious boy," she said, and squeezed my hand.

Uncle Stuart's keys were in the tray on the kitchen counter, but I didn't feel like being presumptuous at the moment. I called a cab and waited outside the attorney's office for my family to show up. They arrived just before one o'clock.

"I'm glad you're alive and well," Sam said, spitting out her words as though they burned her tongue.

"I apologize for the mix-up," I said, and offered no further explanation. "Shall we go inside?"

Oliver Wortham had been my mother's attorney for as long as I could remember. He was a short man with snapping brown eyes and a bushy mustache. His thick shock of white hair was combed straight back from his forehead. He was impeccably dressed in a tailor-made suit. I couldn't help noticing his platform shoes as he stepped from behind his desk to greet us. He seemed anxious to get started, and didn't waste any time.

"I see everyone is here but Mrs. Giles," he said. "My secretary will see to it that she receives a copy of the document this afternoon."

As soon as we were seated, he took a seat behind his expansive desk and made eye contact with each of us. He cleared his throat.

"We are gathered here for the reading of the last will and testament of Mrs. Eloise Matthews Stevenson," he said in a resonant voice. He wouldn't have needed a microphone if he had been addressing a large audience.

If this had been handled my way, we would have all gone our separate ways after the service. The attorney could have faxed each of us a copy of the will, but my sister and my aunt would never have agreed to that.

"This document is very straightforward," Wortham intoned, as he opened a large envelope and distributed a copy of the will to each of us, retaining one for himself.

As I had expected, there were no big surprises. Mom had left a decent sum of money to Trudy. She had bequeathed her double string of pearls and ten thousand dollars to Aunt Lela Maude, and the rest was to be divided equally between Sam and me. Notwithstanding all of Mr. Wortham's pomp and circumstance, the formalities were completed in less than twenty minutes.

We went back to the house to make final decisions as to what should be done with the contents of the house. Sam had agreed to let me buy her out, and I was prepared to do that as soon as we could have the house appraised. I told Ron that I wanted him to have the piano, and he was delighted.

I had told Wortham I would be glad to deliver Trudy's copy of the will, but he insisted that his secretary handle it. She followed us to the house and did her duty. Trudy couldn't speak after discovering the generous amount my mother had left her, but tears gathered in her eyes as she clutched her copy of the will to her chest.

Everyone went to their respective rooms to pack. My bag was ready to go, so I went to the living room to be alone and reflect. I could hear Aunt Lela Maude crying through her open bedroom door. Uncle Stuart was attempting to calm her, but it didn't seem to be working.

"I can't believe my baby sister is gone," she wailed. "None of this feels real; it's like a bad dream."

I understood how she felt. The only thing that had felt right since I got here was the connection I had felt with Sydney Edelman.

Trudy came into the living room. She sat down beside me on the couch and took my hand in her warm ones.

"I guess everybody's about ready to go," she said. Her eyes were red, and I had never seen such a sad expression on a person's face. "What do you want me to do with the house keys?"

I hadn't told her my plans for the house, and I wasn't sure this was the best time to tell her. It might be better to tell her after everyone else had left.

"Would you mind hanging onto the keys for a while?" I said. "I don't want to leave them with a stranger. I thought maybe you would be able to open the house for the person I get to sell the contents on consignment."

"I'll be happy to do that for you."

"Mom didn't make many changes to this house since I left," I said.

"No. The only thing she changed at all was your daddy's study."

I got up and walked across the room to the study, and when I glanced out the front window, I saw Joe Bob coming up the walk.

"Here's Joe Bob," I said. "I'll go outside to talk with him."

Joe Bob had his arm stretched toward the doorbell as I stepped out on the porch.

"Have you been to see the lawyer?" I said.

"Yeah, I've been there."

"How'd it go? Did you retain him?"

"Well, yes, and no."

"What does that mean?"

"I told him I wanted to hire him, but I haven't signed nothin' yet. He had some kinda emergency come up while we was talkin'. I told him I couldn't come back to his office later today, because I had some business at the police station. We agreed he'd meet me there at 5:30."

"Did you tell him what happened that night?"

"Part of it. Actually, I'd just got started. I told him I was involved in a car accident a little over a week ago. That's when he got the emergency phone call."

"Did you tell him a man was killed?"

"I was tryin' to, but he wouldn't let me finish. He was all upset about that phone call. The caller was on hold. He told me what I had to say would have to wait. Told me not to worry."

"Did he agree to represent you with that little bit of information?"

"I told him I wanted to hire him, and he said he'd bring the contract and meet me at the police station. That's all I know."

"This doesn't sound very realistic," I said. "What kind of

attorney would agree to take a case without knowing what it is? Maybe you should go see the other attorney."

"Nope. I've made up my mind. I'm gonna meet this guy at the police station and tell him everthing. There's no use draggin' this thing out any longer. I feel better already."

I looked into my friend's eyes and saw a peace that hadn't been there since before the accident.

"Joe Bob, I wish you the best, man. You're a good friend. I hope you've made the right decision."

"I wasn't absolutely sure 'til I was sittin' in the lawyer's office. Just when I was gettin' ready to tell him everthing; that's when I knew."

"When you knew?"

"It's the right thing to do," Joe Bob said with conviction.

Chapter Thirty-eight

My family and I had said our goodbyes, and they had gone their separate ways. We all promised to stay in touch, but I doubted that would happen. The only time we had contacted one another until my mother passed away was at Christmastime.

I called Bernie to tell him what Joe Bob was about to do.

"Hey," he said, "I'll pick you up and we can go with Joe Bob to the police station; let him know we're with him all the way. I'll drive you to the airport after that."

"That's a great idea. I have to make a few phone calls and tell Trudy goodbye. See you soon."

I made arrangements for three different people to appraise the house, and talked to a couple of guys about selling the contents on consignment. I would make sure Sam got her fair share of everything. Then, I went to the kitchen to tell Trudy my plan.

"Child, why don't you sell this house? I can't imagine why you would want to buy Samantha out and keep it. You don't live here," she said.

"No, I don't live here, but you do. Unless you feel some

attachment to your house, I'd like to see you sell it. It would make me immeasurably happy for you to live in this house the rest of your life, if you want to."

Tears gathered in Trudy's eyes, and she shook her head back and forth as if she couldn't believe what she was hearing.

"You'd better think about this offer before you make it," she said. "This couldn't have anything to do with my acting a fool about the house the other day, could it?"

"No. It has nothing to do with that. I've thought about it a great deal, and it's what I want. Nothing would make me happier. You can keep any furniture you want, and I'll sell the rest. I'll have what furniture you want from your house moved into this one."

"Here's what I want you to do: call me after you get back to Denver and have time to think it over."

"As you wish, but my mind's made up. Give me a hug. Bernie's coming to pick me up. He'll take me to the airport."

We embraced, and I felt the warmth of the woman who had loved me as her own flesh and blood.

Bernie got to the house at five o'clock. We called Joe Bob from the car to tell him we were coming to take him to the police station. He was waiting outside when we drove into the trailer park. I thought he looked awfully calm for a man who was on his way to jail. He slid into the back seat, and pulled his hair into a ponytail with a rubber band.

"Thanks for the ride, Bernard," he said.

"We both want you to know we're here for you," Bernie said. "If there's anything either of us can do for you, just say the word."

"I 'preciate that," Joe Bob said.

He was leaning a bit forward, taking what he probably thought would be his last look at the place he had called home for a long time.

"Who's cat-sitting?" I asked.

"Lucy. She's got him so spoiled. I think he's already attached to her."

Minutes later, we were at the police station. Bernie parked across the street from the station in a shady spot. There was no point in Joe Bob's going inside until he had a chance to talk with his attorney and sign the paperwork. Besides, he wanted to spend the last few minutes of his freedom with Bernie and me.

"Hey, did you guys hear the one 'bout this ninety-year-old man?" Joe Bob said.

Bernie swiveled his head to watch something across the street.

"No. Why don't you tell us," he said absently.

"Bernard, just what is it that's so almighty important that you can't give me one minute of your attention?" Joe Bob said.

"Sorry. I was just watching Freaky Fred. He's pacing back and forth in front of the police station like a zoo lion."

We turned our attention to Fred, the joke forgotten. Fred was wearing holes in the pavement, and something about him seemed peculiar. He wasn't exactly limping, but his gait wasn't normal, and his upper body looked askew.

"I'm telling you, he is one weird squirrel," Bernie said. "It's got to be ninety degrees in the shade, and he's wearing that stupid coat. If he ever takes a shower, he probably does it wearing that old coat."

"Let's go over there and find out what he's doing," I said.

"Okay," Joe Bob said. "It's almost 5:30. The lawyer oughta be here any minute."

Fred stopped pacing and sat down on a wooden bench in front of the police station. His body started rocking back and forth the way it did just before he blurted out the right answer to a math problem ahead of the entire sixth grade class. Joe Bob sat down beside him. Fred's lips were moving, but no sound emanated from his mouth. He rolled his eyes upward, then rubbed his temples.

"Hey, Freddie, how's the world treatin' you?" Joe Bob said.

"Don't call me that," Fred said, his eyes still cast toward the sky. "Told you not to call me that."

"It's your name," Joe Bob said.

"Name's Fred."

"Oh, yeah," Joe Bob said. "That's right."

When we were kids, Joe Bob used to call him Freddie to get a rise out of him. I had forgotten all about it.

"Well, what's up, Fred?" Joe Bob said.

"Police station."

"Yep," Joe Bob said. "This is the police station all right."

"Gotta go inside," Fred said, massaging his shoulder.

"What for?" Joe Bob said.

A high-pitched, hyena-like laugh escaped Fred's lips, the same one he always demonstrated when he was nervous.

"Gotta tell," Fred said.

"Tell what?"

Neither Bernie nor I had said a word, but Fred had just gotten our undivided attention.

Fred got up from the bench and began pacing back and forth, massaging his shoulder in rhythm with his step.

"You know," he said.

"Now, how in tarnation would I know, Fred? I just got here," Joe Bob said.

"You'z there," Fred said solemnly, and swallowed.

"Where?"

"Jimmy Banks."

Bernie, Joe Bob, and I exchanged glances. We had been certain there were no witnesses to the accident, but it seemed the sleazy lawyer had been right. Fred Peyton was the mystery witness, and he was here to tell the police what he saw that night. Even though Joe Bob was about to confess, he had planned to tell his own version, hoping he wouldn't have to drag anyone into it but himself.

Bernie looked sick. The color was draining from his face. He pulled a handkerchief from his pocket, jerked off his glasses and began cleaning them. Joe Bob had started taking deep breaths.

"What about Jimmy Banks, Fred?" I said.

Fred sat back down and looked up, seeming to notice me for the first time.

"Hey, Matt," he said.

"What's this all about, Fred?" I asked.

"He's dead." Fred looked like he wanted to cry.

"I know. I read about it in the paper."

"Seen it," Fred said.

"You actually saw it happen?" I said.

"Police station's got seven thousand, one hundred and twenty-eight bricks in it. Just the front side," Fred said, ignoring my question.

"What's that got to do with what we're talkin' about?" Joe Bob said.

"Why you guys here?" Fred said, chewing his lower lip and rubbing his shoulder.

"We saw you, and just stopped to say hello," I said.

Fred nodded as though my response made perfect sense to him.

"So you're here to tell the police what you saw that night?" Bernie said.

"Yeah."

"Why did you wait so long?"

"Been stove up."

"I thought I saw you picking up cans and bottles a couple of days ago," I said.

"Somebody's gotta do it," Fred said. "You mad at me, Joe Bob?"

"Nah, Fred. I ain't mad at you."

"Gonna tell on me?" he said, his green eyes filling with tears.

"What for?"

"I was tryin' to help him, tryin' to pull him out of the street. Swear it."

"Who?" Joe Bob said.

"Jimmy Banks. I didn't do it, Joe Bob."

"Nobody said you did."

"Didn't hurt him neither; just tryin' to git him out of the street."

"Wait a minute," I said. "Let's back up a little bit. Why don't you tell us what you saw that night."

Fred closed his eyes. I assumed he was silently rehearsing his speech.

"Okay," he said, and swallowed. "Peepin' Tom. Sister's scared. Stayin' the night with her. Dark."

I wasn't sure where Fred Peyton was going with this, but I wasn't about to interrupt him to ask.

"Red Oldsmobile, Alabama plates, license number MOV-167. Movin' fast."

He paused to take a deep breath.

"Jimmy Banks. Traffic cop. Car didn't stop. Hit Jimmy Banks; kep' on goin'. Fishtailed."

Fred spit out his strange laugh again.

"You saw the red Oldsmobile hit Jimmy Banks?" Bernie asked.

"Yep."

None of us could believe what we were hearing. Joe Bob was going to be a free man.

"You mad at me, Joe Bob?" Fred asked again.

"Naw, Fred. I ain't one bit mad at you."

"I didn't kill him. Swear it. Mad at him, though. Been pickin' up my bottles; cans, too."

"Why did you think Joe Bob was mad at you?" I asked.

"Hit me with his Buick. Knocked me in the ditch. Stove up my shoulder."

So if I was understanding what he was saying, Fred had seen the Olds hit Jimmy Banks. Joe Bob had bumped into Fred; he hadn't killed anyone. He had been in a living hell, and all the while, he was innocent.

"Fred, my man, you have just made my day," Joe Bob said.

I could almost see the lines disappear from his face.

A gentleman in a dark suit came hurrying from across the street. He was carrying a briefcase. Joe Bob stood to shake his hand.

"Mr. Murdock," he said.

"I apologize for being late," Murdock said. "There's a room inside where we can talk and take care of the paperwork."

"Well, sir, that won't be necessary," Joe Bob said. "It's all worked out. I'm afraid I won't be needin' your services after all."

The attorney looked puzzled.

"Here's somethin' for your trouble," Joe Bob said. He took out a money clip and handed the lawyer a hundred-dollar bill.

"I wouldn't hear of it," Murdock said. "You haven't even signed the contract. Good luck to you."

He shook Joe Bob's hand, turned, and walked across the street to his Mercedes.

Fred appeared to be rehearsing again. His eyes were shut tight, and he was silently moving his lips.

"Go on inside and tell the cops what you told us, Fred," Joe Bob said. "We'll wait here for you."

Fred Peyton did just that, and when he'd finished giving the police his statement, he came outside looking relieved.

"I done it," he said, grinning like a proud child.

"Fred, I'm gonna buy you the biggest steak in this town," Joe Bob said.

Fred frowned.

"No, thanks," he said.

"Come on," Joe Bob said. "You deserve it."

"Red meat'll kill you," Fred said, and walked off, massaging his shoulder.

Acknowledgments

I want to thank my husband, lawyer, and soul mate, Ralph Shelburne, for his love and support while I holed up in my girl cave to write, destroy, and rewrite this novel. Many thanks also to my editor/proofer, Martin Coffee for his keen eye. Last, but not least, I want to thank Barbara Lanham and Rennie Langman for their support and constructive criticism. You are invaluable.

www.ingramcontent.com/pod-product-compliance
Lightning Source LLC
LaVergne TN
LVHW041207250326
834689LV00016BA/152/J